Metal

Magic and Metal, Volume 1

James K Spring

Published by Magoo Sells Books, 2025.

Table of Contents

1. Dreams and Dungeons...1

2. A Punt Gone Wrong...8

3. Aftermath at Acae 23

4. Histories and Conspiracies 29

5. The Captain's Arrival 46

6. A Paired Connection 62

7. Spies and Lies 86

8. A Testing Planet...94

9. Mothers' War...103

10. City of New Axe 117

11. Missing Paired 127

12. A Cunning Plan..137

13. Hidden Rooms, Secret Thoughts 143

14. Accidentally Mostly Successful 155

15. The Facility 161

16. What Now?..170

17. Duck 178

18. Mother, Daughter, Lover...........................185

19. Observing Tuja 192

20. War and the Whooomp 200

21. Best Laid 216

22. Arena of Death 220

23. Controlling The Room 241

24. Great Escape..246

25. Never Ending...252

1. Dreams and Dungeons

The screaming starts in darkness. What's with all the dark?

"You are screaming!" you think to yourself. Stop the racket and run. Trouble's a-coming, and it's after you. Hunters are moving swiftly behind you across the bleak land amongst these biffen spiky, low shrubs. You cast a torch push and immediately turn towards a likely escape route in the distance.

You run towards it, but the possibility of escape leaps beyond your grasp. You glance backwards. Great! So that's what's with all the dark. Naroozie are after you, the aggressive planet-killers and ever-present war bringers, obviously enjoying this hunt on a darker planet, befitting their low-to-the-ground manner.

With their five legs, the usual four plus one in the middle of their back, they look humorous when they are standing on two legs, but when they use their fifth to change direction and roll during combat, all humour takes an exit from the senses.

In fact, you aren't finding it funny right now as they neatly roll and jump using that cursed leg to lurch towards you. The cliff edges closer, and you can smell the disgusting presence of the creatures behind you. The cliff is the only way out of this. You jump.

The screaming continues as you fall into more darkness.

Hengway woke up in his rickety wooden bed in a tiny, yet considerate room. The room was considerately cool during the height of summer and warm during the depths of winter. Considerate magic was quite rare throughout the systems and was usually confined to armour or single rooms, but the Acae family had a complete and functioning, considerate, architecturally created castle which had been the family home for hundreds of years.

Most of the rooms in the castle had their own considerate design functions; for example, the kitchen considerately cleaned itself each day, the storeroom refilled itself, and the very considerate bathroom had unlimited hot water and, on rare occasions, cold water.

Hengway always felt considerate architecture to be thoughtful but not very practical; sometimes, for example, towels turned up soaking wet, or entire rooms might turn upside down all because someone could not reach a book on a very high shelf.

Hengway and his siblings enjoyed life in a system that had not seen the likes of the naroozie or other planet-killers in some time. The rules of this system dictated that your magical and technical ability would determine what you studied and where you might end up later in life.

Students with exceptional skills were called enchanters. They studied at the Enchanter Dungeons, whereas students with what was considered average magical and fighting skills studied at the Traveller College, commonly known as Trav-Coll. Hengway, being almost sixteen years old, should have shown signs of talent by now. Unfortunately, he had not; however, he would still attend Trav-Coll, like his brother, but in a support class until his eighteenth year.

Hengway found himself beginning to think about making the motions needed to exit his bed. He stumbled out of bed and fumbled at the warm basin of water conjured by the considerate room and washed up, ready for the random craziness that no doubt lay ahead of him.

"Another day in the grind," sighed Hengway, as he put on his dark purple Trav-Coll shirt and deep brown pants. The pants dropped to the ground around his ankles, being a hand-me-down pair from Jay, his older brother. He sighed again, pulled up the pants, and fastened an old brown rope around his waist in place of a belt. Hengway seized his well-worn college bag and shambled through the hallway, down the stairs and into the kitchen. *This bag has probably been in the family longer than the castle*, he thought.

The kitchen had been considerate enough to prepare bread and ham for lunch. Jay, using magic, had two forks fighting with each other whilst he turned sugar grains into cubes, forming an arena for the battling utensils.

"Stop mucking about, you biffhead, and get ready for the punt!" Hengway chastised his brother with a hint of jealousy.

"Why don't you join me in a fork battle?" teased Jay, knowing that Hengway's lack of magical ability was a sore point to him, and the rest of the family. They lived on Yurning 5, a planet which was highly structured and culturally protected by strict social rules. Decrees stated everyone had to have an officially examined skill by age eighteen or they were to join the workers.

Being sent to the mines for life was far from the future Hengway wanted for himself. Yurning 5 was part of the Yurning system, which existed in the middle systems and was predominantly occupied by humanoids like Hengway and his family.

"Just get ready! Where's our sister?" barked Hengway as he was startled out of his thoughts when the fighting forks' sharp clashing prongs went hurtling through the kitchen. The defeated fork performed a death scene much like a poor stage actor, eventually falling to the table.

"*I'm* not her minder. *You* are. Fetch her yourself!" insisted Jay.

With a huff, Hengway took the winding stairs that led to the dungeons, where Trinni's experimental chamber could be found. He wished he had a lit torch to light his way, so the nearest torch on the wall considerately lit itself before floating over to where he was standing. His parents gifted his sister the chamber on the day she became an enchanter. For some reason known only to them, enchanters preferred the confines of dungeons. The damper and creepier, the better.

On finding Trinni absorbed in a book the size of a dwarf planet, he yelled, "Hurry up! Let's get going! You know we need your help for the punt jump!"

Trinni attended the intersystem Enchanter College, located underneath the main library on the planet of Yurning 7. The library was established to distribute knowledge freely, and to unite magic, science, and culture. Enchanters studied laws and rules to find ways to harness and interpret them, or even break them, for the good of all. This, of course, caused conflict between the systems and the various species living therein.

Trinni closed the book and followed Hengway back into the kitchen and carefully set her books on the table.

"What are you doing today, Trinni?" Jay asked.

"The usual enchanter activities. We must practice moving large, heavy objects through the systems."

"You could move Hengway, then." Hengway did not react. Jay's bullying usually started in the morning, and then extended to other students at Trav-Coll throughout the day.

Hengway shot his older brother a glance of fraternal hate, though it could have been perceived as a creepy half-smile. "How do you deal with bullying at Enchanter College, Trinni?"

"Bullying doesn't happen. We are able to turn each other into frogs or sea slugs, so we try not to torment; instead we try to help each other. Ours is a spiritual sect." Trinni disappeared. She always did this before school, and Hengway never got used to it. Whenever she conducted this push, it was to retrieve something from her dungeon for the day's study, but she did not dislike that it annoyed her brothers.

Jay had already been accepted into the section of Trav-Coll that taught only the best students, infamously known as the Chosen. Jay had the requisite grasp of mind control and possessed natural fighting skills.

Students who studied with the Chosen usually ended up becoming elite warriors, spies, or envoys for the system. The Chosen reported to the highest levels of government and had always been honoured with a member of Hengway's family among their ranks.

Even though Jay was the oldest sibling at seventeen, Hengway was stuck with caring for Trinni, who, despite turning twelve next season, really did not need his help. Hengway was not sure whether he liked his brother. Jay certainly did not help him at Trav-Coll and never assisted him with his fighting skills.

"You have a spear exam today, remember!" Hengway told Jay, who stared back without blinking. Jay's dream-fuzzified brain was operating as a utensil-hardened warrior, not a student. Slowly and painfully his brain returned to the land of the living and kicked into life.

"Oh, biffle," he replied as his brain joined the party. He huffed, turned around, and moped back to his room. Achievement badges adorned his immaculate college uniform. This created friction with his brother and many older students at the college who were yet to earn a fraction of Jay's awards.

"Father will go crazy if Jay misses another exam," Trinni pointed out after reappearing.

Hengway's hair prickled. "No punting in the house!"

"Sure, Hengway." Being smarter and nicer than Jay, Trinni did not tease Hengway about his lack of magic or fighting skills. She was quite sure it would come to him over time; with lots of practice.

Her own story was complicated. Trinni went missing one day at the age of six. She was found in a library by the local enchanters, a few planets away. They immediately perceived that she possessed unusual technical and magical abilities. Neither Hengway nor Jay could punt jump, so they needed Trinni's help each day to get to Trav-Coll.

"Let's get going! We'll be late!" Hengway shouted into the kitchen.

A fork flew through the smell of cooking vapour and stuck firmly into a corkboard the castle had considerately placed there as a target during the night. "That only scores as a seven," Trinni said to Jay. He shrugged his shoulders and accepted the score, even though he thought it was an eight. There was no arguing with Trinni on matters of fork target wars.

"You two are insane. Get ready for the jump!" Hengway checked that his annoying siblings had packed their bags with the lunches supplied by the very considerate kitchen, which had already begun cleaning itself in a no-fuss, considerate way.

There were no special words or magic bits and pieces needed for a short punt jump. It happened when the enchanter, or person who could make it happen, decided it would happen. Trinni once had her brothers believing they had to place dead spiders wrapped in rags over their heads for each jump to work. This went on for months until their parents let them in on Trinni's secret. The whole family, along with the people at Trinni's school dungeon, still made fun of them over that.

"Do you know where Mum and Dad are?" Hengway asked Trinni, given that she normally woke up stupidly early to plan the overthrow of the universe or something just as evil. This was not entirely accurate, but Hengway thought it wasn't impossible.

"They left very early with some of the Chosen, and they were in a big hurry. There was a lot of adult talk and adult words, then they all punted after collecting weapons from the armoury." Hengway was reminded daily that his parents were senior members of the Chosen, and how he was expected to follow their path, just like Jay. "They spoke of something called a long-punt. I was very much awake from the effects of the punt blast, so I went to my dungeon to study," Trinni added.

"What the biff is a long-punt?" Hengway asked. Trinni shrugged her shoulders and headed for the double doors to the open area outside the kitchen.

Trinni liked to stand in an open space for each jump, and this spot had always worked in the past. She was dressed in enchanter kit, which consisted of an armoured chest piece, arm and leg guards made of leather, and pouches swinging from webbing over her back. She wore this webbing because she was too young for the sought-after enchanter belt. The pouches were full of bits and pieces unknown to Hengway, though he noticed the odd hairy beastie trying to escape every now and again.

Jay joined the duo, taking in the blue sky that always had a red haze along the horizon. "The moons will be a vision of beauty tonight. Yurning 3 is at its closest point to us in quite a while," Jay explained, expecting someone to enthusiastically converse with him about the wonders of their solar system. Sadly, information regarding the planetary system, or three-mooned planets in general was not foremost on his family's mind

"Okay, Acae family, let's get educated!" commanded Hengway.

2. A Punt Gone Wrong

A figure stood over the hearth, poking at it in an annoyed manner. The fire was also annoyed at being stabbed with a sooty iron poker, so nothing was done to improve the individual's warmth, or indeed cool down his mood. "You are an ungrateful brat. We take you into our hearth and all you do is complain," the father said, not to the fire, but to a child who took the term 'ruffled' to the next level.

The mother took her husband's rant as a request to help with the ritual daily beration, "Twyette, you should be more thankful. All you have to do is to be up before the sun, muck out the sty, milk three cows, of which the milk you benefit thereof, then feed the hens, clear the coop, conduct the mandatory seven house cleaning chores before properly preparing breakfast for the family. Not much to ask, I believe."

"You didn't pick the vegetables for dinner. This is not the first time I had to do your chores," said the brother, who was the laziest lad Trinni had ever met. The unwashed, stinky twelve-year-old continued his attack. "My mummy and daddy found you and gave you shelter. You should be more respectful."

With that, he shut up. Trinni, or Twyette as they called her, continued with clearing the breakfast table and preparing for the multitude of tasks the family known as the Kents demanded her do on a daily basis.

Her last memory was punting her brothers to the academy and ending up here with the Kents. That was over five years ago. She was somewhat miffed at the fact that her magic was so poor on this planet; however, she had been working on what she liked to call her cunning plan.

The Kents believed they had found a lost child. Upon arrival on their planet, she realised she was stuck, so she picked a family that was near enough to a medium-sized village where she could hopefully attain the help she required.

There was one reason she had not killed the Kents and moved somewhere more palatable. That reason was knocking at the door of the small cabin. The knock was hard and unmistakable. "Your stupid enchanter priestess is here," shouted the snotty brat. Trinni had been there for years and had not said a single word to any of them. This was the reason they called her Twyette, the name of their favourite surviving pig.

The father stormed to the door and yelled, "She will be out when she is finished with her chores."

The looming figure at the door raised her hand to speak. "Before I turn you into a tiny insect, get that girl out here now. She already does all of your chores, and it won't hurt for you all to get some exercise. I might add, the enchanter's chapel has free soap for villagers, of which you should put to use down at the washing stream."

The father knew the enchanter could not turn him into anything other than angry. However, the entire planet respected the enchanters, and the Kents' little village was no exception. He stepped aside.

"Well, there she is," said the enchanter as Trinni approached the door. With reluctance he said, "Be home on time to do your afternoon chores." He then spoke to the enchanter. "I don't know why you bother with her. She is good only for farm work. Can't talk, read or write. Only good for me farm."

"I am well aware of your appraisal of Twyette's skills. You are, as usual, perfectly wrong. I bid you farewell, family Kent. Trin... sorry, Twyette, let us go." Trinni walked past the room full of Kents with her head bowed.

The pair walked in silence until they could see the village. "We have collected the books and people you requested from other timelines. Working together, we should be able to get you home."

"I do thank you immensely for your help. That family needs an attitude adjustment."

"As you are aware, they were our best choice to hide you away. The people here are not as accepting of magic as in other systems and planets. Your ordeal shall be over soon."

"I hope I can travel back to the moment I created the punt jump. My brothers may need my help."

"Do they know of your predisposition for long-punts?"

"I didn't even know about long-punts. I hope I gain more control over them. The last five years have been an experience for me. Possessing minor magic is difficult to get used to." The enchanter nodded in agreement.

Approaching the village they first encountered inns and stables. There were occasional steam-bots patrolling the streets but nothing as advanced as on Yurning 5. This village still had horses and carriages, and most machines, including bots, ran on steam.

A building designed to be inconspicuous concealed the enchanter's chapel entrance. The enchanter's symbols were etched into the second step, noticeable only if you knew what to search for, where and, more importantly, how to read them.

The rooms were used for sleeping, cooking and other lodge-type activities. The main room, however, was the practice room, and there stood Trinni wearing farm overalls stinking like every farm animal the Kents had ever owned. Also in the room were people clearly from foreign parts, probably even other planets.

When the room's occupants saw the person they had been trying to help secretly for five years, some sniggered, and some cursed in disbelief. They had never met her, and they all expected someone older and more, well, easier on the nose, and possessing a more *magical* appearance.

The person they really should have been mocking was the wearer of a purple robe topped with a ridiculous ceremonial headdress. It was too big, floppy, and had a feather sticking out the left side. "A bit lost, lass?" the robed man said.

"It's about time you got here, Professor. Can I go home now?"

"It took me five years to find you, so I understand your sense of urgency. To answer your question, home? No. Back to your brothers? Certainly. Luckily, your father and my good self alerted the others on the morning of your departure. Enchanters from a different timeline told us that a long-punt would occur, but we mistakenly thought it was going to happen at the Enchanters College," said Professor Smeltzit.

Trinni dipped her head to one side in deep thought. "That explains you lot running around in the wee hours that morning. During my time here, I have heard about an event called 'the pairings'. Have you heard of this?"

"I have not. Magic is evolving quickly; therefore, be prepared for anything. There is a rumour about an artefact, though," the Professor responded. Trinni remained quiet and intensely resolute.

The Professor bent down to Trinni's ear and whispered, "Danger lies in wait for you and your family. Whatever it takes, follow the light!" Trinni glanced at him and processed his request. She sensed the sensitivity of this information and nodded her head to acknowledge she had heard his statement.

The Professor stood up slowly and turned to the others. "Well, everyone, we need to prepare for the push that we have been practising. Trinni was the first to experience a long-punt. We need to send her back. Be ready. You, Trinni, will appear as though you have not spent the last five years away. I would get used to these long-punts given your enchanter brood are still unaware of what causes them."

"Your study here over the last five years is about to become very helpful. On another note, it has been discovered that someone else caused this long-punt and has arranged a jump-cross to punt you and your siblings to a dangerous planet. Be alert! Here are some goodies to play with." Smeltzit gave her a belt. It held two pouches brimming with vials and herbs typically reserved for advanced travellers.

Trinni glanced at the belt and was suddenly less miffed about the long-punt or the study she had to undertake. The professor's cryptic message and her new kit made her feel ready to follow this metaphorical light. She was still wearing segments of the enchanter armour she had arrived in, which was now adjusted to fit the new pieces of kit. After equipping herself with the belt, she finally felt untethered. The quicker she re-entered her world, the better.

The enchanters, executants and other hangers-on thrust out their hands and created a small but useful push that broke Trinni's five-year long-punt, sending her back to the exact moment when she vanished all that time ago.

Well, hopefully, she thought as she felt the punt take hold.

The three siblings focused on each other, and the punt began. Noticing the physical impact made Hengway curious, as usually there would be no start or stop. They usually arrived a split second before they left, as if a moment vanished before their eyes.

This punt felt somewhat different, as Trinni could attest to, but she decided to keep long-punts to herself at this stage.

Punting was always a strange feeling. The creepy sensation occurred as expected. This jump, however, displaced more than it should have. From the almost noiseless blast, this punt jump was not going right.

As Trinni moved towards Jay in a slow, sleepy motion, Hengway was thrown into a thicket of short shrubs, becoming alarmed at the screaming from a few feet away. The shrubs were a metallic yellow with an unhealthy green tinge, and were not from his planet.

He tried to move and was at once cut on the back of his hand by the sharp, extended leaves of the alien bush. He decided not to call out. Trav-Coll and his parents had drilled into him: "Stay low and still; assess and plan; take swift action!" He could almost hear his mother's words. He wished she were there with them now.

He believed her words were particularly relevant in this moment, so Hengway extracted himself from the biffing shrub and edged towards the screaming.

"Keep quiet!" he heard a young woman hiss. He locked onto the location and crawled as quietly as he could towards an unmistakable voice. Hengway was in assessment mode as he examined the dusty ground and saw two figures lying next to each other. Trinni lay low in her bulky enchanter armour, which was far too conspicuous. Jay was beside her, fussing over his no longer pristine uniform.

"Is that you, Hengway? I could hear you from a mile away," murmured Trinni. Hengway crawled into the space his siblings were occupying and scanned the surroundings for threats.

Not seeing any immediate danger, he whispered, "You weren't wearing that garb when we left. What happened?" Jay was bruised and lacerated as if he had gone ten rounds with a keen street-fighter. Trinni had already applied a bandage onto Jay's facial wounds, after applying medicinal herbs from her many pouches. "What happened to him?" Hengway asked.

"We've been jump-crossed. Someone changed our destination. Jay fell poorly and broke his left upper arm, which I healed with a spell, and now he needs to rest," she whispered quickly, withholding the knowledge of her long-punt, the warning from the Professor and the years stranded on a dreary planet with very little magic. Jay's eyes were half closed. He was conscious, but his breathing was shallow, and his slumped face made him appear drowsy.

This strange world had two suns, both almost setting, nearly concealing a small cluster of moons. Hengway motioned to Trinni by circling his finger in the air, signalling that he was going to conduct a reconnaissance of the area.

He crouched to his knees and surveyed the entire scene. His heart raced when he noticed the large yellow cloud and a tiny figure running straight towards them. Assorted species were fleeing the source of the dust clouds. The primary concern was for a specific dust cloud approaching them.

"Can't you punt jump us out of here?" implored Hengway.

"I have already tried twice. I don't know what's going on. You need to do something!"

Oh, biffle, thought Hengway as the small figure drew nearer. The figure was trailed by attackers through the dusty scrub. Hengway declared the assessment phase to be over as he rapidly picked up Jay and yelled, "Run like a startled bunglebeast from Yurning 2!"

"Grand plan," replied Trinni as she scooped up her pouches and Jay's spear. For someone so small, she could move quickly and seriously look after herself if events needed it. Using enchanter magic as much as the situation allowed, she was jumping and darting, though despite her efforts, something was still preventing a longer jump. Hengway wished that he could float Jay the way Jay floated kitchen forks and sugar cubes, but he had to carry his brother the hard way.

The small object of the dust cloud's attention scurried past, revealing herself to be a dwarf. A dwarf in a particular hurry. She was armed with a warrior's dwarven axe forged in the Cellfast System. The dwarf slowed down long enough to say, "You must be quicker than that; these naroozie want blood." Sure enough, Hengway spun around and saw an unwanted nightmare headed straight for them. His dream was creating its own existence, complete with the dreaded five-legged naroozie. Lots of them.

Cleavie swept through the dense alien scrub, keeping her eyes on the uneven ground, moving one leg in front of the other in a well-practised motion designed to keep her alive. The training in the Cellfast system consisted of a lot of sprinting and swinging of axes. So, this chase might yet end in her favour.

The dwarven-tailored pants kept her safe from the harsh shrubs and sharp grasses that bestrewed the landscape. She might have been sent into this system on purpose, she reflected. Nonetheless, she had no idea where she was.

She was due for a test hunt, another achievement thread braided into her beard. These tests were usually quick and relatively easy. After some reflection, she relied on her father's teachings: *always be alert, be calm, and then be ruthless!* Others should have been present to ensure she was not harmed, at least not excessively. Judging that this pursuit was too challenging for her current level—she was now in the calm phase, which included a stage called 'assessment'.

Given the circumstances, she had to implement the final part of her father's mantra, so she took a moment to conduct an internal tactical assessment. After a brief period, a calculated plan emerged.

The sudden rustle of bushes alerted Cleavie, who slid behind a shrub, keeping low and turning around to get a better view of the scene behind her.

Cleavie was born into a dwarven culture that valued technology and fighting. Different levels of technology existed, including weaponry and self-reliance kits. Some good, some not so good.

"Up. Up. Get out there and tell me what you see," she whispered quickly into the air.

A tinny voice chirped through the chip inserted in the back of her ear, "Hold ya horses there, sunshine! I'll whip up and have a squiz."

I seriously need to upgrade my PSSA if I get out of this with my head intact, Cleavie thought. The PSSA withdrew from its hiding space in her backpack and elevated itself about sixteen dwarf-hands off the ground.

The 'Personal Surveillance/Spy Apparatus' was essential to all travellers, especially those who wanted to avoid the more delicate traps of the job, being: capture, torture, death or all three. PSSA was a low-system device usually used by children and workers who could not afford the better 'spirit-generated' magic of the higher-system science factories. PSSA was about one dwarf-hand wide and featured all the appropriate swirly bits that a personal drone ought to have. The unit was equipped with an outdated lower-system artificial intelligence and knowledge-access construct, which required a significant update by Cleavie's measure.

"Relay my visual," Cleavie whispered as she peered through the sunset, trying to establish whether the naroozie hoard had followed her. A live stream of the scrub appeared on her right retina, showing her the PSSA's field of vision, which included the advancing naroozie.

"You are royally biffed here, my dear," the unhelpful PSSA observed as Cleavie tightened her grip on her battle axe. Dwarf warriors from Cellfast 5 were usually given a personalised axe after passing the challenging exam aptly named 'Pass or Die'. Not in Cleavie's case—she had stolen this axe on her way to the system transporter just before she was sent into this ambush. Her practice axe was light and blunt, so she opted to procure one that happened to be un-dwarfed at the time.

"Go over to the taller trees on the right and create a diversion!" she directed. The chatty apparatus swooned over to the trees, silently humming to itself, enjoying the drama a bit too much. Cleavie was glad she had worn her battle gear on this hunt, even though it was supposed to be a simple reconnaissance test.

"This will be a simple recon mission, Cleave Hammer Petafelt III, so no need for an escort or firearms," explained the chief just hours earlier. He knew she preferred 'Cleavie' and hated her formal name, so he called her by her full name to get her riled up.

This was very wrong and very deadly for him, should she ever get back to that sorry sack of dwarven blood and bones. The current situation felt like a setup to get her out of the way. Earlier that day, a special test was scheduled. She suspected the chief had tampered with the transporter, sending her to this system, time, and dusty planet with its undesirable sharp leaves.

She surmised the test was arranged to decide whether she would be allowed to sit for the 'Pass or Die' exam and, of course, add another coveted braid to her beard. Finding who sent her here instead would be a difficult mystery to solve. There were several dwarfs who would be happy not to have her as competition.

When she appeared on this planet, she found herself amongst a group of other species, which consisted of all known types, including, most surprisingly, naroozie. More naroozie dressed in red armour appeared in front of the group and immediately ran towards their confused victims.

The naroozie in her group stood their ground, assuming they would not be harmed by fellow naroozie; they were wrong. The majority of them ran into the scrub, panting and surveying for a likely escape route. As she reached a tangle of low shrubs, she turned around to watch the ill-fated war fighters who stayed behind participating in a one-sided fight with the naroozie wearing red armour.

Three naroozie separated from the horde and followed Cleavie into the shrubs. Cleavie quickly worked out she was in for an absolute biff-fest. Her quick and barely adequate tactical analysis revealed that the naroozie in red were there for some kind of game or hunt. She intended to turn the game around.

Hidden by the harsh shrubbery, Cleavie watched the three naroozie in red advance towards her.

A naroozie's front legs were capable of adjusting to changes in direction made by its back legs. This forward momentum could reach an alarming velocity, but would often result in the naroozie flipping over mid-turn. The fifth leg would then do its job, since it was three times as strong and protruding from its back. It could correct the fall by pushing the muscular torso back onto its other legs.

The three naroozie stopped suddenly. They could smell the presence of Cleavie. The naroozie were heavy, vicious, intelligent, and deadly.

"This little one smells like an easy win. Let's kill it, or capture it, win this hunt, and go for tea!" suggested the lead naroozie as he applied his keen senses to detect the defiant dwarf. He stood on his back legs to reach the sword strapped to his thick waist.

The other two naroozie waited. Motionless, silent, listening, smelling, and feeling for any presence of prey. The naroozie's greyish, heavily furred skin glistened in the light of the moon cluster as relative silence enveloped the small glade.

The noise of hundreds of humans came screaming through the scrub, right where PSSA was headed. The three naroozie turned while simultaneously drawing their weapons. From years of training, they effortlessly established a three-pronged defensive stance. After a brief pause, they directed their attention toward the stand of humans, all in a line with weapons in hand.

"How did humans make it this far into the system without help?" laughed the lead naroozie.

"Let's concentrate on surviving this first!" a somewhat nervous but well-armed and well-footed naroozie replied.

Cleavie also had no idea where the humans came from, though she could have made a good guess. The implementation of her father's mantra entered the third and vital phase–be ruthless.

She stole some time to activate her dwarven 'kill all nasty things' protocol with the words, "Kill all nasty things, farfeltwood!" This incantation allowed the installed nano-pharm factory to inject her with the right amount of dwarven chemicals needed to magnify her speed and strength.

It also gave her a shot of dwarven beetroot juice to spice things up a bit. Cleavie quickly positioned herself behind the third naroozie (yet to have a speaking part) jumped up onto his fifth leg, giving her a firm platform to swing her axe neatly in a low arc, perfect forcleaving the unimportant minion's head from its thick, hairy neck. The emancipated head sped through the thin air, fresh purple blood spreading behind it.

A human on horseback fronted the warriors, face painted in cobalt blue, wearing a loose wraparound garment made from loomed yak fur. "Ye can take our lives, but ye canna take our freedom," echoed throughout the gully as the man yelled towards the naroozie. The humans were lined up shoulder to shoulder with their blue face paint and clad in what appeared to be the battle skirts worn by lower system inhabitants. Their weapons were smithed primitively, and the lack of armour made them appear weak. The moonlight glimmered off steel axes and other fragile implements adorning the jostling throng of humans.

Weapons had not been made from this metal for thousands of years, so they were completely out of place in this system. The remaining two naroozie stared at the line of humans, waiting for an attack, unaware that Cleavie had already despatched one potential killer and was behind the other two, nurturing a cunning plan which had eluded her thus far.

The warriors were being given a speech by their leader, the man on the horse, when their horses lunged forward, thus beginning their advance. Cleavie used this distraction to stalk her prey from behind, quietly and swiftly.

"Let's sort these humans out so I can have my tea and crog-crog sandwich!" the hungry naroozie whined.

"I can't believe you like crog-crog. Do you know they eat their own—wait, what was that?" The humans, all as one, flickered, their noise modulating, beginning to dampen and become faint. This process occurred again and again. Some humans completely disappeared, intermittently reappearing at random like the flickering of a light bulb.

Cleavie moved so quickly that the head of the tea-hungry naroozie hit his companion on the back leg before he could know an attack was taking place.

"Sorry about the poor playback. I am getting short of power. I need to generate more," said the almost battery depleted PSSA. And with that, the humans completely disappeared, bewildering the remaining naroozie, who turned around to find a furious dwarf with a bloodied axe. The dwarf was giving him a smile fit for murder, undoubtedly his.

"I do love lower system pre-invasion human projections. Well-displayed," Cleavie grunted to PSSA as she moved swiftly and lethally towards her last would-be killer. Her adversary evaded her by creatively using all five legs. With one concerted hop, he distanced himself from her vicious advance as she slid into a low, sharp bush, firmly gripping her axe.

The bush exploded, in keeping with the legendary burning bushes of Waiface 3.

Watching from a short distance, PSSA activated Cleavie's single-use anti-death field. With this last surge of power, PSSA dropped to the ground with its battery completely depleted.

In fireside chitchat, Cleavie had heard the legend of Waiface 3, a high-system planet with spiky flora prone to exploding when it came in contact with blood. Cleavie finally understood which system and which planet she was on. Evolutionary craziness at its best caused the blast to briefly lift Cleavie, propelling her away from the startled naroozie. As he was trying to escape the exploding shrub, a new tinny voice in Cleavie's head spoke, "Shield deployed. Thank you for using anti-death three thousand."

The shield took the rest of the blast then dissipated, allowing Cleavie to swing her body and axe around towards the injured naroozie.

"Wait! Stop! Don't hurt me!" implored the remaining killer. Cleavie eyed the last combatant wearily and slightly lowered her axe to a defensive position. She was well aware that she had no more combat tricks left, and that her lone defender was recharging on the ground.

"Who sent me here?" she growled.

"I don't know. We were paid to kill whomever or whatever came through the system transporter. We don't ask questions; we just kill things."

"I think you are lying, and you need to tell me who sent—"

The naroozie had already pounced with his back leg and had all front claws in ready-to-kill mode. Cleavie instinctively leant back, swinging her axe as hard as she could.

The approaching legs were severed and fell to the ground, sploshing loudly as blood rushed from the naroozie's flailing body.

Without pointless conversation, Cleavie swung the axe into the annoying killer's head. The axe cleaved with a thud and entered the brain cavity without prejudice, instantly killing the paid assassin.

"PSSA back online and ready for operation," cheerily informed the personal drone.

Cleavie extracted her axe, cleaned it on the naroozie's fur, and straightened her armour. A worrying noise startled her. She and PSSA turned towards it. A large mob of naroozie was barrelling towards them.

"We need to go, ma'am," PSSA said to the open air because Cleavie was already sprinting in the opposite direction while quietly planning a way out of the ambush.

Cleavie sped through a section of high grass and nearly ran into three humans huddled behind a shrub. "I would be quicker than that! These naroozie want blood," she scream-whispered at them. *Why aren't those bushes exploding around them as they did with me?* Her feet were moving more quickly than her brain, *quite considerate of them*, she thought, as the three humans behind her followed in a mad rush to avoid the assassin army that was catching up.

"Keep moving! They are right behind you!" informed PSSA. Cleavie ran straight into a castle wall, sending her into a state of befuddlement. PSSA slowed down and avoided a collision, of which Acae Castle was quite appreciative.

3. Aftermath at Acae

"This line of questioning is getting boring and is not helping us get answers."

Cleavie recognised the impatient voice; her father was here. She now wished she were back dealing with the naroozie; much more pleasant. She respected her father, and when he was not dealing with dodgy traders, he was humorous and gentle, but she thought the murderous naroozie may bring out the war fighter in him.

In her head, events were as muddled as a municipal council monthly meeting. Piecing together the bits that made sense to her was a slow exercise. She decided to pretend to be asleep and see what else she could learn.

"There is a lot we are keeping from each other. How did your children avoid the burning bushes of Waiface 3? How did they all get back here in relative safety and why have the naroozie become so interested in all these children across the systems?" enquired Kalle, Cleavie's father, who preferred nights of quiet drinking and loud fighting to interplanetary intrigue.

An unfamiliar voice answered, "The naroozie council has informed us that this was a rogue attack from an unknown naroozie faction. We do not believe this, of course, and all systems and planets that have missing children are demanding answers. Answers we simply don't have."

"What are the numbers of missing and dead?" demanded a third voice. This voice Cleavie knew all too well: her mother's.

"That is a sore point for me, Lyssa, as you know. My wife is still missing; however, my children returned at the same time as your daughter, Cleavie. My daughter Trinni, who is an enchanter, informs me she did not punt jump back to the castle. She is with her dungeon sect, working to determine the magic or, perhaps, 'coincidence' that made the jump possible."

"You can stop pretending to be asleep now, daughter," boomed Kalle. Cleavie opened her eyes to a scene of considerate mayhem.

Two boys rested on mattresses considerately placed to possibly break the fall of someone who might have punt jumped in a hurry. She wished this considerate magical castle worked with dwarfs, her especially. She decided it didn't as she rubbed her skull where the castle had inconsiderately met her upon arrival.

"Greetings, my most respected parents," Cleavie said, giving the formal salutation of her culture.

"Well met," Kalle and Lyssa responded as one.

"I suppose you have some questions for us. Come and meet the Acae family!" Kalle added cheerfully, pronouncing the castle name as 'ahhh chay'. The castle was quite famous throughout all systems, and she had only ever read about it, and never seen it—until now.

None of it made sense. Cleavie rubbed her bruised head again, her father waiting awkwardly for her to speak. Finally, Cleavie put it all together. She was safe in Acae Castle, home to a widely renowned Yurning family highly gifted in military, technical and magical skills.

Hengway was reclining on the mattress hoping to become part of the scenery. Like Cleavie, he wanted to hear what was going on without actually being a part of the conversation. He had seen Cleavie wake up, heard her talking to her parents, noticed that the room had gone quiet, and that everyone was now watching him.

"Hengway, are you all right? Please answer, Cleavie!" said Kalle.

"Wha-? I didn't hear, er, what was the question?" Hengway replied, sitting up quickly and turning his head to the dwarf he had just met on that strange planet.

"Why weren't the bushes exploding near you and the others?" Cleavie asked.

"No idea. I didn't know they had such a volatile, fiery attitude," joked Hengway. The group forgot to listen, and indeed laugh. The intense glare from all within the kitchen remained.

"The last thing I remember was we were with that dwarf," pointing at Cleavie, "running to safety, and then we just appeared back here in the kitchen. Someone left these mattresses precisely where we would land, only that—" Hengway pointed at Cleavie again.

"Her *name* is Cleavie," noted Kalle, his brows raised.

"Cleavie, I apologise, slammed into the wall." Hengway continued the description as his cheeks reddened. This was getting hectic. He would have much preferred having a hot breakfast in a quieter part of the multi-system.

"Jay immediately tried his best to secure the kitchen, and I, was considerately presented with a spear by the castle," finished Hengway.

"Meanwhile; I ensured Cleavie was fully here and safe, that my brothers were safe, and then I left to check in with my dungeon sect."

All eyes darted to a frail figure with white wavy hair, a small nose, and pale blue eyes. Most other systems dismissed her as a myth invented by Yurning's people to boost their reputation, yet here was Trinni, standing in the room, clear to see.

"I was told that you three would come to this kitchen within eight minutes, and that our mother is missing."

Silence once again enveloped the room. Hengway could practically hear and smell all the thinking. The situation was too intense, and he wished it would end as his thoughts led to that of his mother.

"Our mother. Where is she?" he asked, glancing from Trinni to his father. Getting no honest reaction, he drew a sharp breath and looked back to Trinni. The tension in the room thickened; all those present avoided looking Hengway in the eye. He gave Trinni a questioning gaze.

"Hengway, there was another incident like ours, except it happened in space. Our mother's ship got into a clash with an unknown vessel," Trinni explained. She paused for a moment, peering at her father, possibly for reassurance, or permission to continue. Forthwright nodded his assent.

Trinni added, "There are indications that several entities punted from the ship. Happily, our mother was one of them."

"Was it the naroozie? Oh, and no need to thank me for the whole helping to save Jay thing," Hengway said to no one in particular, which was a good thing as no one answered him.

"It was an unknown craft," replied Kalle. "We believe several systems may have been interested in the cargo."

"Yes, it is probably the reason for the children being kidnapped this morning. I have heard from sources, reliable, or not so much, that this cargo is causing a lot of problems between the systems. Rumours have spread that pairings are occurring among the kidnapped children," reported Lyssa while gazing mournfully at her daughter Cleavie.

"Are you all suggesting the stories about pairings are true? That the naroozie rounded up children of all species to see if they could pair?" asked a confused Hengway.

The adults moved to the large oaken table and sat on chairs placed considerately around it. Once everyone was seated, the castle provided bowls of bunglebeast soup, which were keenly received by the attendees. Hengway joined them at the table and waited not so patiently for an answer from someone. *Anyone would do*, he thought, slowly focusing on each adult in the room.

"Exactly one hundred children were taken to the planet you were on. The presence of the legendary burning bushes of Waiface 3 leads us to suspect the planet is in the Waiface system. The bush rarely grows outside of Waiface. After your dramatic return, tribes and clans across all the systems dispatched parties to locate and rescue the other children."

The long speech from Cleavie's father went uninterrupted and was delivered with the steady tone of a seasoned politician or someone who had spent time in the military. In Kalle's case, it was from dealing with nefarious characters at nefarious inns and black markets. He was an entrepreneur in the trade of exports and imports–of what was never made clear, but the less you asked, the better. He had become an advocate for fair worker wages after the Second-Hand War upended countless economies, and was quite offended by tariffs and taxes that planets imposed on true patriots.

Hengway's father, Forthwright, scratched at the short, grey beard that framed his long, bony face. After a thoughtful silence, he spoke "With my wife missing and the abducted children being slowly returned home, we should adjourn for now and meet on Yurning 7 tomorrow. We may learn from the repatriated children which naroozie tribe was responsible. Children, could you see any identifying marks on the naroozie you encountered?"

"No, I did not, sir," Trinni replied. Her brothers nodded to signify that they too, saw nothing.

"My personal protection drone had insufficient power to record the event because I was using him as a distraction during the chase," Cleavie added.

"How did you approach the battle?" Kalle asked Cleavie.

"Alertly, calmly, and then ruthlessly. As did my trusty PSSA, of course."

"I would expect nothing else," her father proudly replied. Kalle had gifted her the PSSA after missing her birthday for a successful round of rocks at the local gambling den.

Hengway's father continued, "I shall call for a meeting of the system leadership council, to summon the heads of the five naroozie tribes. At least one of them is responsible and, until the truth is known and accepted by all systems, those tribes will be difficult to trust."

"I wholeheartedly concur, Forthwright!" responded Kalle. "Cleavie, Lyssa, let us travel home! It is a long trip."

"I can jump all of you if you would like?" Trinni suggested, knowing that dwarfs could not punt jump. Dwarfs did not like accepting jump favours from other travellers, especially humans, however on this occasion, and after such a strange day, Kalle agreed, so Trinni prepared to punt the three dwarfs to their home planet of Cellfast 5.

"See you at Trav-Coll," said Cleavie to Hengway, who stared at her not knowing what to do. "I already know you didn't recognise me from school. I'm a grade above you and study combat, mostly." Hengway fidgeted as he nodded goodbye.

To an outside observer, punt jumping looked straightforward enough. The person, or persons, involved in the punt ceased to be there, presumably entering a new existence elsewhere. The experience was somewhat different for the one jumping, who felt as though time and space itself had stolen from them a very brief moment. Microseconds before the jump the surrounding objects, people and the landscape flashed on and off like a lamplight in a strong breeze.

I hate this punt jumping thing, Cleavie lamented inwardly. She closed her eyes to avoid the nauseating flashes. Which she saw anyway.

They disappeared, leaving the castle to itself. The considerate castle said nothing and was quite proud of its achievements.

4. Histories and Conspiracies

Transcript of Video : Introduction to Travelling the Systems
Traveller College: Year of the Inverted Avocado
Presented by: Head Teacher: Professor Smeltzit

Start.

This is an introductory session on the systems. As the teachers' lounge has free cake in ten minutes, I will make this short. There are many systems, and within those systems, there are many planets. Ancient terminology called these groups of planets and a sun, 'solar systems' as they revolved around a single sun. Over the centuries many systems were found to have more than one sun, and the term solar system was reduced to 'system'.

Question from student: "My father travels to a system he says is part of the lower systems. What does this mean?"

"Please keep all questions until...well, the next lesson. Other teachers will leave not a scrap of that delicious cake for my good self. Quickly though; systems are placed in groups to attempt to identify proximity. For example, Earth is one of the original planets and was grouped in the lower systems. As other species and systems were discovered, they were grouped chronologically into middle and high systems. For instance the naroozie live in the Waiface system, one more recently found, which is grouped into the higher systems. I shall continue.

Planets do not exist in all systems. Some may or may not have life, and others may be populated with various creatures that have evolved to live amongst varying atmospheres.

Magical and technical means have made travel through these systems possible. Creatures that can travel through space without the use of interplanetary machines are known as travellers.

There will be a four-hour exam. You will need to read my award-winning textbook, *The Complete Thesis of Travelling the Systems*. The exam is next week. Thank You.

End.

The jump fleet of the Yurning system was small compared to other systems' fleets, though they were considered masters of the craft. Years ago, the Second-Hand War started when a Yurning fleet ship was caught carrying more than the allowable weight of cargo; five hundred metric tonnes plus twenty warriors per ship. This, of course, was a lot of cargo to pay taxes on, so the Yurning leaders decided that smuggling was the better option, even though it was forbidden by many inter-system treaties.

A ship had been stopped by a naroozie captain named Enfki, who searched the ship and found merchandise that he maintained had exceeded the treaty's weight restrictions. Captain Dwain Hartog of the Yurning vessel argued they were used goods and were not covered by the treaty. "What you have here is a vessel delivering second-hand goods. We are *not* in violation."

Captain Enfki was a naroozie not to be messed with; he quickly turned, lashing out his fifth leg, cutting off Captain Hartog's right hand.

"Now *you* need a second hand," Enfki quipped as he and his soldiers went about their usual business on a ship; fighting, yelling, screaming and general mischief.

The naroozie plundered all of Hartog's cargo and kidnapped forty ship hands. During the terrible battle, five Yurning sailors were killed, and one naroozie disappeared somewhere in the ship's inner quarters, being tucked away by the sailors for later questioning.

Dwain Hartog's hand could not be saved. When he made it back to Yurning's main port, the council summoned him to explain the whereabouts of his cargo. If he could not explain why he was not at fault, he and his crew would have to repay the council the value of the cargo, or be executed. Captain Hartog debriefed the council and was met with doubt from some of the senior members.

"You will have to explain this a lot better," directed a council member, "and also provide appropriate proof of how the naroozie allegedly wiped your on-ship security recorders."

"All of us in the Yurning system, I hope everyone agrees, have long been against anyone having total control. We have tried to purchase and free as many farmers and workers from unfair employment in as many systems as possible. The cargo we were smuggling consisted of supplies and insta-housing kits for the freed people. The naroozie took all the cargo, and only a few crew members remained alive," explained Captain Hartog in a thorough, military-like manner. "Fortunately, members of the crew took a naroozie captive."

"Bring him in!" The Captain shouted at the closed door. The two soldiers guarding the entrance glanced at the senior councillor for guidance, who nodded her assent.

The fortified door opened with a light hiss. In trudged four guards, an eclectic mix of species. Between them, a naroozie was restrained. The guards doing the restraining were dressed in various types of detailed armour and were very much the real deal. All guards pointed their personal choice of sharpened metal at the captive.

"Surely you don't need such silly, overplayed security measures for one prisoner?" posed a council member. The prisoner moaned in immense pain from being bruised and battered. He was also missing two legs from his starting number of five. Almost on cue, to be difficult, the prisoner jolted to the left, then violently swung back to the right with one of his remaining operable legs. A reptilian guard jabbed him with a steam-powered stun rod. He collapsed into the hands of his angry guards.

"The prisoner is quite a handful and has needed encouragement to stay on the right side of death. Furthermore, this *individual*," explained Captain Hartog, "was caught killing some of the crew, but was stopped by these brave people."

The Captain pointed at the guards, who then threw the prisoner to the floor before the Council. "You have one chance to stay alive for another day. Answer this: What was the purpose of your raid on my ship?"

The prisoner mumbled in his native tongue, promptly receiving another shock for his efforts.

"*One* more chance, Mr Three-Legs. Tell us *now*!" The prisoner's hairy shoulders slumped forward as he lifted his big, battered head. The Captain continued his interrogation.

The naroozie have long sloping heads with eyes that appear to a non-naroozie observer far too small, noses far too large, and overly-toothy mouths framed by leather-like lips with barbs pointing inward towards their throats. The prisoner's remaining teeth were now mostly broken, making his next words hard to say and harder to hear.

"Our orders were to make an example, embarrass Captain Hartog, and capture or kill as many workers and sailors as possible. We were also to search for an artefact called 'the light', something like that," the naroozie gasped through the sharp enamel and dribbling blood.

"Take him away and make sure he is *un*comfortable! We will deal with him later," said The Captain. Without any further noise from the door, the naroozie was dragged out the door into a most unpleasant future.

The council drew back in their seats. The Senior councillor contemplated Captain Hartog.

"What is it you would like us to do now?" she enquired.

The Captain reached into his jacket with his technologically enhanced replacement hand and retrieved a package wrapped in expensive cloth bound by a thick leather strap. He opened the package carefully, and approached the council. Slowly and methodically, he placed his severed hand on the table.

"We must end this hiding and swiftly liberate workers and families from unfair conditions. The era of suffering caused by the naroozie, and others, will cease today. The attempt to control and dominate working planets must cease. This hand represents an injustice that will be redeemed. Justice and safety will drive us into a new era of freedom."

The council could not help but stare at his lifeless hand. As Hartog spoke, many were waiting for it to move, explode, or do something horrifically morbid. The Captain would have loved to have made it dance, but he was from long generations of military stock. Humour had almost always defeated him. Metal was his main game.

"This hand represents courage and the right to freedom. Not one more hand will be removed from anyone in the Yurning or the Cellfast system. Let not the naroozie cut a *second* hand from the warriors of freedom!"

Hence, here began the Second-Hand War, with the memory of a horrific event and a bizarre call to arms, or perhaps hands, for all to heed.

Naroi knew the story of the Second-Hand War better than most and was sick of hearing about it day in, day out. Captain Enfki was Naroi's father and a hero of the naroozie. This was indicated by the plastic stripe he wore on his dress tunic, showing the battles and wars in which he had fought. They also denoted that he was a secondary naroozie leader who had performed repeated acts of bravery.

"The five Gods be honoured. Begin the meeting!" The formal method of starting a command meeting was given by the head of the naroozie council, usually a member of the Heidzi tribe. In naroozie culture, the Heidzi represented the right front leg, the leading leg and usually the most agile. Being naturally suspicious, since ancient times they believed the number five held spiritual merit. Each leg had its own name and god association. The most revered, of course, was the powerful fifth leg.

They used the number five in a nefarious way to organise fighting teams. Given that five is an odd number, it prevented the formation of equal factions within the group, thereby ensuring that each member could monitor and report on every other member. Self-regulation and power plays were supposed to keep everyone in the group honest.

"Do I really need to attend Traveller College?" asked Naroi in the Room of Command on Waiface 5, the main planet of the Waiface system.

Will I get out of this ridiculous request? thought Naroi as he gazed around the sparse room. The table was made of stone, the chairs made of marble, and each leading naroozie wore garments that differed according to his or her status and tribe.

"There are five reasons you will do this, Naroi," explained leader Akash of the Conzu tribe. The Conzu represented the fifth leg, found on the naroozie's back, which they believed gave them superior stability and cunning.

"First, the Council gave you a command. Never question this council again!" An uncharacteristic pause, one intended to make Naroi nervous, worked.

"Second, you will learn at Traveller College. You are ignorant. The council needs you to be wiser and more cunning. Third, we have many missions for you to undertake at this school, and you will seek what information the council needs from the students and staff as the council deems necessary."

"Fourth, the Council gave you a command." Another pause.

"Fifth, and most importantly, you will honour the five gods by being obedient and by being victorious."

A speech from Akash was always weighty and contained no mirth or tricks with words.

Enfki added, "When you are properly trained and have finished your education at Trav-Coll, you will be assigned to a team of five and placed in service to our great naroozie culture."

Oh! The great naroozie culture? Naroi knew this meant if he stuffed up this strange assignment, he would be allocated to a bunglebeast farm out in the lower systems, picking up droppings and milking the beasts in the early hours.

Bunglebeasts can be milked only in the mornings. There are many suns in the lower systems, making mornings alarmingly haphazard, and long shifts common. Work allocations are lifetime-bonded, and Naroi desired to follow his father and grandfather into a ship fighter regiment, the equivalent of an interstellar navy and the prestige that comes with it. Thus, Bunglebeast milk was out of the question.

Naroi had brothers and sisters much older than he; however, all those that had not been killed were missing in action. MIA sometimes meant that not even the smallest body part could be found after, say, a horrendous explosion or a not-so-nice interaction with an enemy. Naroi was imagining a time when considerate architecture was transferred to inconsiderate weapons. "Answer me! Are you listening?" Enfki's booming voice broke Naroi out of his wayward train of thought. Naroi was known to deftly 'become one within', which meant he daydreamed–a lot.

"I am at your disposal, faithful council." This was something he would always say whenever he was caught 'becoming one within'.

"Yes, you are. Pack and get ready for a system transport!" Naroi's neutral mood gave way to despair, which slowly sank to a mixture of regret and reluctance. The system flights were rough on the ship but rougher on organic occupants.

"Don't mope like that! If we do this right, you will be able to punt jump as they do in the Yurning system. Go now, study hard, learn everything, and report your progress every fifth day!" Enfki ended the instruction, then stood rigid. The rest of the council stood after him and bowed to one another. Following ancient protocol, they bowed at Enfki last. They turned and shuffled off to a door behind them, leaving Naroi standing alone in the room.

Off I go to Trav-Coll, his brain sang as it sorted through all the issues he would encounter. It became a list too long to maintain.

Hengway, Trinni, and Jay stayed in the castle for the next few days. Many people came and went, persistently asking them, and all the other 'paired' who were abducted that day, the same three questions in a variety of different ways: Where were you before you got kidnapped? Could you identify the tribe that those naroozie are from? How did you escape? Where are your injuries?

Many sources called the event 'the Paired One Hundred'. Identifying specific marks was crucial, and the exploding bushes and defiant scrub led them to a planet with signs of a massive battle. Despite hours of patrolling, no bodies or signs of inhabitants were found. The fact that it was a naroozie planet rarely got a mention.

Once the adults believed they had everything under control, they got to planning and tried to keep everyone busy and distracted.

Hengway's parents, Tuja and Forthwright, were usually the binding element of the daily routine. They made life a little boring but also made it safe. With Tuja missing, the castle took on the day-to-day routine. Trinni helped when possible, including talking to the castle to encourage it as much as she could, whilst Jay and Hengway were virtually useless.

Weeks flew by. Each family member dealt with what they had to. A few more weeks had passed when Forthwright said to his daughter over dinner, "Thanks for helping out more than usual, Trinni."

"Thank you, Father. I am worried about the boys, though. Jay has gone quiet, and Hengway has some major exams at Trav-Coll coming up. I fear that this will be a distraction." In moments like these Trinni would have liked to have spoken to her father about ancestors, long-punts and the mysterious light she was tasked to follow. *Not just yet,* she thought. *I need to know more before I can truly trust anyone in these bizarre times.*

Hengway was in the corridor outside the large kitchen. He had made his way there from his bedroom after he could smell the aroma of food cooking and wanted to sneak in a quick meal by himself. He needed time and, of course, food, whilst he tried to work out how to pass these ridiculous tests. Since their short respite after the Paired One Hundred, he had attended school and tried to maintain a relatively normal existence. He still had many questions and believed he might find a little more information from eavesdropping on his sister and their father.

Trinni was doing her best not to appear to be reciting a rehearsed speech to her father. "I have heard that the search continues for

Mother and the missing others. My sect has discovered that certain tribes of the naroozie, mainly the very annoying Heidzi tribe, are searching for an artefact they believe can create pairs. It is rumoured to be as rare as critical thinking from a naroozie council, and possessing it may result in enormous magical, technical, and fighting abilities. The belief is that one of these traits will be enhanced more than the others."

What a load of bunglebeast nasal hairs, Hengway thought. *Surely they cannot think we believe such an outrageous story.*

"I understand that you have been a big part of the search. Thank you, Trinni," stated Forthwright, who habitually settled into his quiet thoughts. Once composed, he continued, "Most of the systems are scared of provoking the naroozie, especially the Heidzi and Conzu tribes. I wish we could launch a rescue mission of our own, however the council has forbidden it until negotiations have been completed with all five of those tribes."

"We should stop this silly charade and launch an attack immediately," the voice of Jay filled the kitchen. Hengway was not the only eager eavesdropper. "They have shown their colours by kidnapping people across the systems. Gods only know what they really wanted to do with us," Jay added.

Hengway could hear a chair being pulled across the stone floor, and maybe a clink of a saucepan being placed on a solid bench. A short time passed before he heard the noise of an angry, shaky slurp from a cup of something that smelt awful.

"Hengway was of no use, as usual. Lucky that dwarf, Cleavie, swung by and jolted a bit of action into him." Jay stated for the hundredth time. Forthwright stared at him with a frown, worried for both his sons—the face of a father who wanted his kids just to get on without all the fuss.

"He is quite useless, Dad. He is a bit too fat, and really, not particularly liked him at Trav-Coll. Everyone asks me why he is so odd," Jay stated plainly.

Trinni sat next to Jay and got his attention by slapping her hands together as if she were about to cast a spell. Trinni and Forthwright laughed as Jay, after a short bewilderment, was propelled a few inches into the air.

"We are all good. Sometimes we can be bad. Sometimes we have greater skill than others, and sometimes we have less. Learning to work with inner positivity and to harness positivity in others is the enchanter way. You could glean much from our books," explained Trinni, gazing at Jay with a tender smile that only someone of Trinni's learning and natural behaviour could muster.

"All jokes aside, the rumours of the Party One Hundred don't help Hengway's cause," asserted Jay.

'Paired One Hundred' was an incorrect name because no actual pairings had been made. 'Party One Hundred' is what the youngsters across the systems called the day of the kidnappings, accusing those involved of having a perfectly arranged riot.

"Come in from the shadows, Hengway! I have something to tell you all," exclaimed Forthwright, who was aware his son was listening and wanted him to be involved in the conversation.

"It's about time you joined the family," scoffed Jay. The older brother glared at Hengway who approached the table, selected a seat at the end, and made use of it. The table was unexpectedly and considerately packed with their favourite food and drink. In the far corner, a strange brown substance with crusty green edges bubbled softly to itself. The Acae family was gathered around the table, with the notable absence of the mother. Despite most of the family being physically present, they were distinctly separated in their thoughts and approaches to the current situation. Trinni lowered her head to recite an incantation, though it was possibly more of a prayer.

Hengway and his father stayed still and reverent. Interfering in Trinni's sect and their discussions with the Gods was futile and disrespectful. They wondered if Trinni was trying to find her missing mother, or why all of this had happened in the first place. The real reason for this spell was to recharge the castle and keep its considerate magic up to date; the castle also liked a magical pat every now and again.

"Your mother was carrying an object that probably caused this whole mess. Only a handful of people know of her main mission to take it to a safe place, possibly on the same planet where the Paired One Hundred were sent," explained Forthwright.

"We believe the object is an artefact called the Chaos Light which, in the wrong hands, could create Pairs who could be extremely powerful," he continued.

Hengway digested this news while keeping an eye on the bubbling substance in the corner that smelled strangely delicious. "Still sounds a bit over the top. Is magic evolving at such a pace that this artefact can do all those things?"

The Chaos Light? Follow the light? Trinni was most intrigued. "On one hand, I hope you are more than correct. On the other hand, if this artefact fell into good hands, rather than hands desiring to conduct dirty deeds, it could still make extremely powerful pairings."

Forthwright gazed at his children grimly and picked at the plate of meat beside him. "Either way," he concluded, "we need your mother and...," he looked at Hengway, sensing his light cynicism, "we need that object back in our hands very soon, otherwise things will get worse." He looked to where his wife usually sat. "We may lose your mother." The room turned quiet as they all contemplated what had just been discussed.

I could lose my wife, Forthwright reflected in sorrow as he finished his meal. He eventually left the table and lumbered towards his room high in the castle.

Hengway was convinced his father did not believe his mother would be misplaced then found some time later. After the meeting ended with some less-than-helpful comments from Jay, and a long, thoughtful glance from Trinni, Hengway heard Trinni mind-speak to him, "Come to my room!"

The secrecy amused Hengway. He probably should have been mildly alarmed, at the very least, but he knew Trinni had a fondness for drama, so he played along.

Trinni's room, which others called the dungeon, was in the part of the castle rather cleverly known as The Dungeon Section. It was damp and cramped, consisting of several levels where any invader trying to break out, or in, would be considerately led back to their cell, occasionally called 'a hard cell' by witty interrogators, to meet an unpleasant end, or a very interesting start.

The magically considerate design allowed known, liked persons to have well-lit, clean and well-heated rooms if they so desired. It was also interestingly considerate that Trinni now had a larger-than-normal room with the same facilities of a huge, over-equipped kitchen on a luxurious steam cruiser.

Before Hengway could knock on the door, it opened, embarrassingly leaving his fist in the air as he stepped into the world of his genius younger sister. She wore enchanter overalls made of sturdy yet lightweight fabric from the middle systems, tough enough to withstand the strongest blast or poisonous mishap.

"Is it true that the fabric has considerate magic in it like this castle?" asked Hengway, scrutinising the new section of multi-coloured bottles and jars containing Trinni's anonymous things. Some entities within the vessels were visibly interacting and audibly blooping. The jars were displayed on what he presumed to be a new bookcase made of a silver substance that did not shine like pure silver. Instead, it absorbed light, though occasionally a dismal hue would arrogantly escape across the surface.

Ignoring his question, Trinni declared, "I need information about considerate magic for my brother." She reached into a front pocket, which Hengway was sure had not been there a second ago, and handed him a scroll.

"Oh, wonders will never cease! A paper on the properties of considerate magical items, and a complete equipment list," she murmured with a hint of humour.

"So, the answer is yes, then? When are you going to make me a considerate brain? This one is broken."

"There is nothing wrong with your brain or your attitude. Confidence can be built by facing the unknown..."

"And being kicked in the bum two seconds later." Hengway finished Trinni's speech with a smile.

"The castle can, if he likes the individual, be somewhat considerate in times of need. You may think yourself fortunate sometimes, but as a castle familiar, the castle may help if the need arises."

"Well, that does answer a few questions about how lucky we have all been lately," Hengway mused.

Trinni gazed at her brother. Others called him fat, stupid, short and without skill. Most of the Acae family had given up on him, especially their brother Jay. "It could just be luck and not the castle. Either way, we need to be patient with what is happening. The council is incompetent and may not want to start another war with the naroozie or the other unruly sects. My sect has discovered alarmingly strange things that occurred on the so-called Paired One-Hundred day."

Trinni paused as she watched her brother poking at one of the jars. *Always inquisitive but never asking questions*, she thought with a smile. "For a starter, the day was poorly named. Of all the hundred different younglings who were taken, only a very small percentage were knowingly paired after the ambush."

"Most were under sixteen years of age, though. About my age, right?"

"They were. That was one thing I thought you would find interesting. Almost none of them had shown signs of magical or technical ability. They, including you, have displayed no real sign of improvement in magic, technology or military tactics so far." Trinni studied Hengway's face, hoping for a reaction. Her sect considered that some of those present did pair that day. Being smarter than most, or very scared of repercussions, they were likely keeping it to themselves.

"Nice trick talking to me in my head."

"What do you mean?"

"When you asked me to come to your room," Hengway explained, with a slight tremor in his voice. Trinni appeared to be learning this for the first time.

"I presumed you did that to me?" Trinni thought he was hiding skills from her.

"Nope, you did it to me," insisted Hengway, shrugging off the strange interaction with a poke at an interesting, reddish-purple jar on the bookshelf.

"Hengway, things are about to get serious. The sect knows where our mother is." Hengway swung towards Trinni. Now she had his full attention.

"More to the point, we know that she was with a group transporting the Chaos Light who were punt jumped to the same planet we were sent that day."

Hengway nervously scratched his chin and silently stared at the floor as Trinni continued, "Designated parties from several systems are searching for the lost team, but especially the Chaos Light. It is suspected that it has not been discovered as yet, otherwise unnatural pairings would have started to show."

Unnatural pairings were created by using the Chaos Light to enforce a togetherness with amplified abilities. This magic was dark, and legend had it that although it could create strong positive pairings, it could also create extremely strong negative pairings.

"Father and Jay have already been informed. Father is waiting for the council to develop a plan of action, and Jay is just as brooding and angry as ever."

An alarm triggered quietly, creating a soft shield over the two of them. A calm voice declared, "Two visitors."

This place is becoming more mysterious than usual, thought Hengway. Trinni placed her hand on a knob right as it appeared on the table, then the room brightened. The door to her room opened, and Forthwright and Jay entered. Judging by the swagger on Jay, he had assumed they were barging in unannounced, and smiled smugly at the intrusion.

Forthwright walked over to a chair, sat down, and scanned the room. "Trinni, I hope your sect pays for all of this equipment. There are some truly rare ingredients and samples here."

"Father, I assure you; everything is on loan at no charge, or legally obtained," explained Trinni as she straightened her tunic. Even Hengway did not believe any of it, but who would dare argue with Trinni? Hengway thought he briefly saw a slight smile on Forthwright's full, fat and cracked lips, but the expression changed too quickly to be sure.

"We all need cool heads. Your mother is missing. We may know where she is. We cannot, and I say this with regret, we cannot get involved. Jay, you will keep attending Trav-Coll as planned. Hengway, you have exams and the skill assessment coming up, and Trinni—well, I don't know what you do; but keep doing it, and be safe!"

"Please keep out of the way of the investigation. When everything goes as planned, things will work out for the best!"

Forthwright finished dramatically, examining his children from oldest to youngest. Jay nodded in a surprisingly upbeat manner. Hengway took the cue and nodded when his father's gaze settled on him.

Trinni mumbled a few words. Petals, leaves, feathers and butterflies appeared, floating around the room. They swirled in the middle of the room, forming a love heart roughly two hands high, which hovered in front of Forthwright.

Hengway thought it was awesome and applauded. Forthwright closed his eyes in quiet personal thought. Hengway turned towards Jay, who had been standing nearby, and was not astonished to see that he had already left the room.

Professor Smeltzit could have just said, 'Go and retrieve the Chaos Light', Trinni thought, amused and miffed at the same time.

5. The Captain's Arrival

From the outside, the lone building on Yurning 4 appeared to be a glass object with no tangible form or distinguishing features. Trav-Coll was one of the finest colleges in all the systems. Aside from the college, the entirety of the planet was an open training ground for the many skills and abilities the college needed to develop in its students.

Trav-Coll held about five thousand students, though you would never know because their movement around campus was considerately timely and well ordered. It was universally known that herding students into their allotted lecture theatre was as difficult as milking a male bunglebeast.

Fortunately, the college's powerful, considerate magic aimed to maintain the safety of the students, and expeditiously prodded unruly pupils in the general direction of their next lesson. The building moved students and teachers around with precision, so no difficulties with crowds or blocked walkways ever occurred. Students never bumped into each other and were rarely late.

Hengway knew he was going to be a failure. The skill games were scheduled for six weeks' time, and he had not won a duel in all the years he had been at Trav-Coll. Since Waiface 3, he had seen Cleavie occasionally in the hallways or the refectory, but he had not found the opportunity, or courage, to talk with her.

Cleavie was now on the duelling mats in front of the vast audience of students called in for a lecture on duelling etiquette.

Hengway felt a brief pang for her because if he were selected for a training bout, he would feel a great dread that would leave him shaking in his socks. It was to be a duel in front of a huge group of people, and against a naroozie, the new student called Naroi, who was older and probably better trained. Hengway was surprised by the inclusion of a naroozie at Trav-Coll. They had not been taught at the college since the start of the Second Hand War, when the last naroozie students were expelled.

"This is going to be a massacre," chortled Chorlie, Hengway's only friend. Chorlie was a human from a solar system within the lower systems, with only one sun and eight planets. Chorlie was in a support class with Hengway and attended Trav-Coll only through a scholarship awarded to senior families, whether from political, military or artistic cultures.

Chorlie's parents were senior political figures in their far-off system. Transporting people from the lower systems without the aid of punt jump magic was inordinately expensive. Because of this cost, Chorlie and his two siblings never left Trav-Coll during the term, returning to their planet only during college vacations.

"I heard this new naroozie is pretty good. I can't see it being a fair fight," agreed Hengway as the umpires took their positions around the middle of the arena. The duel would use personal weapons, and it would be a fight to the death.

The activity was a warm-up to the skills test all students had to take at this time of the year. Hengway was glad his name had not been drawn for this 'friendly' duel. Each duellist could choose any weapon he or she liked, though each clan, sect or tribe had a favourite.

Cleavie appeared smaller than usual, her thick hair tied tightly under her helmet. She wore a hardened leather breastplate made from a sacred beast reared specially for dwarven armour, and she tightly clutched a two-handed axe.

She appeared uncomfortable, or so Hengway thought. He felt she might be frightened but was trying to conceal her rational fears for tactical advantage. Well, he at least knew that he was frightened, but given he was safely seated, she was probably a tad more concerned.

A silence settled over the hall as Naroi entered the arena. He walked on his regular four furry feet, with his hairless fifth foot held up behind a metallic shoulder piece designed both to protect the fifth leg and to make the duel fair for others.

The naroozies' feet could grip weapons just like his opponent's opposable thumbs, but the feet with their hardened knuckles could also be clenched to form a strong hoof in order to sprint on all fours. Naroi stood on his rear legs, the fifth secured in the shoulder harness, and grabbed two spears from the weapons rack.

A spear's reach was far superior to that of any axe. He held a long spear in each foreleg hand. Each of the expertly crafted weapons had an extended, flat blade sharpened on each side. Naroi performed a fast spin with both spears in his front hooves-hands, making the entire crowd gasp a collective "Ahh!" followed by hushed whispers and coy smiles from some admirers in the crowd.

"Your dwarf girlfriend will have to move like a bunglebeast on quick juice," commented Chorlie. Hengway flinched but tried to hide it. Chorlie knew that Hengway was having problems talking to Cleavie after the Paired One Hundred, but he always took pleasure in teasing his friend as much as he could get away with.

The contestants took their positions at either end of the arena mat, which flickered on and off as though it were an excitable living entity, filling the room with even more tension and excitement. One of the three umpires raised her hand, allowing a line of light to escape her palm high into the roofless arena.

Naroi moved quickly, as naroozie did, but Cleavie's well-trained reflexes allowed her to dodge the clumsy first charge with ease.

Naroi's spear missed her by a large margin, so she allowed herself a quick smile before acting with her instincts and training; she lashed out with her axe, turning quickly to bring it back to her body, protecting herself from a responsive defensive strike. Cleavie's attack proved as clumsy as Naroi's, and both ended up rolling out of each other's way. Gasps and laughter could be heard from the stands.

"This is going to go on forever if they keep dancing about like that," complained Chorlie as the fighters circled each other seeking an opportunity for the best chance to strike.

"You get in there and do better!" suggested Hengway as he poked his friend in the shoulder. The crowd roared. Hengway turned his attention back to the arena where Cleavie was lying on the ground, thrown down or struck by a spear. Cleavie instinctively rolled backwards, losing her helmet in the roll. She bounced to her feet and searched for an advantage. Naroi was grinning, *cockier than he should be*, Hengway thought. Since this was a fighting duel, magic or other technical abilities could not be used.

"I could really use PSSA about now," Hengway said. Chorlie shot his friend a bemused look, then kept his eyes locked on the action.

I could really use PSSA about now, Cleavie thought to herself at the same moment. Through the fear of defeat she was trying to remember the theory concerning weakness and effect. She could hear her old fighting teachers: find the weakness, hit hard and hit often, hit where the fragility exists.

Well, that's great, she thought. This naroozie was twice her weight and probably twice her height. What could she do to—*wait, I think I've got it*. Cleavie rolled to the left, giving her extra time to formulate a plan.

Before she could implement anything, Naroi threw a spear at her face. It narrowly missed Cleavie and the umpire standing behind her. Pointing at Naroi, the umpire sent a bolt of blue light into the sky, signifying that he had received one penalty point. Three penalty points lost the match. This interruption provided Cleavie a welcome opportunity to get her plan moving.

"Is it true you naroozie have to live with your parents until your fiftieth name day?" It was the best jibe she had. Naroi scowled angrily, the reaction she wanted. He attacked wildly and left himself open on his right. She rushed forward, ducked, and swung at Naroi's unprotected rib cage.

Naroi had known that Cleavie would try some mind games to distract him. He did not expect that it would come as such a feeble, silly remark—one which amused him more than it angered him. He used his powerful legs to jump over Cleavie, landing on his rear legs, and guided the spear from his right hoof right through her back, the armour not slowing down the attack. The strike was ruthless, without anger or malice. Cleavie's body slid down the spear and lay forlorn in the arena.

"Well, that must suck!" exclaimed Chorlie in his usual sarcastic tone and manner. The hushed crowd stayed in their seats, waiting for the conclusion of the match. Lessons would always be learnt from duels to the death, and the umpires and teachers meticulously detailed each tactical decision for learning points.

Naroi moved back to the starting position in the centre of the arena. The umpires took their time with their discussions before slowly walking over to him. Naroi and the arena mat flickered twice, and Hengway could hardly discern what he was seeing before Naroi and Cleavie vanished.

The umpires and crowd waited patiently. If you were new to arena death matches, you might not have noticed the absence of blood, frenzy, the lack of screams in pain, or that it was all a projected image.

"I still don't see you volunteering for this nonsense. You will have no way to avoid conflict during the skills test. I bet you won't be so confident then," Hengway whispered to Chorlie. The crowd remained silent as a loud thud came from a small opening at the side of the arena. Heads turned as an elevated walkway appeared, leading from a tall doorway to the centre of the arena mat.

"Aw, biff off!" grunted Chorlie with a droll smile, unable to hide a subtle hint of disrespect.

The crowd applauded as the door opened. Naroi and Cleavie stepped onto the walkway with Naroi, being the winner, entering the arena first. His fifth leg was now free, which he used to wave to the crowd as he walked on all fours. Both duellists had just exited the training module, and still wore the cables and attachments needed for the arena projection system.

Cleavie was not scowling, nor was she dragging either of her hands through her beard. *No visible signs of distress*, Hengway thought.

"She put up a good fight. Naroozie are hard to beat without magic and a few punt jumps for tactical positioning," responded Chorlie. "She should be happy. It could have been a lot worse."

"Yeah, it could have been real, like when I first met her," Hengway murmured, remembering the morning he first saw her running through the low, sharp scrub from the naroozie assassins.

"I bet you both would have welcomed a Yurning training mat that morning," joked Chorlie. The Yurning planets had some time ago discovered a combination of considerate architecture and lower-system technology to create an impressively realistic training environment for duelling. Other training environments were used, but the Yurning training mats were the closest you could get to real combat without actually being injured.

The umpires and a senior teacher approached the two students, clapping loudly and enthusiastically, encouraging spectators to do the same. As instructed, the arena applauded with gusto when, without warning, an umpire raised her hands to stop the clapping.

"Typical of teachers," commented Hengway, "one tells you to do one thing, and another one tells you to do the opposite."

"Right as the other left," responded Chorlie. Hengway stared at him and sighed. Sometimes, Chorlie tried a little too hard and said some really strange things. Hengway continued to stare at a grinning Chorlie. The sound of someone clearing their throat brought Hengway's focus back to the teacher in the middle of the arena.

"We have seen a quick yet educational duel here today. Naroi, our newest student, has brought techniques to our arena that we are not familiar with. Cleavie has shown us she has improved using our style and techniques."

The senior teacher, wearing a gown with the college crest on the left side, paused before adding, "Several students heading into the forthcoming skills test will receive special, advanced instruction. The first of these students will be Naroi and Cleavie, as well as someone already studying in the support class, Hengway Acae." Hengway felt his cheeks blush and braced himself for an unwanted excursion to humility central.

The other umpire stepped up to conclude the ceremony. "Our glorious council has given us an instructor of great renown and supreme knowledge of the three skills. The man who started and finished the Second-Hand War, Captain Hartog!"

The students' faces were like unwritten scrolls. A few nods of recognition were given, especially from the older students who had already studied war history and a separate subject called 'Contemporary Criminals.'

"The Captain?"

More voices reverberated across the arena.

"The *Captain*?"

"Oooh, *The* Captain!"

Finally, the wave of recognition hit all of the students. The news of this new instructor was exciting and welcoming. Students were to meet the notorious saviour of many worlds, and a warrior who fought against repressive and irrelevant government rules.

The Captain appeared on the stage. He was no longer a bunglebeast, for which he was grateful. He then realised he had not showered, shaved or sha–that is to say, he had not been in a clean environment for five weeks. On the other hand, he pondered, *one does like to play the part of a legendary hero.*

"Hengway, come down to the arena mat!" commanded the senior teacher.

All eyes burned on Hengway, his greatest dread. Then he could hear the comments: "Tubby on stage," "He doesn't deserve the effort," "No-good-Acae, they call him," "Come on, short arse."

After walking through the bullying rabble, he ended up next to the two duellists. Cleavie didn't even nod his way. Naroi was glowering at him in a manner he did not understand. Was it hate, or was he just tired? Naroozie are typically stolidly quiet just before they rip your head off, so their expressions were complex to read.

Words were uttered, deeds promised, and more clapping followed. Hengway was mentally at a loss for what to do, so he did what all experienced students do: nothing, until someone told him to do something. He heard voices blurring together until one voice cut through time itself. He peered up at The Captain. The Captain spoke some words that were lost to Hengway. Then came more clapping, and the students stood up and filed out of the arena with much noise and excited conversation.

Hengway saw the legend before him–the person who some believed was a terrible criminal. On the other hand, most knew that he was a generous and kind man who understood inequality and did his best to fix it. He was human, surely. His shirt was loose and torn, holding weeks' worth of grime, smells and encrusted mud in splotches up here and down there.

Hair stuck up or out from every place. His clothing had many holes, revealing a lot of red hair. His pants were of a rugged leather design with a missing piece on his right knee, which, amazingly, had a tuft of red hair poking from it. *Knee hair? Red knee hair? Eww,* thought Hengway.

The Captain gazed at the three students with a big grin shining through his crusty, red hair-ridden face.

"Jealous 'bout the hair, hey?" he sputtered, with the resonance of a bleating bunglebeast. "Sorry, just getting da hang of da humin tongue," he sang out quickly in a high multi-toned pitch. "I was a bunglebeast for a while. Can anyone of you mind time? Try for the last fifty-seven minutes."

The Captain indicated that he wanted all of them to clasp hands, so they obliged and formed a circle.

No one can mind-sit in this group, Hengway thought. He was incorrect in his presumption. Without notice, the mind time of The Captain's last hour began.

Mind-sitting was much like a dream. The participants saw everything through the eyes of the individual whose memory was being tapped. Some mind-time executants could perform these events so powerfully that you could feel their pain and emotions emanating from the deepest pits of their soul. Sometimes, you could talk to the person being tapped, and even engage in events as they happened. Of course, you could not change events that had already occurred. A capable mind-sitter could investigate and walk around a memory, finding information they had not realised could be extracted.

Hengway had never been involved in a mind-time event. He was apprehensive, but decided to watch this one through and knew not to try anything fancy.

It began.

"Wake up, you smelly creature!" A complimentary kick to the ribs prompted this rude awakening. The Captain was not accustomed to such disdain and disrespect. The prison guard, who had failed to bathe for quite some time, did not care about The Captain's discomfort and kicked him again.

"Actually, on further consideration," The Captain confided to his surprised students, "I am definitely used to being treated like this. Concentrate a bit more, and you should be able to hear my thoughts at the time of the event without my interrupting." The students were delighted to be part of something like this. It involved complex magic, and their hero. Refocusing their attention, the students continued to watch The Captain's recent past.

A prison was a prison. This one had a few additions to the stereotypical prison, but it featured the basics. They built it with the expected impenetrable walls, tall fences and food and light deprivation measures to keep people inside. It even had the mandatory cold floor, seeping walls, metal bars on the windows, and magic field blocking the doorway.

This door was not the usual shock or laser beam captivity door. It was a special evil — humorous evil if you were not the intended victim. If you touched this doorway field, you were transformed into a bunglebeast for a few hours. The Captain knew this because he had tried to run through the field yesterday, or was it the day before?

Time was hard to tell when the only illumination came from a dim wall light on the other side of his cell, which never flickered or gave any indication of whether it was night or day.

He spent hours as a bunglebeast before he got bored, deciding he would seek another way to escape. Bunglebeasts had awful teeth, pus and blood leaking from their gums. This poor dental hygiene left a bad taste in your mouth when you eventually changed back into your normal form.

Normal form? Ha! The Captain had rarely seen his standard form since he had become a man of independent means. Independent means, in this case, meant smuggling food and insta-housing kits, which were desperately needed in the poorer systems. Unreasonable restrictions such as law and order, taxes and safety regulations ensured he was in disguise for the majority of his waking hours.

Naroozie liked to ensure that systems and their planets were reliant on them for protection and continued trade. The downside of this was that they were usually protecting systems from other naroozie tribes. It was a circle of lies and deceit that only made systems poorer and chosen tribes richer.

The Captain's form changed from human to dwarf to naroozie as often as possible. This was to avoid unnecessary dealings with the law and to trade amongst the systems with anonymity whilst gathering information of great importance.

The unique concoction he used for the transformation into other species was expensive and used rare ingredients. Luckily, he knew where to steal–or more rarely, actually purchase–the very best products.

"Wake up, I say!" Three guards stood staring into his cell, not standing within it, which meant they were not there for his daily beating.

The Captain slowly untangled himself. He was in his original human form, which was a relief; hair matted and unwashed, wearing a jacket made of considerate armour and pants designed to hide many things. Unfortunately, all his weapons and technical gadgets had been taken from him upon internment. He could not recall whether it was four or five weeks ago.

A technically enhanced hand was the only piece of technology they let him keep. He regretted the time when a few months back, when he was on Cellfast 5, he had not installed the optional escape kit.

"Getss a movess on!" yelled a guard. The guard was an impfish, an amphibious race from a very high system that had evolved from both fish and reptiles. Impfish had long, thick tails and walked on two hind legs; they were slow of movement and massive of strength, which gave The Captain an idea for a little trick. The other two guards were human, a male and a female. The female guard was standing under the only light in the hallway, ready to engage the door-containment field.

The Captain was shoved into the hallway by the impfish. He glanced at the guard under the light and timed his next move. As she raised her hand, he stopped suddenly and pushed back into the impfish, who was now standing in the middle of the doorframe. The field was activated.

"Oh, bifffff—" cried the impfish as it mutated into a bunglebeast. The Captain and the two guards stood watching the newly created bunglebeast trapped on the other side of the containment field. The male guard laughed. A laugh that started at his feet and exited his mouth through clenched teeth and quivering lips. The Captain nearly laughed too, but kept as quiet as he could. He thought another stint as a bunglebeast would not be in his best interests right now.

"You'd better leave it there. That's the third time you have turned it into a bunglebeast this month."

The guard tried inadequately to stifle his laughter as his female colleague snarled, "We must get him to the council!" She grabbed The Captain roughly and shoved him down the dark, damp hallway. "This day is going to get worse for you, troublemaker."

Screams emanated from other cells. *This is going to be a bit rough,* he thought, as he passed caged prisoners of different species, cowering, standing, or semi-conscious, waiting for their next violent interaction with the guards or stint as a bunglebeast.

The guards brought him to a room that The Captain recognised as an old technology-driven punt jump room. A huge orange gem was glowing from within a transparent box in the room's centre. *These coveted large gems could contain millions of punt jump spells, not to mention what they'd get on the black market*, thought The Captain.

He recalled his training concerning the gems. According to standard procedure, this advanced magical technology was operated by designating the destination of the punt jump, specifying the number of travellers followed by engaging the adjacent steam-powered lever to activate the punt spell. Once everything was prepared, an electric charge was generated and directed toward the gem.

The Captain waited for the split-second backwards sensation. The feeling came, then went, and he found himself on a platform in the middle of a large, green-tinted dome. The guards had not travelled with him.

At first he thought he was alone and wondered where the nearest tavern was. Much to his dismay he found himself not in a tavern. He squinted and saw the Yurning council, as well as naroozie from all five tribes with an impfish dressed in a royal gown. They did not seem impressed.

"How's it going, folks?" The Captain yelled at the assembled politicians and leaders from most of the known systems, and even some humans from the free systems.

"Gentle species, may I have your attention?" Forthwright's voice moved across the room, demanding awareness.

Once he had the silent regard of the assembly, he began, "As you may be aware, Captain Hartog has been smuggling technologies and housing kits to systems in need. He has done this at the Yurning council's request."

Those present did not react to this news, so The Captain reasoned that they had indeed already known. The situation was hairy, and not in a good way. *How the biff do I get out of this one?*

"Captain Hartog, although you started the Second-Hand War, of which we are most grateful, the naroozie requested you perform one last task on our behalf, to formally complete your mission," said Forthwright in a voice that exceeded formality. The naroozie from the Fanich and Donpha tribes chuckled and were somewhat pleased with themselves. The Captain and Forthwright had worked together in the war and he had even conducted many smuggling missions on Forthwright's behalf.

"Don't I get a say in this? Is this even a fair trial?" The Captain spoke to Forthwright directly.

"Captain, you have done a great service to all. My system owes you more than one debt of gratitude. Your colourful ways of avoiding the more aggressive units of pirates and corrupt military have also put you in the favour of most of the representatives here," explained Forthwright.

"I accept some things went wrong. How was I to know that impfish couldn't eat weeds from the Yurning system or drink the gum-buster concoction of Upia Red? I certainly didn't know the combination could make them pregnant. It's a live-and-learn kind of thing, saving planets from starvation. Just trying my best."

"I would like to believe you," Kalle said to The Captain, offering a broad smile. His appearance was marked by a distinctive single eyebrow, deep black eye sockets, and reddish-brown eyes that resembled pools of dried blood. His beard, extending to half his height, intricately knotted and twisted, served as a testament to his experiences, reflecting the vast adventures, travels, and battles he had experienced.

The beards of Cellfast dwarfs were highly sacred. Touching them without consent meant death or, at the very least, a terrible slap. The

Captain could see the braid signifying the Second Hand War and its battles which helped secure imperilled systems. Now, of course, this business about missing children and military personnel was making the systems unsafe, once again.

"Are you going to sentence me to a diplomatic post in the impfish system, or perhaps as a waiter serving gum-buster drinks in a last-chants saloon?" Laughter failed to be forthcoming. A good joke was lost on this lot. A bad one was less well received, often with punishment.

"Evens worsse," growled an impfish wearing military garb. The Captain peered at the impfish and realised it might have been one of the impfish he got pregnant. He knew he was in trouble now.

"We shall make you a teacher."

The horror of such a punishment! Children scared The Captain more than one hundred Fanich naroozie on the war hunt for captain flesh. The children were too fit and far too inquisitive.

"You will be given your orders once you arrive," instructed Forthwright, smiling and laughing and squinting with delight.

The Council is enjoying this too much, he thought. Two guards, who considerately appeared before him, grabbed him gruffly. He was dragged back to the punt room, all the while clapping and laughter continued behind him. "Off to Trav-Coll with you, impfish daddy," chuckled one guard. A backward moment, a seeming pause caused by the punt jump, destination; Traveller College on Yurning 5.

The three students and their new teacher stopped the mind time and stared at each other in amazement on the arena mat.

"Wicked," gasped Naroi as he pranced like a young child off the mat. The Captain grinned at them and walked away towards the staff room and its cache of complimentary biscuits.

Cleavie and Hengway gawped at each other in bewilderment, shrugged their shoulders, and slumped down, overcome by fatigue.

"Mind-sitting is quite an effort, in my honest opinion," declared Hengway.

"To be sure it is great fun though," Cleavie replied, closing her eyelids for a wee moment.

6. A Paired Connection

"This is all the fault of the humans, yet we got stuck with cleaning up your good intentions. This type of geo-political nonsense always ends poorly," yelled Cleavie.

Hengway held up his hands in a defensive, if not apologetic, manner. "What are you going on about?" he asked. "How does this connect with the fight against Naroi?"

"Well, it doesn't. The Captain is part of my problem. You know dwarfs were planet-takers of the past, and if we had our way, we would own the systems."

"All of them? Of course, you would," Hengway mocked.

"Yes, *all* of them," she hissed. After loosening her clenched fists, she continued, "That man made planet-taking a bad memory, causing a conflict between the three 'red' tribes of the naroozie and nearly all of the dwarf planets."

An uncomfortable silence passed between them before Cleavie dramatically rose to her feet. Taking a deep breath, she continued in a slower and calmer voice, "My father blames you bunch for forcing peace and for compelling almost every species in all systems to obtain this silly Chaos Light thing. I'm troubled about the skills tests, and it won't work out well if–if things don't—" Cleavie sat down, still exhausted, nearly sitting on her axe.

Hengway noticed for the first time that her beard was not braided nearly as much as that of other dwarfs her age. Her cheeks were puffed, and he could see her long nose and dry, thin lips through the flowing, thick red hair obscuring the rest of her face. When she sat, her armour crumpled neatly beneath her.

"Is that considerate armour?" he asked, trying to diffuse the anger. *The anger*, he thought, which was redirected incorrectly at him. He had not started or ended silly system wars.

"The armour doesn't matter. I have heard that your sister, the wicked witch of Acae Castle, and her cult know where the lost ship and the crew might be." It was more of an accusation than a question.

"The wicked, what of where?" The Acae family was unaware that Trinni's enchanter sect was less popular than they imagined.

"You know why they are called enchanters, right?" Cleavie was shaking, unable to mask her growing anger.

"Not really. It's a fancy name for someone who can use all three skills in an exceptional way. Or so I remember from skills history class." Hengway sat next to his dwarf friend and began to feel he might be way out of his depth in this conversation. And swiftly discovered that he was.

"Certain aspects of history are kept from people by the ruling class to ensure a happy working class. You will discover, Hengway, that your council has not told you everything about your historical wars. And if that be the case, what aren't your leaders telling you now?"

"That could be the same for your council as well."

"Oh, definitely. Don't you find it odd that all of our sets of parents are high in each of our councils, and yet both of us are falling deep into whatever game is being played?"

"Well, I have thought about it," he lied, then tried to avoid the topic, "So, back to why they call them enchanters—"

Cleavie snapped out of her rant-fuelled diatribe of wrath and calmly explained, "The enchanters–those who transgress or create trouble. Hundreds of years ago, no inter-system travel existed. Species stayed within their systems. The Enchanters learnt to punt jump, to control minds, and to create technical gadgets and spacecraft that upended all of that."

"That's right." Hengway's brain kicked in, and he remembered fragments of what he had always considered boring ancient history.

"It's not boring, and it's certainly not ancient history. The masses might love the enchanters, but they are kept close by the political classes and spied on by the military."

"I never said that!"

"Yes, you did. Or you put it in my head." *This boy is a lot more unusual than I thought.*

"Oh, is that right? How did you read my mind? Just how *usual* would you like me to be?"

This is getting strange; they both thought, and heard, at the same time.

Cleavie clicked on to a train of thought, instantly forgetting her passionate fury. "Your mother and some dwarfs from my planet were on the same mission when they went missing. We will need to explore our new magic what-nots in depth. Especially mind talking. Maybe we can do some really great magic trickery."

"A very good idea," Hengway replied. He took a pencil out of his coat and began to stare at it. It moved ever so slightly at first. After minutes of intense concentration, he had it standing and moving. *Jay's forks had better look out!*

Cleavie was trying to punt jump, but Hengway's thought made her laugh. The technique alluded her for now. "Practice makes perfect," Hengway mind-spoke to her.

"Apparently," Cleavie replied in a sarcastic tone.

The arena was empty. They sat alone in the middle of the considerate fighting ring practicing various pushes and spells. Light shone down on all sides, making the whole combat zone easy to see from the stands.

A side door crashed open. Naroi leapt through the doorway and rolled down the first few steps. "You'll pay for that," he sputtered with a thin, mean smile on his mean, thick lips.

"Give it a go then!" came a new voice that Hengway recognised, as did Cleavie. Jay burst through the door dressed in training armour with a training sword in each hand.

"Oh." stated Cleavie, raising her eyebrows. "They became friends quickly."

Hengway nodded and responded, "Trust Jay to make friends with the tribes of death."

"Let's move!" suggested Cleavie to an absent Hengway who was already rolling to the other side of the arena. The lights hit the main training floor as the outer lights dimmed. This was an excellent cue for Cleavie and a confused Hengway to continue into the safety of darkness amongst the seats.

There were no more voices in each others' heads, so they used military field signals to silently indicate they would stay and listen. Cleavie rummaged in her pockets and threw a small object into the air. It turned sharply, raced towards the ceiling, and came to a dramatic stop three human lengths above the arena mat before turning invisible.

Cleavie was controlling PSSA through small, delicate movements of her fingers taught to her by dwarven artificers after the mishaps on the day of the One Hundred.

PSSA began recording and checking for any other technologies or magical fields that could be causing the telepathic events between Cleavie and Hengway. He told Cleavie he had seventeen minutes left of charge, also that she had to be home before dinner or her axe would be confiscated for good this time.

Jay and Naroi leapt onto the main fighting mat without using the training system. Jay tossed a sword to Naroi, and they moved around each other, seeking an opening to launch their attack. They were sparring for real with no safety equipment or considerate safety magic at all. One wrong move could be fatal.

Hengway noticed they were both good–very good. Neither used magic or technology. This contest consisted of pure skill and form as they thrust and jutted their way into each other's space, practising fatal blows with ease. They fought hard, occasionally complimenting each other on good moves and rallies.

"You are going to have fun with my brother and his girlfriend training for the skills test," muttered a tired and sweaty Jay.

"I will teach them a thing or two, don't you worry," Naroi said with a wink.

"Ha! The Acae family has been trying to teach Hengway simple things for years. You and some one-handed freak from the war won't be able to get his brain to function any better than we have," Jay said, swinging a sword at Naroi's neck.

Naroi took this moment to roll onto his fifth leg to quickly sweep at Jay's leading foot, heaving him into the air. He flew like a sack of bunglebeast droppings and hit the mat hard. The move was performed quickly and expertly. Executed with intent by a larger, older naroozie, this move could knock four or five smaller fighters out of a conflict.

"Don't lose concentration, *ever*!" Naroi offered a hand-like hoof to a stunned Jay, who was aware of his error. Accepting the hoof-like hand, he stood up and patted Naroi on the shoulder. Naroi's fifth leg whipped around and slapped him on the back. Jay shot Naroi a nervous grin.

"Good work, hey?" Naroi asked. He wrapped his fifth leg behind him to hide it, and to keep it out of the way.

The pair hiding amongst the stands exchanged worried glances. Hengway could not believe Jay would be friends with a naroozie. Most of the conflicts of the last one hundred years had been with at least two of the naroozie tribes.

Hengway watched on in disbelief as Jay and Naroi continued to congratulate each other. Naroi was playfully wrestling with Jay on four legs. *They seem mind-numbingly close,* Hengway thought. Cleavie continued her plan, disregarding Hengway's obvious distress from witnessing the murderous naroozie that chased Cleavie on Waiface 3 play with his brother.

Cleavie hailed PSSA, who reappeared above the arena and quietly floated towards her.

Hengway glanced at Cleavie with the sly grin of someone about to commit mischief. He examined PSSA and quietly assessed the skills this little 'I-Life had to offer: floating and invisibility. He grinned and narrowed his eyes.

"What terrible idea have you devised?" Cleavie asked with more questions ready as soon as the answer was given to her.

Let's find out what Trinni is up to!

"Let's go find out what our local enchanter sect is doing!" Hengway said. "Does that flying thingy use old or magic energy?"

Cleavie did not answer as she accidentally punt jumped into her changing room, surprising herself somewhat.

Hengway and Cleavie, now his partner in discovery, planned to spy on Trinni to discover what she knew about the Paired One Hundred and the disappearances of family members.

It was a long burdensome journey of mental gymnastics to develop their plan. No amount of failure could impede their determination to become magically stronger. Persistence and luck helped them in their endeavours. After many, many long and arduous trials, their skills improved. The scheme was now ready to unfold.

Hengway had been somewhat critical of the artefact's power but now wanted, and more appropriately needed, to understand the impact to magical evolution, why they were forced into classes by an unkempt smuggler, and what these new magic skills meant. He chose to keep his questions to himself until he figured things out.

At this stage he had no idea of the extent of his new powers. Yesternight, he could not get to sleep and wished he were by the lake down in the valley far from the castle. He felt that now-familiar backward sensation and punted next to his favourite thinking and swimming place. He sat there for a while in his thin night clothes and wished he were back in the warmth of his room. Nothing happened. "Just great!" he said to the chilled night air.

This nothing kept happening for quite some time, and it was getting colder.

He considered his options. Walk back to the castle? The walk was long and uphill, a journey he rarely enjoyed making, though the lake's views and solitude were at times worth the pain.

Who would believe him about random acts of magic?

He had to walk back. At least it would warm him up.

For the two hours it took to get home, he pondered on all he knew about the enchanters. The sect began as a group of troublemakers and dissenters. They were supposed to stop the poor treatment of those with technical and magical abilities by others who did not understand these skills.

Magical skills comprised mind reading, mind control, and object manipulation. Training began with moving small objects, like Jay did with forks, and could progress to advanced abilities such as mind control, mind sitting, or mind swapping.

Technical skills, though powerful enough to be recognised as a necessary category, were the oldest and least regarded. They were used to build machines or artificial intelligences to perform mundane or dangerous jobs. Enhancing technical objects with magical solutions provided beneficial innovations, such as punt jumping and considerate architecture.

Enchanters possessed almost all of these skills. They had the added ability to mix them in different combinations, creating captivating results. Their sects evolved from totally unwanted and misunderstood enchanters to completely wanted, yet still misunderstood enchanters. Over time, their behaviour and knowledge were shared with all the systems, giving the Enchanters political power among system councils and legitimacy with all involved.

PSSA was a fine example of a combination of magic and technology. He was a very high-grade artificial intelligence trapped in a two-hundred-year-old drone, which by itself was barely adequate to calculate food bills, let alone house such a remarkable intelligence. That was what PSSA thought, anyway, as he and his inadequate body appeared in Trinni's dungeon.

"I hope PSSA is invisible in there. I have asked him to record and send feedback to this view screen," said Cleavie apprehensively.

The equipment was ancient and it had taken them all afternoon to install and calibrate. They had told their parents they were studying at Acae Castle. Nobody else was around, so they locked themselves in Hengway's room and started the mission. A strong table had considerately appeared after Hengway's long trip the evening before, and as soon as he saw Cleavie's heavy old technology, he understood why.

The substantive table looked just as ancient and was as high as Cleavie's hip, so Hengway had to squat on a short stool to comfortably view the collection of silver boxes with their varying stages of rust and damage. They were stacked on either side of a big screen made of an unusual combination of wood and glass.

Hengway fiddled with the knobs and sliders surrounded by coloured flashing lights until he was slapped on the wrist by Cleavie and told to biff off. Hengway had heard of these cumbersome technical and non-magical machines, but assumed they were extinct. Cleavie asserted that this technology was used in 'many other less rich or politically aware' systems.

"And it works without needing magic, which suits the two of us just fine," she scolded as the screen buzzed to life, showing an angled view of the dungeon room. Or rooms. The screen had not stood the test of time, so details were difficult to see. On hearing Cleavie disparage his magical abilities, he tried a floating push on her that he had been practising in private.

She turned around to talk to him and noticed he was no longer there. "Up here," he said, blushing from his mistake.

Her laughter rocked the almost unmovable table. She concentrated, created a gravity push, and he fell to the floor with a magnificent thud.

After dusting himself off, he waited for the laughter to stop before looking at the screen. Trinni's old room had grown into a massive workspace with hidden crevices and larger areas branching from all sides. Some of the spaces may have considerately grown all by themselves, but Hengway couldn't shake the feeling that Trinni had something to do with it. *This castle gets stranger by the day*, thought Hengway.

"Can you move the drone thingy into one of those side rooms and see if it can find Trinni?" asked Hengway.

"My name is PSSA, and I am quite alive, dear," replied the drone. His voice could be heard from a set of wooden boxes covered in a kind of knitted mesh, through which PSSA sounded distant and tinny. The drone could display a certain arrogance, especially for an artificial intelligence.

"Is that you, Pisser?" Hengway said.

"Hengway, stop it. I will use thermal imagery and determine whether I can spot her." PSSA replied curtly, whilst moving towards the right side of the main room. A small map appeared in the upper right corner of the screen, and on it were blotches of blue and green, which meant little to Hengway.

"We are seeking heat from living creatures. It will show up in thermal imagery depicted with the colour red. Pale red to dark red, depending on how hot the creature is." After fiddling with more knobs and producing steam from within the machine, Cleavie said, "It looks like this dungeon has been there for centuries."

This statement was a fair inference, but it was false. "I was there yesterday. It felt uncanny and had lots of colourful potions and beasts, but it definitely wasn't that big," Hengway explained.

"Perhaps considerate architecture did its job?" suggested Cleavie.

"Considerate architecture alone is not equipped for such a rapid expansion, especially with all the new technology in here," answered PSSA. The thermo-image screen presented a hint of red. It was a Trinni-shaped blob. PSSA moved towards it using a technical stealth field, which was helped along by a little bit of recently acquired magic from Cleavie.

Hengway recognised a voice.

"My family is getting restless. I was assured that no harm would come to any of them." Trinni was always a straight and confident talker, except this time a little twang of nervousness crept through her words.

"Your mother was caught in an unfortunate situation," came another voice, emanating from an unknown origin. Cleavie leant over Hengway, nearly pushing his head into a sharp bit of a silver console in an effort to detect any magical happenings. Frowning, Cleavie toggled a switch and twiddled a different knob. "A conference is evidently occurring, probably using magic," Cleavie said in a hushed voice as the small thermal-imaging screen displayed green blobs around the room where Trinni stood.

"They are using a magical conferencing system, projecting themselves into the room. Only people tuned into that magical frequency would see the other figures," said Cleavie as she stepped away from the table. "This should pick up magic-fluence. The voices must be projected through these portals," she surmised.

Trinni's confident voice came back into force, "I cannot demand the safety of my mother. I know this. I knew the risks before we started the search. What should we do next?"

"Patience and commitment to our sect. Two important personal measures to which we all must adhere," another unknown voice originated from an older sounding individual. Once again, Cleavie barged past Hengway to twiddle with knobs that made no sense to him.

"Seriously, a bit of courtesy."

Ignoring his whining, she turned a knob and the box fizzled and farted as they tended to do. Hengway clenched his lips, not daring to comment on the sounds the boxes were making.

On the main view of Trinni's room, several shapes began to take form. Slowly they transitioned into images of enchanters. Seven of them, each in a similar style of robe, with representatives from almost all systems in the strange gathering.

The room fell quiet as the enchanters contemplated their options. "We must find the missing ship with the Acae woman and the crew she had with her," said a new commanding voice. Neither Hengway nor his pushy companion could tell which of the shapes was talking.

"Perhaps they are mind-speaking," proposed Hengway, staring intently at the screen, where the conversation had now slowed.

"We know where the ship is, and we know where the Chaos Light can be found. It is on—" The green orbs on the screen fluttered and flickered. "Wait, don't say anything else. This meeting has been compromised. Trinni, your security is weak. You should have prepared for this. We must meet at our alternative location!"

The coloured orbs disappeared, the screen went blank, and PSSA reappeared in Hengway's room without warning. For a moment Cleavie was stunned. Then, coming to her customary senses, she darted to the rear of her pile of silver and wood boxes and started ripping out the mess of wires.

"Help would be nice about now," she grumbled. Hengway jumped from his stool and ran towards the door to await the almost assured arrival of his sister. *We are way out of our depth*, thought Hengway as he struggled to think of what he might say to Trinni.

"Which way to the room?" came a screech from someone whom Hengway recognised as one of the speakers from Trinni's dungeon. He assumed that one or more of them had punt jumped into the castle after the incursion was discovered.

"I agree with you," said Cleavie out of nowhere. The mind-speaking was getting unsettling and needed to be resolved, probably a bit later, though. Trinni and her sect needed sorting first.

Cleavie mind-spoke, "Okay, *okay*! Let's just face this." She came to the door and stood close to Hengway and, as though they were thinking in unison, they wished they were both invisible.

The door disappeared. There was no crash, tingling, or sparkles. It was simply no longer there, instead replaced by a solid stone wall.

Three white figures of different heights and widths stood at the threshold. Trinni extended her right hand, palm facing to the cobblestone floor, and raised her right foot off the ground whilst slowly rotating her foot counter clockwise, ever ready to react to whatever they had sensed behind the now non-existent door. Trinni's stance may have given a casual observer the impression of a comically executed yoga pose, but it was the signature move of a well-trained enchanter.

Trinni, along with her angry sect members, could now look through the new wall that was once a door.

Before them was an empty room.

With only a few weeks left before the mid-term examinations, Hengway and Cleavie joined The Captain for pressure training. The Acae family had a long history of not only passing these tests, but also being best in class for at least one of the skills: magic, technology, or fighting tactics. Naroi underwent his advanced training separately, so they rarely saw him—which was just fine with Hengway.

Hengway had no doubt he was going to be a floor sweeper for the rest of his life. He was constantly bested by the most basic fighting combination and could not successfully cast a pot-boiling spell, let alone force an opponent out of the way. *Although things may be getting better*, he thought.

Hengway and Cleavie were walking through the Trav-Coll halls towards the training mats when Naroi and Jay crashed through a door in a playful and needlessly bullying mood.

Two impfish who were talking to each other near the door instantly became the centre of undesired attention from Jay and his new best friend. Naroi pushed the smaller of the two into the wall. Not wanting to miss out on the day's bullying, Jay slapped the other one over the back of his scaly head, causing the victim to fall forwards.

"You two should watch where you are going," Naroi snarled. He turned around and came face to face with Hengway. "Have you come to learn to be a real fighter?" he sneered.

"We need to get out of this without getting killed," Hengway mind-spoke to Cleavie. Their new skill worked intermittently, and they had not entirely worked out how to get it to consistently behave.

"Jay, your dumb brother is a jerk. Let's fight anyway!"

Before Hengway could send back a response, Cleavie hunched down and ran straight at Naroi. She hit him with her shoulder and stretched her short arms around his broad chest. Her intention was to pin his fifth leg behind his back. She failed. Her arms were too short for his bulky chest, so she grabbed prominent tufts of his back fur.

"Not the biffing back fur," Naroi cried. He was startled and could not use the entire power of his fifth leg. He stumbled backwards onto Jay. Cleavie let go and the two startled bullies fell backwards, hitting the ground hard on top of each other.

Hengway flinched at the gristly sound as he waited for his brother's reaction. Jay reached for his weapon as Hengway raised his hand and wished that they should be still whilst he figured things out.

The two bullies froze. They remained stuck in time, still and breathless. Cleavie turned around to see that Hengway had somehow conjured a time-stop spell. She regrouped with Hengway in front of the motionless bullies. Nearby students had been attracted to the fight and were milling around the scene.

"What lovely work you have done here," boomed the voice of The Captain. "You wouldn't happen to know how to reverse this spell, would you, Mr Acae?"

Hengway knew that feeling well; when a teacher or coach asked him a specific question that he did not know the answer to. "I don't even know how I did that, Captain," admitted a bewildered, though highly amused Hengway.

"Don't tell him anything!" Cleavie mind-spoke.

"I don't have a lot to tell," he replied.

"Are you two mind-speaking? Wait, don't answer that! Go and get ready for our training session. Remember to practice magic more. I will fix this lot, have at it!" The Captain commanded. He spoke into his Trav-Coll communications device, which burped steam after he released the button. An enchanter promptly appeared, dressed in what looked to be regularly issued armour; however, this one unusually featured a badge marked 'Trav-Coll Magic Unit'. The enchanter raised both hands, reanimating the bullies. Animated, but not happy.

"What happened?"

"Where are they?"

"I will kill them," they spoke in unison.

The Captain's eyes narrowed before he said, "Let's just say you deserved what you got! As a lesson, you will both write a five-hundred-word essay on how to avoid combat spells." The punishment suppressed their complaints, and they slouched off to a place that was far away from The Captain.

When he reached the training mats, Cleavie, Hengway, and the other Support Training students were lined up, ready to start the session.

"You two slackers appear to be doing your best sack-of-rotten-potatoes impersonation. Get off ya enhanced buttocks and go to the object room to practise some old-fashioned fighting—forks, sticks, shoes and anything else you can get your minds around," barked The Captain, pointing at Hengway and Cleavie.

Hengway broke into an embarrassed mope towards the object room. Cleavie sighed through her beard as she followed him with a drag and shuffle across the training mat. They had tried this age-old teenager technique of sulking many times over the last few weeks, but each time, the ploy failed.

Now well behind them, The Captain was still yelling orders in the distance as they entered the object room after the long walk down the depressing, bleak corridor. They were shocked to see The Captain already in the room, standing at the back nowhere near the only door. The object room was used to practise moving objects in a close-to-real combat simulation.

"Think quickly, ya bludgers!" The Captain spoke rapidly before throwing two large chairs at the pair of daunted students. Cleavie disappeared.

"I'll get him from behind. You keep him busy upfront!" Cleavie mind-spoke to Hengway. Time expanded, his body and mind slowed. The chairs were coming directly at him. The Captain had by then launched four wooden boxes, leaving six large objects soaring at Hengway.

Hengway was calm, astonishingly so. He knew what to do, once again, astonishingly. This situation, as confusing as it seemed, was under control, a feeling new to Hengway.

The Captain noticed Cleavie's absence and in response, also vanished, only for Cleavie to appear a few steps behind where he had been.

"Move, Hengway!" Cleavie's voice was swift and sharp, and, like him, she felt more astonishingly confident.

Hengway bade the six objects to stop and change into sweet patties. Patties typically came in fruit or vegetable flavour, and were delicious. Six perfect patties dropped to the ground, and Hengway disappeared. His visual perception turned monochromatic. He could see the outline of two figures moving to where he was, one tall and one short. This was mind-moving at its best. He had heard that some executants could do things like this, but had always thought it was a myth. Cleavie turned her head towards him, and he indicated they should turn around and move to where The Captain was expected to appear.

"This experience is eerie and funnily fun," he mind-spoke to Cleavie.

"Slow down and wait for him to appear! Then we'll cleave him," Cleavie replied with a wry smile.

The Captain's outline changed from shades of grey into solid colours, and appeared where Hengway had been standing moments earlier.

"Nnnaaaggghhh," The Captain moaned as the two would-be warriors appeared and ran straight into him, knocking him backwards towards the door.

A short time-loss occurred as Hengway punt jumped all three of them. They landed on soft grass near a lake by the side of Acae Castle where all three fighters crashed to a stop.

"Ho boy, that was greatly enhanced, brother and sister. Greatly enhanced indeed!"

Cleavie was on her stomach with one arm pinned under her torso and a rather confused snail in her mouth. Her head was at a very uncomfortable angle, her eyes pointed almost at the sky. She untangled herself, gently spat out the snail, and checked for personal and, more importantly, equipment damage.

"Greatly enhanced?" questioned Cleavie. The lake was placid, with a gentle breeze creating subtle ripples upon the light blue surface. The only sound from the forest was a soft susurrus as the leaves fluttered in the light breeze that flowed through the treetops, making the place calm and peaceful.

The Captain lifted a sleeve and showed a video tattoo of a replica hand being built on an injured arm. Tatt-vids were popular for soldiers during the Second-Hand War but lost favour when people realised that they were not reversible, leaving them stuck with tattoos that looped every ten seconds or so. The last few seconds of his tatt-vid featured a slogan, 'Greatly Enhanced.'

"I can't say that's very catchy," commented Hengway, who was enjoying the soft, green grass by the water.

The Captain frowned at the remark and, instead of lecturing them on how awesome and 'greatly enhanced' he actually was, he turned to matters at hand, "Now, have you any idea what's going on?"

"No," they both replied, anxiously glancing at each other.

"Well, you two are in for a biffer of a time!"

The afternoon was a haze of teachers and adults seated in front of Hengway in a small room at Trav-Coll. The room was about fifteen feet square, had no windows, and smelled like mouldy wood and wet naroozie fur. Hengway thought he would probably be in a lot of trouble if a naroozie heard his assessment; however, it was widely known that a wet naroozie usually smelled like overripe oranges, five-year-old farm boots and library dust in sour milk.

"That's not very nice." Cleavie's voice was clearer than it would have been had she said it aloud.

"You can't argue with me, though. They always need a wash after the rain." The two were still mind-speaking, which Hengway accepted as he was glad for the company. They had not caught a glimpse of The Captain since Cleavie punt jumped them all back to the college.

"Wait—The Captain has just arrived," mind-spoke Cleavie from whatever room she was within.

Before Hengway had a chance to respond, his father walked into the room; Hengway feared he was going to be reprimanded and made to clean the castle's toilets for the rest of his life.

"Well, this is interesting," said Hengway's father "Grab your stuff and come with me! We are heading back to Acae Castle to have a chat with Cleavie's clan." Forthwright was wearing the usual Chosen armour and red cape that came down only as far as the belt on the back of his trousers. His sword hung loosely at his right side since he was left-handed, and his bunglebeast-hide boots were well worn and tattered, though still functional.

They walked out of the sparse room into the hallway and sauntered into the next room. The Captain and Cleavie were laughing at a private joke as they entered.

"Well, then, you two. Stop mucking about and jump us to the castle before we die of boredom in this wretched college," said The Captain as he leapt from a seated position onto the table whilst Cleavie remained happily perched on a chair.

"What is this about...," Hengway started to say as they appeared in the Acae kitchen. The castle had considerately constructed a large room next to the main dining room. A suitably sized table stood in the centre, well-lit with candles and some light sticks that ran on older technology from a lower-system.

Fresh food covered the table. Fruits which were yellow, orange, and something that could possibly pass as purple in a certain light. All types of roasted flesh, some prepared as small chunks on skewers, ready to nibble on, some large joints, and even whole creatures steaming and ready to be carved. Hengway was starving and found himself in front of the familiar named meats whilst standing far from the colourful but unknown fruits.

Hengway started contentedly feeding himself when he noticed an accusatory silence. With a stick of meat in one hand and a fresh bun in the other, he gazed around to see the other people in the room glaring fixedly at him.

"I believe you should have waited to eat; everyone is staring at you, including me," Cleavie channelled.

Hengway stepped back from the table and found comfort by the cold stone wall behind him. His father was there with two dwarfs and an older enchanter dressed with an orange belt over her traditional armour, indicating that the wearer was a senior sect member.

Once Hengway was at a respectful distance, everyone moved to a seat. As this was Forthwright's castle, he sat first, with the others following his lead, sitting quietly in huge wooden chairs that Hengway had never before seen. He surmised that the considerate castle probably ensured that he and his siblings never got the chance to ruin the carefully crafted legs and backrests by keeping the chairs well hidden.

Hengway noticed an empty chair directly in front of him. He waited for others to move, but impulsively grabbed the chair with both hands, one on each ear of the stiles. He dragged the chair towards him, unintentionally making a scraping noise; the particularly irritating screech made by well-polished wood on hard stone cobbles, attracting further glowers despite so desperately wanting to avoid attention.

"You are becoming quite the popular boy," Cleavie mind-spoke with a suitably smug look.

The god-believers spoke their prayers, while the stomachs of the godless waited patiently. The dwarfs never understood any of the religions; however, each dwarf, including Cleavie, would grasp his or her braided beard and whisper low, mysterious words. These utterances were particular to each dwarf, phrases based on unique experiences and ancestry.

The human inhabitants had long ago discarded the gods. There was talk that humans came from one planet deep in the lower systems, and when they began to travel, they became free of their gods and relied only on technology for resilience.

The disparate group dined in a formal but expeditious manner. After they had completed their meal, Forthwright neatly placed his cutlery on emptied dishes, pushing them to the centre of the table. After he loudly clapped his hands, he declared, "It would be considerate if all the crockery and cutlery were removed from the table, then cleaned and placed in the appropriate cupboards."

The tableware dutifully shifted a second back in time and disappeared. The table was soon cleared, and a slight clatter of cleaning, sorting, and the closing of cabinets could be heard from a nearby scullery.

Hengway sensed a punt blast and found himself in the same room, on the same chair, but at a different table. This table was smaller and featured a two dimensional representation of the middle systems and all the planets within. He had seen this before, but he had always been told to leave the room because he was too young.

The table was made of a stone-like material with a black glassy top. Depending on the size of the sitters, it could seat up to five on each of the long sides and three on each short side.

"There has always been much tension between certain groups of naroozie and most dwarfish clans..." Forthwright paused. "...and other species." He turned toward his son and stated, "Hengway and Cleavie have been through a lot since the Paired One Hundred and probably have a lot of questions."

"Your father is the master of the blatantly obvious. Was he trained?" Cleavie quietly quipped.

"Shh," responded Hengway through their intermental connection.

Forthwright continued, "Cleavie's parents and I have spoken at length regarding the possible impact of the pairing. Since Cleavie and Hengway are now evidently growing some advanced magical skills, we thought they should be a part of the solution, not part of the problem."

On hearing this, Hengway's face flushed red. He listened carefully for any mention of his mother. His father proceeded as though his wife's absence was a given that needed no more discussion. Forthwright believed there were matters of greater import to be discussed. The councils of each system were either keeping things secret or did not actually know anything new and relevant.

"Hey Forthwright, you did promise me some ginger beer with somewhat of a mean spirited kick," spoke The Captain for the first time. He was seated at the other end of the table, facing Forthwright, and taking up the whole of his side with his unique way of sitting. His right leg splayed across the expanse, occasionally aquiver and shaking in a fierce display. Such was the dodgy leg-violence, the seat next to him remained vacant. His left leg behaved just as rowdily, but it lacked the uncontrolled shaking that the other would flaunt.

The Captain leant forward, grinning through grey, gold, and purple teeth. It was not easy to get dental work where he had been for the last few years, so he had persuaded a piratical companion to fabricate some dentures for him from a purple rock they found in a dark cave while running from the Death Pirates of Cellfast 3.

He had engaged a blacksmith to nail them in, and there they were, perfectly good purple teeth amid gold and decaying dentition. His mouth was a party of colours that was either funny or frightening, depending on his mood and the immediate situation.

A mysterious enchanter broke the silence. "It is quite clear that Cleavie and Hengway are paired. We see no connection to the boy's missing mother and other missing dwarfs." The only two people who were astonished by this statement were Cleavie and Hengway.

The Captain smiled his multi-coloured grin. The parents remained quiet and inactive.

The tinkering going on inside Hengway's head would have made an almighty racket if it were made of metal. He started to piece events together. Paired, they had a heightened level of skill, when they were close to each other, they were far more powerful than when they were alone.

Hengway thought about the first time they met; he had moved and fought better. Lately, they could render themselves and objects around them invisible, and they could also punt jump at random times, usually when it was to help them make a timely exit.

"Makes sense when you think about it," Hengway mind-spoke to Cleavie.

"I thought something momentous was happening. I didn't want to put you in danger," responded Cleavie, who remained as motionless as the adults around the table.

The Captain stood up and made a dramatic gesture with his artificial hand, causing the table to project a new scene. The images of several younglings from various systems scrolled across the screen.

"These are the paired youngsters we have identified so far. They have shown unforeseen talent."

"When can we meet them?" asked Cleavie.

"These are disturbing and complex times, Cleavie. Being paired is a great, complicated gift. As wonderful as that is, it is a curse and a burden interwoven with immense personal responsibility," explained Cleavie's mother. Hengway noticed Lyssa had many different braid patterns in her beard, indicating a colourful and experienced past.

"Most of the paired ones have been captured. There are systems, clans, or almost any group with an instinct for power that would pay handsomely to have the paired under their control. Some of these groups would even have pairs killed so they could not be used for criminal means," said Cleavie's father with a grim countenance. "In fact I wouldn't mind a bunch of them myself. Would make my business dealing a bit more positive," Kalle said, triumphantly leaning back in his chair.

"Stop it, now!' Lyssa interjected with a sharp glance that not only spelt trouble, it smacked you with a wet fish that had 'trouble' written on it—in your own blood.

"Why haven't we been bothered by those bunches?" asked Hengway.

"Good question. Your existence is known only to us," the enchanter said in a low, song-like, harmonious tone. "We originally assumed it was your brother and that naroozie boy who were paired, though it would seem they are simply talented in their own way, and have matching temperaments."

She glanced at the others, then continued, "Your talents are as yet unknown. The Captain will lead you through simple martial training, and other teachers will give you the more magical and technically aligned skills."

"Lyssa and I will coach you in technology and lower-system skills," said Kalle. Cleavie was not sure how to feel about her parents being involved in whatever this was. What she did know was she and Hengway needed to talk privately, and very soon.

"The skills test is in eighteen days, after the school break. Perhaps Hengway could come and visit the lower systems to learn a bit more about intelligent technology and the customs of planets therein?" suggested Kalle.

The adults agreed with a nod, sealing the fate of Cleavie and Hengway for future endeavors. Hengway heard voices and noises jostling inside his head. The most loud and sincere voice he heard was Cleavie's.

"This is all greatly enhanced, as The Captain would say. At some stage, though, we need to go and fetch the missing dwarfs and your mother."

7. Spies and Lies

The Yurning system revolved on a four-hundred-day cycle where the two seasons of 'hot' and 'not as hot' passed each other without acknowledgement. The seven planets with two suns were mostly habitable, though the closer the planet was to the suns, the less predictable the seasons became. Yurning 7 hosted the Capital building, the library and the enchanters' dungeons. The enchanters were experiencing problems for the first time in years. They were forming opinions amongst themselves as to where the blame lay–or, more importantly, for the bureaucrats among them, on whom to lay said blame.

Enchanter sects were broken into odd numbers, so there was always someone to create a balance of opinion. The concept of arranging sects into odd numbers was 'borrowed' from the naroozie. In the enchanters' case, they had no great spiritual or social attachment to their sects. Through their studies, enchanters mainly supervised magic lore and endeavoured to ensure the advancement of all.

Enchanter society began with a sect of three, creating the first building block of their culture. The three sect members were part of an outer sect of three groups, making nine members. Those nine were part of a grand sect combining another eight outer sects.

Trinni considered it all a bit silly. She would joke: "Why do enchanters have six legs? Because they are in-sects." Such a jest was dull, and perhaps unoriginal, but her two brothers thought sect humour was hilarious.

"When can we have your brother killed, Trinni?"

"Any time *we* can also openly slaughter *your* siblings, o trusted friend," Trinni chastised Nosu, a fellow One of Three. 'One of Three' was the name for the smallest sect. They usually did all of the mundane work, but once they were of a high enough grade, they could work on almost any project they desired. Until then, they were only called to do sect duties when their particular skills were needed.

"You two need to get on a bit better, Trinni. The events at your castle have placed us in a dark position with the other sects," said Garis, the informal leader of these three apprentice enchanters. Garis was taller, somewhat older, and came from a relatively unknown culture from the lower systems. She was human, some would say from the oldest branch of that tree. Garis used antiquated technology, but used it exceedingly well. There were only a few multifaceted enchanters from her system, and Garis was a leader amongst them.

"The event at the castle two weeks ago has gone unexplained. When Nosu and I investigated Hengway's bedroom, we found no indication of any wrongdoing."

"I was hoping to find that fat, stupid oaf there with his ridiculous girlfriend so we could deal with whatever they are doing to hinder us reaching our objective," barked Nosu, refusing to break eye contact

"Whom is she calling an oaf?" asked Hengway.

"Shush, keep listening!" hissed Cleavie. They were listening to the conversation through a device PSSA planted on Trinni during the 'events' at the castle. They had planned this from the beginning, and regularly listened to Trinni's private conversations. After many boring hours, nothing interesting was heard—until now.

"We are getting closer to the Chaos Light, but no closer to identifying why the pairings have stopped nor why the naroozie want it as much as they do." Garis spoke slowly and awkwardly.

"All three of us are aware of the personal sacrifice we have made to ensure that we, and only we, control the power of the Chaos Light. Trinni, if need be, are you willing to–" Garis drew a sharp breath, "take care of your two brothers, should they get too close to the truth?"

"If my brothers need 'taking care of' then I will do it, and I will do it alone," declared Trinni.

The conversation stopped. Hengway and Cleavie held their breath as they heard the sound of a door closing slowly, producing a high-pitched scrape characteristic of castle doors.

Then came Trinni's steady breathing, pages being turned, and the scratching of a rusting nib on paper. These were the only noises to be heard for an uncomfortable stretch of time.

Cleavie turned a knob on the greying wooden box balanced on her knees. "Well, that's all we will get for today. It's the best information we have so far," said Cleavie pointedly to Hengway, who had his thinking face on. This face, for all intents and purposes, gave observers the impression that he was either on the toilet, or that his toe had been thwacked with a sledgehammer. Nobody could ever tell which.

"Take care of us? Well I'll be biffed. I would have never guessed Trinni was in this so deeply. Those horrible beasties have turned her into some kind of evil enchanter."

"Sorry to say, Hengway, Trinni is most likely involved in being more than a simple sect member. Those three are leading the search for the Chaos Light, and they know things about the pairings that not even my parents and your father can see or even dare imagine."

The bell in the main tower tolled thrice, encouraging students to clamber back to the dark halls of Traveller College.

"We shall talk about this after school. As for now, we have to get to the training mats in the arena. I wonder what The Captain has planned for us today."

News about the missing paired was making the rounds through the systems. On the lower systems, information flowed through a technological network of outdated artificial intelligence, like that of PSSA. Messages were passed from unit to unit. A PSSA to PSSA protocol, if you will.

The units, or T-Life, as each liked to be called, automatically communicated when they were within a couple thousand feet of each other, so long as nothing got in the way

T-Lifes eventually became a recognised species in the middle systems, hundreds of years after humans began to travel. This recognition granted them all the social and economic rights (and wrongs) that such a designation entailed. It also meant they could be directed to perform military or political duties if a council demanded it.

There was no standard monetary charge for sending a T-Letter; however, if a T-Life within the chain did not like you, it might charge you whatever it wanted to keep the message moving. If the endpoint T-Life felt wronged by your message or mere presence, the negotiations may involve the sale of precious belongings or body parts, not necessarily yours. The T-Life believed everything was on the table, including the odd limb or two.

Hengway was waiting for Cleavie outside the library.

"I have a letter for you," announced Cleavie's PSSA. *Here we go,* thought Hengway. *I wonder what he wants this time.* For the previous delivery, PSSA compelled him to clean all of Cleavie's ageing boxed technology, for which he was still getting grime out of his fingernails.

"A burner is located in the master teacher's office," said PSSA. "We shall go there, and I shall create a film-based copy for you."

In under a minute, PSSA and Hengway were spying within the office. Two haughty and menacing administration T-Lifes were by the far wall behind a row of tall filing cabinets, which was fortuitous as the film burner was on the side closest to the door, far from the pernicious office guardians. These drone staff were known for their angry approach to students. Rumours circulated that they could freeze anyone who made the unwise decision to cause an upset.

"Do we shut them down?" asked Hengway, hiding behind a glass partition that separated them from the administration room.

"You really need to catch up on your T-Life information, young man. That is not possible with that species of T-Life."

"Try to perform the invisible magic again," Cleavie chirped via PSSA from her desk in the Trav-Coll library.

"Sure, and I'll turn everyone into a bunglebeast whilst I'm at it," scoffed Hengway, who was beginning to find the whole exercise unnecessary. "We could just go to the castle and burn the film there."

"Go on, try it!" joked an amused Cleavie. She wanted to stretch him a little to see what bounced back.

Hengway thought it would be nice, or even considerately excellent, if he could not be seen. He inspected his arm but could still see it.

"As I have suggested, this is biffed up beyond all recognition."

"Excuse me, Hengway. What?" asked PSSA.

"What does that even mean?" Cleavie said, putting her question on the table for the team to process.

"You two aren't helping," Hengway dryly noted.

"Hengway, you are not visible to me or my heat detectors. I ascertain that you are quite invisible to technology, magic and almost all species," said PSSA.

Cleavie added, "I told you it would work, Mr Confidence. Get in there and burn this film!"

Hengway slinked into the room, finally feeling like a chosen one of the highest rank. PSSA activated his invisible field, hoping there was enough juice to raise the shield and follow Hengway into the room. He did so, though not as confidently.

Hengway took the film from the envelope and placed it onto the burner. PSSA spoke with the device through the magic of wireless technology. The T-Letter was burnt onto the film silently, PSSA let out a small chuckle as the device had relayed a particularly ribald limerick.

"Get out of there and meet me in the library!" This time, Cleavie mind-spoke in order to avoid PSSA's intermittent and overly cranky transducer revealing their presence.

"You know," said one of the T-Life administrators, "The Captain is a complete menace, and those paired brats should be sent off to the farms to muck out the stables."

"Quite! If the family knew there had been a sighting of that stupid woman and those silly dwarfs, there would be trouble from them all."

"Luckily, Trinni and her silly witches are keeping the truth well hidden, so we have no problem."

"Though if they ever locate The Planet, they will find far more information than they need."

What, where and possibly who, is The Planet, Hengway thought.

Instead of making a run for it, he kept listening and hoped that PSSA and Cleavie were listening too. This needed discussion and action. As his mum always instructed, 'Stay low and still; assess and plan; take swift action!' He had stayed low and still quite long enough. Hengway's mind was now focussed on getting to the action part.

After waiting a few moments for more information, but hearing only silence, Hengway slipped the film into his jacket and left, with PSSA following close behind.

The T-Letter was in a language that even PSSA, with his limitless knowledge of system linguistics, could not translate.

"We need to tell someone, Cleavie," said Hengway as they walked toward the training rooms.

"Who is going to believe us? We need to find that planet. We need to do all of this whilst being watched by your traitor sister and her friends, my parents, and your father!"

They passed through the entrance to the training arena to find The Captain was alone. Hengway and Cleavie walked cautiously, waiting for some training trick The Captain would normally pull on them. They reached the arena training mats. They waited. Nothing of interest occurred.

"Time for us to get serious," boomed The Captain. "When are you scheming kiddies fetching the taken ones?"

"What do you mean?" faltered an uncomfortable Hengway.

"Let's tell him," mind-spoke Cleavie. After giving a lengthy explanation of the events of the last few weeks, Hengway produced the sheet of film for The Captain, revealing the strange letters.

"Bless me! What do they teach at this college? Don't answer, Cleavie; it doesn't need an answer!" Cleavie closed her ready-to-shoot mouth and scratched her beard in annoyance. She was itching to inform The Captain of the unmanageable schedule the college had imposed on them.

"This is a cipher. The numbers at the bottom are the key to decoding it. PSSA, use these numbers to crack the code and read the message to us!"

"It is, I now realise, a fundamental code," intoned PSSA as he read out the message, "System 6, the fourth planet from the Suns."

"It has to be the planet where they have my mother; let's go!" urged Hengway.

"I would say yay and advance, lad, except this may well be a trap! You two aren't ready for a stoush of this level. Besides, you have more to learn first, and I'm due a nice beetroot beer," The Captain mused. "Time for a bit more arduous training!"

They both groaned as The Captain smiled at them with his gamut of teeth.

8. A Testing Planet

"This is seriously biffed," grunted Hengway as he ran through a fine example of a Cellfast 5 forest. The pair of T-Life trackers whirred loudly, tracking him from behind. Without fail, the T-Life-Ranger would stop and closely sweep Hengway's track for threats, no matter how careful he had been to conceal them.

The Trackers were basic models trained to fight, capture, and detain, but they were expressly programmed not to hurt Hengway. He wanted to try a short punt jump by himself. He was finally starting to get the hang of combat-jumping, and although Cleavie was not with him now, he tried to launch into the jump as though she was. It worked, and he began a new course of evasion.

Where is Cleavie anyway? he wondered.

Since learning the basics, he had punt jumped between planets and systems a few times. Expansive jumps were more manageable to him than the short, aggressive jumps needed for combat. The jump ended with him behind the T-Life-Trackers, where he shouted, "Boo!" thus, defeating them in his formal test.

The trio had punted back to camp when The Captain appeared behind them, clapping vigorously.

"As you just learnt, although you are paired with Cleavie, that doesn't mean you need to always rely on her," The Captain said as he sat on a mossy fallen tree.

During many wars, the dwarf clans often built tree villages as a base for their resistance. From their network of tunnels hidden in crowded forests they could keep invaders at bay for years.

"Speaking about Cleavie, she was summoned by her elders to sit the Pass or Die examination."

"She's been wanting to do that test for years," replied Hengway, who now understood the feeling of emptiness since Cleavie bade farewell that morning without hinting at her destination.

"This is an important event for her. I would suggest finding a nice spot to get comfy to try mind-speaking to her. It would be a lot better if you could mind-sit, though we haven't properly practised that yet."

Hengway took the cue to punt jump himself and The Captain to a nearby house. It was a simple log hut made from the forest, with a bunk in each room and a main room for meals and social gatherings.

Hengway sat on the soft, mossy ground and spoke, "Do you have the new braid symbol for your beard yet?" He was trying to coax Cleavie into a quarrel. This approach wasn't working because Cleavie remained suspiciously silent.

Refusing to play nice, he concentrated harder. Surveying the surrounding forest, he could see particles left over from where Cleavie had jumped into another system, so he focused his senses on that path. Intense path analysis led him to discover that the trail ended back on this planet.

"Captain, I followed her path. She tried to evade someone, or many *somethings,* then she ended up about an hours' walk from here."

"Well done, boy. That's the way of it. Now, think about her and her safety! Think and mind-sit with her. But don't speak to her straight away! She could be in a dangerous position, and you might help her opponent!."

"Where's PSSA?" asked Hengway, trying to be positive. "He would be a great help right now."

"PSSA cannot help with the test. I don't even know whether your interference is allowed," said The Captain while smiling, his polychromatic grin only working to make his demeanor move one step closer to psychopathic.

Today, he was wearing a hat that a pirate from the watery and gaseous planets of the higher systems would be deeply proud of. Occupants of most systems grew up with tales of space pirates capturing weary travellers and giving them a choice to become privateers like themselves, or, to become dinner.

"Concentrate, lad! My hat is not as interesting as helping Cleavie. Keep your mind on the end game!" insisted The Captain in a controlled and deliberate way, knocking Hengway back into focus. He concentrated on Cleavie's helmet, followed by her beard.

Mind-sitting turned out to be like punt jumping. The transition jerked a second behind itself creating an aggressive flicker of space, not time—never time. The sitter slipped into the target's very existence. Hengway could sense everything Cleavie could, while maintaining complete control of his mind and body.

Ever heeding the advice of The Captain and his mother, he remained silent and assessed.

Cleavie dangled over a long drop above a deep gorge, her axe in one hand as she barely held on to a bulbous root protruding from the slippery shale cliff. The sound of incessant steam whistles pierced the air, moving towards the gorge. Over the cliff came the added sound of lasers and vintage weapons, shattering the solitude of the forest. A shockwave just above the dangling dwarf roared across the clifftop, causing dazzling red and yellow flame to arc across the now blackened sky.

"I bet ya she's danglin' over a cliff," said The Captain, his horrifically shiny smile still lighting up the surroundings. He put some brown weed into a pipe and lit it with a burning twig. After a mighty toke, he sat back and smiled even wider.

"You're spot on, Captain. She should jump out of there."

"Calmly speak with her and fathom what help she may care to seek."

Hengway gave their mind connection a bump, imagining Cleavie and himself beside each other in the same place.

"It's about time you got here. I can't punt jump. Get me the—"

Hengway gave one more push, imagining her physical presence beside him. Cleavie shifted back one second before appearing next to The Captain and Hengway.

"What the biff happened?" Hengway asked.

"As soon as the test started the situation escalated into destination biffed very quickly. Loud whistles blasted across the place. There was a huge explosion and steam-bots and T-Life appeared from everywhere. It was what I assume was a co-ordinated attack." She breathed deeply and continued, "Thanks, pair-partner. I need to get back, probably not exactly to where I was, obviously. The test is to capture or kill two escapees and return them."

Hengway wanted to be a beacon in a world of moral darkness, "I hope that's just a test simulation. Really—killing escaped thugs without due process isn't a good thing." He quickly became a weak candle of morality missing its beacon goal by a considerable number of lux units.

"Due process? Surely you jape! The catch is that there are three other dwarfs doing the test. Whoever deals with the escapees wins. We *have* to find them," implored Cleavie. The top of her helmet was burnt, her armour dented, and her cape smouldering.

Hengway was disturbed that Cleavie did not even notice how bloodied and beaten she appeared. Unlike Hengway, she was quite happy to survive an event that was undeniably a fierce storm of dirt, sweat, and fire.

Hengway playfully suggested, "If you were on fire you would make a good candle." The death-gaze from the battered dwarf hindered his jocular enthusiasm. Clearing his throat, Hengway added, "Um. Let's inspect the scene, shall we?" Cleavie raised an eyebrow. Just the one.

They punt jumped to the top of the cliff, immediately becoming invisible. The Captain stayed behind with his pipe, savouring not being a bunglebeast.

Hengway assessed the surrounding area and noticed that there were several points of interest. One location contained several punt jump particles he could not recognise.

"Wait!" Cleavie cautioned. "There is a lot of T-Life in this area. These ones operate on steam. Imagine a lackluster human facsimile, but with rust issues. Let's scout around a bit more." Shots rang out as a villainous T-Life shot at a dwarf entering the clearing.

"This is definitely *not* a part of the test. I think these clockwork biffers have been tampered with. The test is called Pass or Die, however; death does not really happen, well, not all the time anyway. This may be an attempt to kill or detain us," Cleavie said.

The targeted dwarf fell to the ground. Blood seeped from his shoulder. The T-Life fired more shots, with most zipping past, but one bullet hit the leg of another dwarf.

Thwap!

He fell, screaming, gripping his leg as blood flowed from the wound.

More shots were fired at the third dwarf, who was trying to duck out of the way of harm. Her manoeuvre did not help her cause, and she was shot square in the chest. The dwarf did not scream. Falling instantly to the forest floor, she folded grotesquely, helplessly clutching at her mangled chest armour.

Thwap thwap!

The test was careening in a direction Cleavie could not control. She mind-reached for the murderous T-Life units and punt jumped them to the middle of the forest clearing. Hengway seized their weapons while Cleavie mind-moved sticks, branches, and large trees to form a tall wooden barrier around the drones.

Hengway reasoned that it would be considerate to have a force-field around the structure, and the force-field obliged, surrounding the area with a light blue haze.

Cleavie punt jumped the test assessors and her parents into the liberated clearing. Hengway saw this and fetched The Captain to join in the festivities.

"Lad, ya gotta tell me when you do tha jumping thingy."

"Where's the fun in that, Captain?" Hengway jested.

Ignoring The Captain's request, Cleavie vanished. Hengway sensed where she went and followed the jump.

He found it easier to sense her location the closer she was. Being paired made him happier than he had ever known. Being happy was one thing; realising the new skills came with a downside was quite another. Even though unknown miscreants were trying to kidnap or even kill them, and other youngsters were going missing, he felt that right now he and Cleavie could take on the system-verse. *The way this biffed show is developing, we might have to take them all down,* he thought, surprising himself with his calmness under pressure.

The clearing's occupants felt a soothing tranquility drift over them. They were safe once again. Cleavie and Hengway were privately planning their next move. The adults in the clearing were staring at The Captain, waiting for good advice.

"Don't be gawping at me, you lot. Them two are busy with their mind trickery. I don't even have a sword," responded The Captain whilst casually stuffing his pipe with purple and orange plants. He packed in the crushed leaves and took a dramatic moment to rummage through his array of pockets, finally producing a small glass vial. He uncapped it, pouring a measure of powder onto the top of the colourful herbs.

"You can't be serious?" grumbled Kalle, jealous that he had not thought to bring his pipe.

"We can't be letting these children dictate—" Lyssa was interrupted by another dwarf scrambling to a dark green bush a few body-lengths away, and the sudden disappearance of her daughter. The shrub barely hid this well-fed dwarf. He was shaking so much that the whole shrub shook with him.

"Come over here ya daft specimen," yelled The Captain as he realised the absent pair must have made them all invisible with the blue invisibility field. He had heard of invisibility fields before, but never a soundless one. *These kids are probably more potent than they or anybody else might guess,* he realised.

The Captain leapt out of the safety field towards the stricken dwarf. The dwarf had stifled the bleeding from his shoulder wound and was startled further as a ruffled humanoid with exceedingly bad teeth appeared out of nowhere, his only weapons being an ugly hat and a pipe blowing foul smoke across the clearing.

"Would ya like a formal invite, or would ya prefer to stay with ya quivering leaves, and pools of blood some more?" The dwarf knew of The Captain, with his strange magic and assorted mystifying activities that occurred around him and certain others.

"Thank you for helping me, Captain. Do I reckon rightly that I failed the test?" gasped the out-of-breath but delighted-to-be-safe dwarf.

"I think anyone who lived through this complete biffle passes all tests," Kalle exclaimed from behind.

More T-Life appeared in the clearing, jumbling, bumbling and quite seriously making the jump look far more violent that it should. "It was just in here," reported a four-armed T-Life, two of which were laser-destructors built by weapon-makers from the Waiface system.

"Whom are you calling 'it', ya tin-head?" screamed the overly excited Captain.

"Oh, no, we are all going to be ki—"

"Calm down, ya whining dwarfling. The Captain needs a rest and a good slap. We are safe here, for now," said Kalle, who was wondering what was for dinner.

From the right of the clearing came a deep growl swelling into a throaty rumble that randomly changed direction. In tandem with the clinking ruckus of approaching attackers was the trembling of the ground. The rumbling and trembling ceased, stopping behind the barricaded T-Life units. Everyone turned to where the commotion first sounded.

Hengway and Cleavie appeared between the people and the improvised wooden enclosure, stopping time for all but them.

"This", remarked Hengway, "is a major mind biffle." Everything was silent and tremendously still. Dimensions, sound, and colour all froze, yet Cleavie moved around freely. Her first task was to tie up the newly arrived T-Lifes and ensure that every weapon was pointing somewhere other than at innocents.

"Get our parents and all the others to that ridge there!" she instructed, pointing at a high grassy mound about a decent spear throw away. The punt jump happened the instant Hengway thought about it, which both excited and scared him.

"Thank you, Hengway," said the increasingly-polite Cleavie, who had the appearance of one who had been dragged through several animal farms over many weeks on a few too many planets. Hengway didn't say this, but he didn't have to—Cleavie already knew he was judging her.

"Stop it, o paired of mine, or we will have to practice axe management!" she quipped, mocking him with the shake of her fist.

When the clock clicked back into normal time, the T-Lifes found themselves trapped in the middle of the clearing by a force field, with everyone else safe on the nearby mound.

Charcoal burned beneath large metal pots filled with vegetables, a few identifiable meats crept to the surface. The soup, known as 'Better than Nothing' by hungry children, was a crowd-pleaser from Cleavie's home planet.

The group crowded around, quiet and reflective. Cleavie's parents and The Captain uttered words of gratitude as they huddled around the steaming pot.

"Don't you two be peekin' in ta our heads, you little scamps," scolded The Captain.

As the plan to kill or capture Cleavie had badly misfired, she thought now was a good time for a feast and a lie down. After a brief conversation with her parents and Hengway, she punted to more comfortable surroundings. Hengway likewise decided his foray into near–death experiences was getting old, so he punted to his castle home.

"Captain, they did okay today, me thinks," Kalle said as he passed a flagon of what appeared to be a barely legal concoction.

"Saved a few lives and proved they can work together. They may be ready for some real work," The Captain replied, balancing the flagon on his knee, in a weirdly loving way.

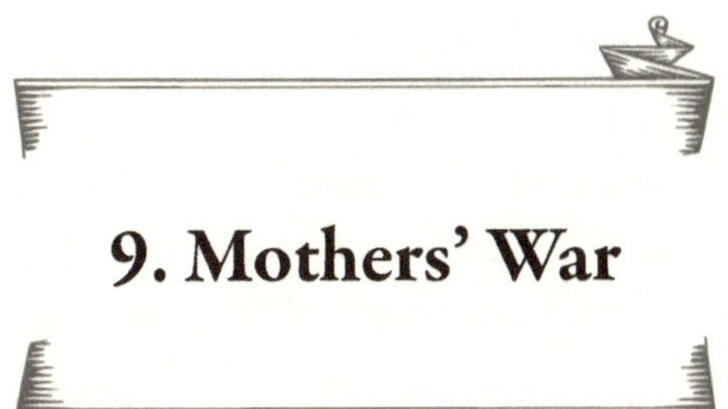

9. Mothers' War

Naroozie planets orbited in a high system known as Waiface. The naroozie were considered wealthy by some standards. Not an 'earned it the honest way' kind of wealthy that is lovely, fluffy, and inspiring. Theirs was the 'saw what they wanted and took it by force' kind of wealthy.

The dwarfs and the naroozie had existed in an unsettled alliance in the domain of planet and system conquest for many thousands of years. Each competed to control and rule planets or entire systems. As the dwarfs tried to move among the systems and make a place for themselves, they had to pay for magic and magic technology they couldn't otherwise acquire

The dwarfs held locations which were not ready or capable of being part of the traveller community. They conquered isolated planets and mined their precious minerals until the planets were stripped bare. Having been left with nothing, the original occupants were forced to move elsewhere, and the whole cycle of nastiness would start once again.

Like the dwarfs, the naroozie also conquered planets and systems around them. This was more for wealth-creation and power than for any desire to better themselves. As far as the naroozie were concerned, the systems were already theirs, and others just did not know it yet.

The Waiface system had seven planets and, like most desirable systems, the standard two suns. After thousands of years of fighting and internal bickering, the five clans decided to take one planet each. The other two planets were for naroozie who were not of any clan. Those without a clan were frowned upon, but not completely rejected. These planets held the social and main market hub for the Waiface system, and for trade between other entities since they were deemed to be neutral from any clan or deity.

The soldiers, traders, space sailors and inter-married naroozie made these planets home. The seventh planet was where most inhabitants had their trading houses. In keeping with trading hubs everywhere, this is where the spies and devious politicians plied their trade.

Naroi's parents were the leaders in their field and were feared by everyone who was smart enough to know who they were dealing with. Underestimating Enfki and Tarlan Fnwah was a deadly mistake.

Although the Fnwah family had an elegant estate on Waiface 5, they traded and spied whilst conducting legitimate business on the seventh planet. The dwellers named the planet a word that was hard to pronounce in naroozan. Roughly translated, the planet of Llffandudofkoffen is referred to in common-tongue as 'Trade, spend and biff off.'

"We understand the dwarfs are preparing to conduct another test for their younger candidates," commented Tarlan, Naroi's mother, who was in charge of assassinations for the wealthier naroozie elite.

"Your attempts so far to destroy the families of the paired have been pathetic and clearly incompetent."

"That's not fair, First of Heidzi," said an annoyed and equally worried Naroi. First is the title for the most senior naroozie of each clan, and in formal circumstances, Naroi always addressed his mother by this important honorific.

Being five-legged creatures, each of the five clans had twenty-five senior members. Every group had a supreme leader whose identity was kept secret among the five-by-five to limit messy assassination attempts, and to keep inflated egos at a minimum.

"Son of mine, the degree of fairness is not an excuse. Results are what they are, not what thou wishest them to be. Results, Naroi, maketh the strong naroozie. Excuses are for the dead, or the workers."

"I await your instructions to make my great mother and father proud."

"Once again, it is not pride we seek. It is the destruction of those unnatural children. You have befriended the enemy's eldest child and converted him into an excellent asset. Have you installed the listening devices in Acae Castle?"

"I have, First of Heidzi. Although our technical magicians cannot receive a signal, we think that the Castle's considerate architecture may be the cause." Naroi thought his mother was being a bigger pain than usual because of her two guests.

The largest room of the Fnwah trading house was tastefully adorned with expensive vases, paintings, and other ornate objects that spoke quietly but haughtily of wealth.

Here were displayed dwarven axes with metals from low systems that gleamed in the light, never dulled, and perfectly balanced. There were vases made of translucent marble adorned with precious stones from planets long extinct. The room stank of money, and of the blood of those who presumed to own the wealth before it was extracted from them.

"Be not disheartened by your mother's harsh words, Naroi," said a senior member of the Heidzi clan. She was old, her silver hair surrounded her long and narrow face. Her fifth leg was half-missing, now a useless protrusion on her back, though Naroi had heard she wore this disfigurement as a sign of honour and a warning to her enemies.

Naroi had always wondered what battle had awarded her that trophy. He did not know her name, even though he had known her since his first fighting test when he was in the second year of his second lustrum—or, as other races would say, six years old. He had always liked her, and thought she conducted herself like a true naroozie warrior. She was a good addition to the other hard-won treasures in the room.

"Orders have changed. You must make contact with the T-Life assassination team. We have been able to–" Tarlan's eyes shifted to a table piled with trinkets, "take care of most of the pairings, and we have successfully kept that stupid Acae family away from the Chaos Light," continued Tarlan.

The other senior naroozie were sullen, yet remained attentive to Tarlan, as it was indeed a good way for them to remain physically intact. It had been rumoured that the Fnwah family dominated the members of The First, with the result being Tarlan became the chosen leader.

"I will talk to Jay about this. He is on board. Do we capture or kill any of the paired if we see them?"

"My dear Naroi, if you could kill any of these paired now, you might be killed thyself," one of the leaders said, more as information than a warning.

"Three of the five clans have forbidden the sacred species of naroozie to be paired," the elder continued.

"Naroozie be pure. Five clans to unite." The four naroozie repeated the chant to unite and remind them of their culture's mission. The naroozie believed that they, and only they, had rights over the three skills, and that they alone should control the multi-system council that ruled over all systems and their planets.

"If you can capture any of the paired, feel free! Your role is about information and disruption."

Tarlan stared at her son, "Be pure." She waved him away with a silver pistol, which he noticed was ready to fire.

Naroi nodded, and exited the room in fear and silence.

It was not easy being the oldest brother in a family with a fat middle brother with no skills and an unnaturally talented enchanter for a younger sister. Surely, Trinni and her sect had sold their souls to one of the naroozie gods, because despite their best efforts, the sect had been impossible to spy on, so Jay and Naroi concentrated their efforts on Hengway.

Jay assisted Naroi by placing sensors in Hengway's room. Annoyingly, whenever Cleavie was near, contact with the devices was lost.

Paired individuals formed a connection, linking their two minds as one. Jay resented Hengway for receiving this gift effortlessly while having to work for his own skills. Helping Naroi and his clan gradually take over the universe, planet by planet, was immensely satisfying.

Their secret meeting in the Waiface system went well. Jay was amazed at how green and lush the planet was. Punt jumping was still a no-go for Naroi and Jay, so they had to catch commercial ships, or sometimes ride along with members of Naroi's family on one of their privately owned jump punters.

These ships were the second-best way to punt jump. Even though the jump itself was immediate, the ship had to move to a safe jump location due to its size as well as the countless number of ships that would jump at once.

The music onboard was the usual naroozie affair—dark and moody, turbulent and sad. Drums made of skin produced a low rumbling beat when played correctly, or as a naroozie would say, aggressively.

There were stringed instruments, made from the rarest trees, which took all five legs to play. Any species with fewer feet had difficulty with the weight, making the technique of playing these instruments a challenge, if not dangerously hilarious.

"Do the Naroozie ever sing, biffle-face?" Jay asked Naroi, who was comfortably seated in a naroozie-designed chair. It had a cut-out in the back with a cushioned rest about twelve inches below it. Commercial punt jumping ships catered for all. "As proud as I am to be naroozie, my young stenchy friend, our singing needs some improvement. I believe our artistic clan, the Fonich, boast that we are fighters, not singers of love songs."

No love songs? That's a shame, mused Jay, as he studied his friend's seated appearance. A naroozie is notoriously dedicated to their tribe, though naroozie and human partnerships are not unknown. Such unions are accepted as long as the relationship is conducted in a discreet and conservative way. *I will probably never have a chance with Naroi*, he brooded.

He gazed at Naroi. "What do we know about the T-Life assassins?"

"T-Lifes? They are a breed of their own. New T-Life have not been built in centuries. The dwarfs and impfish build drones rather like a T-Life, but the intelligence boards are old and based on outdated technologies."

"I heard talk of T-Lifes building replicas of themselves so that they can cover more territory."

"You give them too much respect, my good friend. They are still mere appliances to us naroozie. They will do as they are told, or they will be compelled to do so."

"Makes sense. So what's the plan?" Jay asked, studying the colour of Naroi's eyes.

"You and I set a few traps. Ensure your sister gets a steer towards the Chaos Light, which will be false, and we hope she repeats the lie to your brother. After setting the scene for the capture of that miserable pair, we need to ensure the dwarf's T-Life and all the evidence disappears."

"I do feel some remorse about the backup plan. I'm sure it's for the best, though" Jay contemplated. *What would happen if Hengway and Cleavie were not captured?* he thought. *Death?*

A naroozie wearing long enchanter armour wandered into their cabin. This was a first for Jay since he had never before seen a naroozie enchanter. In fact, naroozie rarely joined any other non-naroozie sect, clan, or service.

Naroi caught the startled expression on Jay's face. Such a beautiful face. His hair had not seen a brush in days, yet to Naroi it was perfect. It fell to one side, only just covering the bruise he accidentally gave Jay in their last training fight. Bright green eyes set above beautiful, shallow lips that glistened with sweat after a practice duel. Small ears hidden slightly by messy, deep black hair. Naroi took in a sharp breath and tightened his fifth leg. He would get himself into trouble if his thoughts about Jay were ever revealed.

Love should be easy, but never seems to be. Get to like someone, get to know them, and be with them when you can. Ah, hopefully, when all this is over, I can discuss this with Jay.

The enchanter raised her hand. "Are you ready, younglings?" They nodded in agreement and were punt jumped to the dwarf testing planet. Forests continued beyond the teal horizon. Low pink clouds obscured their view. They ducked and rolled, landing fifty feet from Cleavie. Naroi, with his fifth leg, was quicker and somehow quieter when on the trot.

"That sneaky witch put us this close to the house on purpose. We need to sort her out when we get back," spat Naroi.

"We should assume a defensive position and plan the attack," Jay suggested as he led the way to the clearing where Cleavie and Hengway were going to be captured.

Planning for the operation took hours and was more difficult than they had imagined. Their first command was for a section of T-Life steambots to open the attack phase, creating a distraction by whistling collectively to initiate an explosion.

The whistles whistled, the explosives exploded, and the hours of planning went straight to the pit of well made plans everywhere. The deep pit of oh-biff-this-is-not-working.

They instructed their T-Life assassins to cause as much trouble as possible and, at one stage, had Cleavie hanging from a cliff, but before they could capture her, she managed annoyingly to arrange a jump to safety.

One of their T-Life drones notified them that Hengway and The Captain were also involved, so they moved their T-Life assassins in for a last push to complete the capture. Unfortunately, the pair were too powerful.

Jay and Naroi were forced to watch as Cleavie and Hengway saved the day, rescuing dwarfs injured by the T-Lifes and thwarting not only their own plans, but those of some very powerful naroozie and their allies.

"Turning themselves into heroes, instead of zeroes," Naroi quipped to Jay, who had already started rolling his eyes.

Naroi gently touched Jay on the shoulder and motioned that they should move out of sight.

"Plan C, I think," said Naroi as he and Jay slid behind a hill.

"Do we *have* a plan C?" queried Jay as he and Naroi left empty-handed for their designated pickup area.

Trinni stood before the senior sect beside Nosu and Garis. The mood was mostly doom and gloom, with a slight touch of whom to blame. She had been consumed by anxiety since her sect of three was summoned to appear before the high council. She did not like how the meeting was going, and it had just started.

The three were still wearing the enchanter day kit, having not had time to dress appropriately. *These outfits are too showy and not altogether functional,* Trinni thought as she stood before the Council of Nine in her armour, with pouches bulging from highly impractical places.

Senior members of enchanter councils traditionally wore orange sashes over white gowns. In the middle of the nine sat a naroozie enchanter with four sect members on each side. Her sash was a fascinating glow of purple that shined and glittered with shades of orange.

The unelected, informal, and very respected enchanter observed, "I'm sure your brother does not realise he is the only non-dwarf visitor invited to that silly dwarf planet in over fifty years." Trinni was the direct object of the naroozie's attention.

Garis deflected the question with her own response, showing her authority, and to help Trinni mentally get back into the game. "Hengway Acae, I submit, is the least of our issues. The dwarfs will no doubt have their own game to play. Cleavie and her clan are smarter than they appear. Which, let's face it, is not a stretch goal."

Through the panic, Trinni found her train of thought. "By using the strength and popularity of their pairing, they could reunite with the naroozie and restart plying their trade. It is unknown what they truly want, except that utilising machines over our magic has always been an objective of theirs."

"There are rumours that the two planets in the dwarf system require immense physical power and resources. We also hear rumours of experiments to force-pair younglings," explained Garis as Nosu, the third member of the junior sect, remained unusually silent.

Trinni knew why Draggi, the enchanter in the purple and orange sash, was not giving Nosu a tough time. Draggi was Nosu's mentor and assessor. Having such a high-ranking connection almost guaranteed that she would rise through the ranks. Trinni's assumption on this matter soon proved to be inaccurate.

Nosu's silence was a ploy to appear to support both sides of the argument. Trinni never liked Nosu, and she needed a way out of this sect and into another. It was not long before her wish came true.

"Unfortunately, for you three, our trust and patience in you has somewhat diminished. We are disbanding your sect. This is not a common decision. Actions such as this require much debate amongst senior members."

There was a strained silence as Draggi drew stares from around the room. She knew that her decision was far from popular. If she saw any body language revealing overt disapproval, she was ready to pounce and pounce hard.

Draggi turned sharply to Trinni. "Please wait outside while we speak to the remaining two!"

Trinni immediately complied by punting to the secure waiting area. Two paintings hung on the wall, artfully made using exotic, natural materials that were near-impossible to obtain in the higher systems.

The first painting depicted the initial contact between dwarfs and enchanters. Several dwarfs were hunched over metal boxes with screens displaying seemingly indecipherable images. This painting spoke of dwarfs and enchanters working side by side. To Trinni, the artist had wonderfully captured the sense of movement on each screen. T-Life assistants, like PSSA, were depicted hovering above the dwarfs.

The second painting portrayed a pair of cities undergoing changes over time, depicted in two halves. The top part showed a city with short buildings of different colours, shapes, and sizes clustered together like a dropped bowl of rocks.

By following the picture from left to right, the city grew in size and architectural advancement. The buildings gained height and formed a planned structure. Denizens could be seen occupying the carefully manicured city. With attentive observation, one could see both enchanters and naroozie in the bustling streets.

The bottom half showed a similar evolution, except it featured more of what Trinni would expect from the higher systems. Like the top half, this part also showed a fledgling city, but with stone castles set amongst simple wooden structures. Traversing from left to right, the viewer engaged with the images of considerately designed buildings growing tall and significant. The buildings were still made of stone, but were far more advanced than the earlier structures.

"This is one of my favourite paintings," said Draggi, appearing behind Trinni.

"I understand it shows the way dwarfs, naroozie, and enchanters changed the course of our civilisations," Trinni stated without turning to Draggi.

To their distant right was a blank frame where the third canvas should have been. "The third painting is the most fascinating. It has been missing for so long that we can only guess what it depicted. What do you think was featured therein?" asked Draggi, moving towards the missing painting's former spot before turning to Trinni.

Trinni paused, and started to formulate the expected answer that all enchanters had to learn. Novices were taught that the third painting represented cohesion between three unusual ways of life. Enchanters with magic, dwarfs with dubious metals and liquids, and naroozie with military skill and strategy.

"I imagine it represented destruction and war, Draggi. The lack of human representation may suggest the painters' disdain for humans, or lack of foresight to presume humans may be a species to help in their domination. These three different nations are too arrogant to exist together, not to mention permit human integration. Even now, we enchanters continuously endeavour to become more dominant. The naroozie want to rule the middle and higher systems, and the dwarfs are getting more and more guarded. I think the third painting would have been a warning to us all."

"That response would mean failure for a novice," responded Draggi. "Not so much for someone like yourself, it seems."

She placed her arms out, palms facing upwards, as Trinni placed hers under Draggi's wrinkled and pallid middle foot. They closed the gap between them. Time stepped backwards, and they found themselves inside a castle room.

Trinni's eyes swept along a large stone table, which was exquisitely finished. Detailed carvings decorated each end. The tabletop was superbly white, as though it had never seen a dinnerplate or a hint of spilled wine pass across its perfect surface. *Indeed, it has not had anyone like my family eat off it*; she thought as a picture stood out to her at the far end of the room. She moved casually, trying to hide her fascination.

"The third picture is exactly what you think, Trinni. The artist had the sight. They could see and depict the future."

Or they could long-punt jump, Trinni thought.

"How old is this painting?" Trinni asked as she realised what she was seeing. The picture showed buildings on fire, human castles, dwarf cities, and punt ships crashing into each other. In the centre of the painting, two enchanters, holding hands, stood before a perfect city. Three buildings like burning castle turrets thrust slowly into the sky, one each of the three colours of the enchanters: brown, orange, and deep purple with fantastical orange sparkles.

"The age or the name of the artist is unknown. This is our destiny. Enchanters started with domination in mind. We will rule with the help of others, or without it. What do you notice about the two enchanters in the painting?"

When Trinni touched the painting, she suddenly found herself within its scene. The two enchanters turned to her and said, "You will not stop us. You will fail."

The image disappeared as instantly as it arrived. "Those two! Well then. My mother and Tarlan cause this destruction?" She gasped. She finally started breathing again. She slowly turned to Draggi. "How... How long have you known?"

"Unfortunately, they discovered that we knew of their nefarious plans. It was decided they needed to be stopped before they went rogue."

"They most certainly should be stopped," she said.

"Indeed," Draggi replied. They continued to examine the painting together in stillness. Trinni considered her next move carefully. After too many questions formed in her mind, she broke the silence.

"What will happen to Garis and Nosu?"

"They have been kept together, and were given a new sect member. They will continue to track the Chaos Light. We believe they will fail; however, we must try every avenue. The Chaos Light will be the key to success for any group that finds it. Some want to use it, and some want to destroy it." Draggi did not indicate her preference one way or the other.

"For the Sect, and for our future, I will stop Tarlan and Tuja," Trinni whispered, feeling an instant loneliness.

"Trinni, very few of our kind have been given a solo mission. You must ensure there are no problems arising from these meddlesome two, and keep the others safe, *especially* your brother and the dwarf.

They are building quite a following in the Yurning and Cellfast systems, and they must be left unmolested."

"The first long-punt tested that you had the fortitude to work by yourself in uncomfortable circumstances. You will have more long-punts, but with specific goals. Good luck, Trinni. Be sure to keep yourself away from your family. Protect them, and more importantly, protect your mission."

"I will achieve both. I will get close to my mother and Tarlan, searching for weakness, and protect the others who are looking for the Chaos Light," she took a deep, nervous breath, "Draggi, I will follow the light and do what needs to be done."

Young Trinni formed a most unique enchanter entity—a force of one.

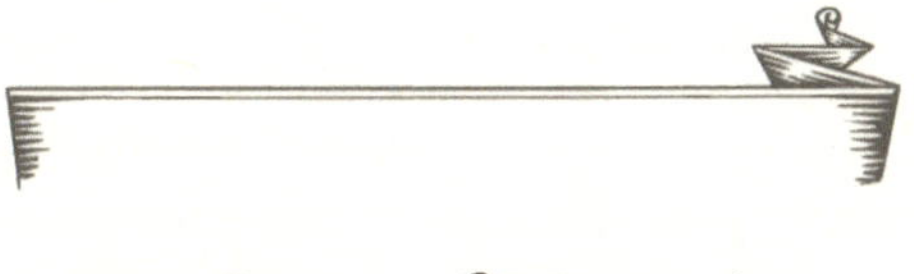

10. City of New Axe

After the series of violent events, the primary councils created a new department to investigate the pairings, the missing adults and children, but, most of all, to gain further information regarding the location of the Chaos Light.

Rumours and strange events surrounding the story of the mystical artefact led to the creation of gangs hoping to find it. It was now common knowledge that the pairings were being used for nefarious causes. Every candidate for a senior role, or in some cases, any role at any level, would claim they were paired and all-powerful, hoping to gain a faint glint of a clue. The fact that only younglings were being paired made these claims from adults comical at best.

"You just made that up," reasoned Cleavie as she examined a long black road.

"No I didn't! I heard that one human applicant insisted she was paired with an invisible being and could work three times as hard as anyone else," sighed Hengway as he followed Cleavie down the major road leading to her home city.

On Cellfast 5 there were designated areas for punt ships, and similar areas for travellers who could punt jump unaided. The magic guided the jumper into the safest area, which bureaucrats endorsed for the welfare of all citizens. Happily, it provided the same bureaucrats an added economic benefit of being able to charge a tax on each visitor.

"When she was caught out, I heard they immediately had her placed in a punt ship's kitchen, peeling and slicing vegetables... three times slower than everyone else!" Hengway shot a sideways glance at Cleavie and laughed his usual laugh. If the joke were funny, he would sound like a toad expelling a quick burst of air through closed lips. If the joke were hilarious, she would have gotten the full, long burst of a giant toad playing the tuba.

Cleavie kept walking. "I will never, ever get used to that laugh."

The surface was hard and hot. It was designed to retain heat to make it easier for vehicles to roll across the roads. The vehicles were almost noiseless, reminding Hengway of farm carts from his planet, but without the occasional wheel flying off and running over a small animal or child, seemingly at random.

"I am glad we could inspect more of your planet," said Hengway as he watched a three-wheeled vehicle hum past. It had no driver, and the occupants were kissing in the back. "I, um, am enjoying getting to see more of the older technologies I kept hearing about."

"Well, I am quite surprised we got permission to spend time in New Axe. We should be able to get some hidden knowledge from their masters."

"How do those carts work? Magic or technology?" asked Hengway as the city's colourful ambiance grew more alive the further they walked towards it.

"Most masters would say it is a bit of smarts and a bit of dark magic," said PSSA, appearing from behind.

"Where have you been!? We haven't seen you since the test," grumbled Cleavie, who was more concerned about how he found them, and where he had previously punt jumped to. Cleavie was worried about PSSA acting strangely since the terrible events with other T-Lifes harming the dwarfs on the test planet.

Hengway marvelled at tall buildings made from exotic materials, filled with incredible colours and shapes that characterised the culture and mood of the planet so different to his: constant, daring, and lively.

Reminds me a bit of Cleavie, Hengway decided as another vehicle slowly approached and smoothly stopped. This was a stunning silver vehicle, shining from top to bottom and from back to front. The door panel vanished, presenting to the group a burly, bearded dwarf. More significant in width than usual. He had innumerable achievements braided into his beard. Pure white teeth like a snowy mountain range jutted out through his thick black beard, beholden with classic tinges of grey.

"Get yer behinds within, then. Stop flappin' aboot. Dinna ye recognise ya Uncle Travis?" the man yelled towards Cleavie, who was digging deep into her memory.

"I don't, uncle. I must confess. My father did tell me that my uncle may be picking us up at the jump point. You are late," she said with steely eyes.

"I am an old, wise dwarf in a very pretty conveyance. I am on time when I arrive. And this uncle's ne'er late. Nor is he early. He arrives precisely when he means ta, where and when he is needed."

"Now I remember you. Didn't you get nicknamed Travis the Truthful?" teased Cleavie, knowing that dwarfish humour meant the nickname likely described the opposite of what it was.

"I dinna appreciate such a silly nickname, niece of mine. I prefer the name I achieved in the Second Hand War: Travis the Most Exceptionally Awesome. A truer name shall ne'er be spoken in all the systems."

"I'm sure that to be nothing but the truth, Uncle."

"Who're ye?" Travis turned his head and gave Hengway a menacing grimace.

"I, I'm, ah, Hen—" stuttered a startled Hengway.

"Ye're a hen? I dinna think so, lad. Hens have feathers. What's yer game here, boy?" Travis continued his interrogation. Cleavie was enjoying watching Hengway melt under pressure, so felt no need to help.

"Is he for real?" Hengway mind-spoke to Cleavie, who remained silent.

"Spit it oot, lad." Travis squinted with his good eye.

"I'm Cleavie's, uh... I'm with Cleavie," he stammered a coherent response, still mesmerised by Travis' sharp accent and rapid approach to speech.

"A servant, then. A bit scrappy; I expect a bit more from servants these days. Hope ye don't pay him much. No much ta look at!"

"Does he ever stop talking?" Hengway mind-spoke, not expecting an answer. A silent Cleavie stood her ground, waiting for the next act of the show.

Travis burst into laughter. It was so great that it scared the birds a furlong away. "I am kidding ye there, lad. Ye two are rumoured to be the next shinin' light. The dwarf and the human, two master magicians. *Paired!* Ye'll be getting a lot of admirers here. Methinks ye should expect some folk who'd think it all a scam an try some hijinks to test yer wits. Welcome, lad!"

"He finally stopped," gasped Hengway, unwittingly speaking out loud.

"Ye two been speakin' to yaselves in ya heids? Fair 'nough, though. I would if I could. Wha da ye think of ma vaaaaaeeeeehhhhhhiiicccccall?" The word 'vehicle' started around the corner and stretched at a momentous pace, snapping to attention on the final syllable. Travis' rendition had far more letters in it than any word should.

The vehicle opened its metallic doors. They cautiously sat down on plush, furry seats. The fantastic silver machine set off in a whisper. *I am definitely going to like this planet,* Hengway thought.

"I know he's speaking a common tongue, but that accent is, well, unique, and takes some getting used to," mind-spoke Hengway.

"Well, lucky for you, I lost my accent when I went to Trav-Coll. You'll hear much thicker accents than his around Cellfast 5. Don't panic, though; you'll get used to it."

During their lengthy journey Cleavie explained how this planet was one of the oldest in all the systems, and some, especially dwarfs, said that humans travelled forth from this system.

Hengway had heard such theories many times. "Oh, *the mystical race that began space travel and movement throughout the systems* story again," he mocked. He was far from the best student in the world, and had not studied system history since he was a youngster. As in all areas of life, Hengway learned that cultures made their history to fit whatever the ruling leaders wanted.

"The second oldest planet was colonised a few centuries before the naroozie came seeking planets to conquer and useful valuables to steal. Instead, they found knowledge of high technology." Cleavie could talk about her people's history until their only sun rose in the east.

"The legends say that the naroozie had to team up with the older enchanter sects, who were even more aggressive than the naroozie themselves, to end a long war."

"You two scared'ns will av all the time ta know tha boring history ov this planet. I knowed magical folks like youse good selves should be setting ya eyes to the future," said Travis, who was pointing at a building taller than the others.

"Wow!"

"Too right, my boy. Wow, indeedy, McSpeedy."

"Indeedy Mcspeedy? Uncle, have you been visiting our cousins in the northern countries again?" asked Cleavie, who was not at all interested in her planet's buildings. She grew up inside them, and even knew how the architecture worked. "And Hengway, before you ask, no, it is not considerate architecture. We've been building these skyscrapers ourselves for thousands of years."

The tallest building thrust skyward, forming a warrior's giant silver spear. From the moving vehicle, Hengway could not see how tall it was. "The stairs must be a real pain if you can't punt between levels," Hengway noted, craning his neck to see the building's apex.

"It is a structure made with well-arranged reinforced concrete, and it is easy to climb the stairs, really, if—"

"Shut up, PSSA," came the unanimous intervention. PSSA found a space on the floor to have a silent, unnoticed tantrum, during which he plotted the end of all beings that were not a T-Life.

All conversation ceased the moment Cleavie caught the majestic view of the entire city.

"I hope the occupants gives youse a nice big hullo," Travis said. "Hengway, I gives ya the city, New Axe."

Hengway was shown an ancient city raised from a seedling, a village of farmers who grew potatoes and made moonshine, to a vast metropolis that was still growing potatoes and making enormous vats of moonshine.

This simple but effective culture was what some historians conjectured to be the beginning of system exploration by humans. The humans discovered a system for travelling by jump-ship, and many years later, the dwarfs came in and took over, that being a fine example of the dwarfs' inclination.

It was far from a friendly takeover, but in the end, the dwarfs and the humans learned to avoid each other. Millenia since, the city's residents were predominantly dwarfs, with a smattering of other species who integrated well enough. This came especially easy, thanks in part to the gross domestic product being an enjoyable beverage accompanied with fried potatoes. The dwarfs were forever wary of humans, and anyone else not a dwarf. They had strict laws regarding access into their cities, and some found it harder to get in than others.

It took a few days of comings and goings, miscommunications, mild argy-bargy, outright lies, and some customary bribery for The Captain to be granted access to the planet.

The Captain and Uncle Travis got along famously, and delighted in tormenting Cleavie and Hengway whenever they were awake to hear it. Hengway started to feel stronger and more thoughtful with each day. He was enjoying the lessons from the masters, and feeling more powerful and skilled, even when Cleavie was not close by.

Hengway and The Captain were the first non-political and non-trading humans allowed into the city for several hundred years, so their visit was clearly quite an honour. Hengway, however, believed the honour was all due to Cleavie's success on Waiface 3, and her esteemed parents. They visited every day, and ensured instructions and lessons were conducted with military precision, except for whenever Cleavie's mother had to drag The Captain, Travis and Kalle out of yet another drinking establishment.

Daily activities: spear work early in the morning, punt jumping in the practice ring, rounded out with training-mat exercises. All of that occurred before breakfast. Hengway's favourite was technical training after lunch in the park near Cleavie's family home. T-Life instructors and highly regarded dwarfs taught them how a force called electricity would power the technology units, including the T-Lifes. Hengway learned how electrified machines could make daily tasks a lot easier. This amazing atomic magic could even be manufactured by T-Lifes so that they could operate autonomously forever.

Humans outside the Cellfast system lacked knowledge of electricity. Travis' history lessons helped Hengway understand this clearly. "Once da considerate architecture made its way to da wealthy systems, da buggers didnae need lower technology," said Travis to a captive audience that included Hengway and Cleavie.

"That's when da naroozie decided ta scarper off with dwarf prisoners an' have 'em work. They had ta muster up military technology to use against t'other planets," Travis explained in his quietest voice.

The news was transmitted differently on this planet. Boxes set inside rooms and vehicles received messages and odd music through circles of black mesh. Apparently, these boxes also informed the occupants of what happened in the cities.

Hengway shuffled over to the foreign device, poked a few silver knobs and twiddled some buttons, making an effective nuisance of himself. The appliance hissed and crackled loudly. Cleavie stifled a giggle as she strolled over, tuned the radio and adjusted its volume.

"We'll have ta give ye a session on wireless use, laddie," snorted Travis incomprehensibly to Hengway.

The voice on the radio was deep and relaxing. Music from the man's planet was played on drums and stringed instruments. The broadcaster's mood was broken with an unwanted transmission disruption, 'Breaking news. The kidnappings of the Paired One Hundred continue across the systems. We have received reports that at least sixteen younglings identified as paired are missing.' The radio fell silent, belching a low hum before the voice continued, 'The enchanter and naroozie high councils have denied responsibility.'

A second voice joined the radio broadcast, "Well, this is remarkable! Many witnesses have confirmed that an enchanter is responsible. Trinni Acae has been sighted at many of the kidnappings. A spokesperson for the enchanters has revealed that Trinni has been banished from their sect. I don't know about you, but this is hard to believe since she still wears their armour, and obviously has access to all of the enchanter magic and technology. Somebody should do something about them."

"You are right, my wise colleague! This repugnant Acae girl could be acting alone, or maybe she's executing a cunning plan with the full backing of the enchanters. Where are our paired children? And what does this mean for the latest attacks in the higher system by certain tribes of the naroozie—"

"Off with that drivel!" spat The Captain.

Hengway was shaking. "What is going on? How long has this been happening?" he muttered through clenched teeth.

"We must be thinkin' dis mess through," Travis finally got some words into the conversation.

"Are we really in trouble? I haven't heard from Dad or Jay in a week. *Are they safe?*" fretted a concerned Hengway, trying to control his growing anxiety. His father's most recent message was brief, saying he was investigating something for The Chosen. Hengway was, at the time, not particularly worried since his mother and father were generally away for weeks at a time before this abnormal turn of events invaded their lives.

"Hengway and Cleavie, you must stay with me!" The Captain ordered brusquely. He dismissed the remaining students, leaving the four of them alone in the park while PSSA hovered above. "PSSA, why didn't you tell us about this? You are the only one that gets any news quickly, you sly rusty slab of tin."

"Captain, I have received no information since landing here. I determined that this lack of news would occur because of the ridiculous restrictions the Cellfast system has placed upon us. Hence, I am very much left bereft of useful information," PSAA replied.

"That may be a ting, but we need more than tha. The knowin' of tings is ya job, an' if you canna do it, ye need tae let us know," Travis yelled, his face reddening.

"This lot is now in danger. Not here, of course. We need to understand just how bad things are before we go back into the higher systems." The Captain was pacing briskly whilst relentlessly stroking his thick beard, as nervous people with newly regrown beards so often do. "We need to speak with the senior dwarfs immediately!" he pronounced.

As their planning began, nobody noticed PSSA flying out of their sight range to punt jump unnoticed to Trinni's room at Acae Castle. Her old room was now a sweeping set of rooms, replete with vials and tomes lining nearly every surface of almost every wall.

"Your brother and his team have found out about your work," said PSSA.

"They're ahead of schedule, but everything should now move along with the plan," responded Trinni in her ever-steady voice.

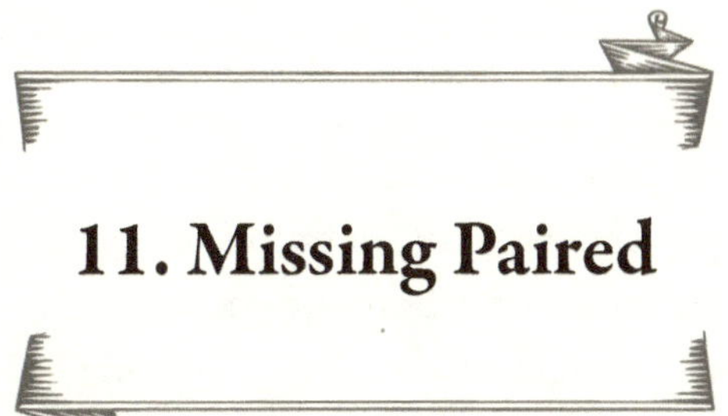

11. Missing Paired

Forthwright Acae sat in a stinky inn outside a stinky town. The battle with the stench started the instant he commenced his mission. Having spent the last week negotiating, fighting, spying, and generally making himself a nuisance across most of the middle and higher systems, he had detected nearly every horrible fragrance imaginable. He wanted, and desperately needed, a long hot bath, with an abundance of high quality foodstuffs to follow.

All questions about the Paired One Hundred, or the Chaos Light, were met with disdain, disgust, disrespect, and, most of all, disapproval.

Using disguises and changeling magic, Forthwright posed as a naroozie and an impfish for days at a time. Living in a different skin was not the problem. The problem was the naroozie and impfish diets and their associated bodily functions.

Humans eat vegetables and meat. Naroozie are obligate carnivores. Impfish are mostly omnivores who generally desire a singular type of blood-thirsty parasitic flying fish that is highly poisonous to most other species. When the parasite cannot find a healthy, fresh source of blood, it attaches itself to any larger fish and sucks the host dry—as long as the host is compatible.

When one uses changeling magic, the internal essence of one's body does not change. Forthwright retained his human stomach, which found itself in trouble from day one. Bodily functions became desperate and disgusting. The stench was enough to melt rocks, so during a rather traumatic evacuation, he promised himself never to use changeling magic again.

"The elders and system councils will deal with this. Don't you trust them?" was the type of question posed by many of the politicians and senior military bores he encountered.

The Chosen should have been helping him with the investigation though, of course, they had not. After much debate and pleading, the best solution they could offer was to grant him leave from his duties until his investigations were concluded. He knew something impish, if not downright disreputable, was going on. The more he poked, the more wasps of information rapidly emerged from their nests, giving him a sting or two.

"I was attacked by two T-Life individuals on Waiface 4. One was pink! Bright pink! The strangest thing I have seen for a T-Life. And the other one was a flyer, like a remote autonobot–definitely a T-Life," confided Forthwright into an old technology microphone.

The voice that came back was broken and faint, "Heng—y says he—o. -—T-Life means suici—-ission. Probably a crim—l—" The radio was as old and as dodgy as the bony fish he had to eat for dinner.

"I get your meaning, Captain. Tell Hengway everything is alright. Even though Trinni is being accused of the most terrible acts, his mother is still missing, and I have had my life threatened at least five times this week!" The radio hissed and splattered, evoking a tap from Forthwright that was less gentle than he had intended. The radio behaved itself, though to be fair, most things behaved after getting a slap.

Forthwright continued, "It is hard to trust anybody. The dodgier criminals follow me when they find out who I am, demand to know where my paired is, or just outright try to kidnap me."

"It is stra—e that they say 'your' paired. I thi—k they are -ink—g you can ow- a pai—d," crackled the response from The Captain.

"Ownership is definitely what most are thinking. I saw some being sold on Waiface 3. An impfish and human are being kept by a naroozie-run village, and they display signs of being a right pain for their captors. I am meeting with the impfish council later today." At first Forthwright was hesitant to mention any of it, but felt The Captain wouldn't let Hengway and Cleavie do anything stupid.

"Mu—-o. -tay sa-e!" Forthwright started to respond to the broken message but the device punt jumped back to where Cleavie or Hengway sent it from. Moments later another small ceramic object appeared and he heard the Captain's mind speak, "Take this and put it in your mouth. It contains some information about your wife." He tried to respond but The Captain did not reply. He quickly seized the object and placed it between his teeth and his gum.

The Captain could have just told me. The petty squabbles of yesteryear must be swept from our minds, he thought as he prepared for his meeting with the impfish council. The vital answers were tangibly closer. The more miscreants who tried to deter him, the happier he became.

The meeting with the impfish senior council was brief, but it had gone a lot better than expected. The impfish were discovered only one hundred and fifty years ago, making them a relatively new species to enter the multi-system parliament.

They were delighted to be a part of decision making and, more importantly, to receive a share of economic trade which came with parliamentary membership. The first pairings came as a shock to them since prior to the day of the Paired One Hundred, they had noticed no magical talent within their ranks.

Forthwright hoped The Captain had taken the hint to attempt to free the pair held captive on Waiface 3. He promised their paired youngling would be freed in return for help from the impfish council in the future. He was sure that Hengway, Cleavie and The Captain were more than up to the task.

Forthwright turned towards the washroom to banish the stink of the planet from his hideously stenchy body when darkness hit. Well, being struck by a chunk of darkness did not cause him to black out. More precisely, he was hit with the blunt end of a spear swung by a large and very nasty T-Life with upgraded arms.

"Cop that, ya bastard," the violent T-Life said.

"Get it wrapped up for punting. I can't stand this planet any longer. And why does he smell so bad? Do something about that!" barked a disgruntled PSSA.

"Yes, sir," affirmed the violent, ugly, and mildly psychopathic T-Life.

"No backchat! *Get it done!*" the PSSA ordered. Unlike Cleavie's PSSA, this was one angry T-Life. "We need to dump the prisoner with the others and continue the search for any paired and other interfering biffers."

This nefarious PSSA was on a good run. He wanted to have at it, and cause as much mischief as he could manage.

The naroozie village sat on the outskirts of a small city on Waiface 3. Having one planet-wide continent meant that cities and towns could sometimes be days apart. In this case, it was by design. The naroozie from the Donpha tribe liked to keep to themselves, especially since most of them were escaping crimes committed in the naroozie system.

The village had a mixture of Cellfast technology and considerate magic architecture. A few generators quietly pumped out a continuous cloud of grey smoke that drifted across the hazy landscape and up into the dark night sky. Decades earlier, the generators had been converted to burn imported liquid fuels after all natural resources were exhausted. They were expensive to run, but were crucial for keeping the lights on, powering cooling boxes, and for charging T-Life varietals.

An older magic technology created a protection field around the village, keeping the nosey away. The fields were created either by magical folk or technology usually contained within a specially crafted box. The size of these boxes would vary depending on the magnitude and nature, defensive or offensive, of the required force field.

Cleavie checked the village using a mind walk technique she had been taught by The Captain. "There is also a very powerful field around the brick building in the middle of the village," mind-spoke Cleavie to a very alert Hengway.

After they found out that Hengway's father had been kidnapped, they had a heated argument. Hengway wanted to chase after his father immediately. It took Travis and The Captain hours to convince him to leave only after all the paired in captivity had been rescued. Hours of talking, yelling, eating, and drawing plans in the dirt.

"Your father has been in worse situations than this and can take care of himself. They will trust you two more than me," said The Captain, which they all agreed was probably true. Scared younglings were never made calmer by a raging lunatic with an unruly head of hair and a multi-coloured smile crashing through their cell doors.

After they arrived the planning for the operation began. Within hours, they were almost ready to take back the captured paired held within the force field. It would be much quicker than The Captain had told them earlier.

"Maybe we could try the old trader-at-night trick?"

"We are almost adults and, quite frankly, appear to be every bit the dodgy two travelling from dodgy town, acting in a dodgy way. In fact, we should have hats made with '*I am Dodgy*' embroidered across the front," replied Cleavie, implying that his idea was quite dodgy.

"Wait, there is another tactic," Hengway added. "Travis made me read a book on very old wars that occurred in and around New Axe. We could create a diversion like you did the last time we were here. Except we don't have PSSA–we do have us, though. Let's try something new."

The suggestion elicited a rare smile from Cleavie, though it was difficult to discern the shape of her mouth beneath her beard. When she did smile, her beard lifted on either side of her face, reminiscent of a carefully groomed poodle. The sight nearly prompted him to laugh, an action he had not engaged in for quite some time. "You should consider smiling more often, or is that more of a grimace?" Hengway remarked, maintaining his characteristically light-hearted approach even in grave circumstances. *The best way to be*, he thought.

"Do take this seriously! I can read your thoughts, you know, and I'll smile when I want to! Snap out of it, and let's save these poor paired! Imagine we were there, and some paired were just joking around instead of saving us!" Cleavie liked giving Hengway a push when he needed it. She was sure he enjoyed the attention. He did not.

They surveilled the area, and created a fire by a disused shack away from the village. Hengway mind-cast a protection field to hide them and the fire. Cleavie discretely checked it, as she always did with Hengway's work.

"Can you not do that anymore?" He exhorted as he glared at her.

"I am sorry. Old habits, and we can never be too careful. You were there when Travis spoke about teams implementing the ruthless independent check on their teammates' work."

"I suppose so. He also said he was going on a mission that would shock all those involved" he replied. He reminisced for a moment about those lessons. "How about we create a diversion using mind control? Making a noise in the east whilst attacking from the west is a good, reliable tactic, or so Travis tells me."

"Good idea. Let's plan this thoroughly!" Ignoring Travis's comment about his clandestine mission, they huddled by the fire and drew a plan in the dirt with a smoldering stick. It was the oldest and most trusted method of planning and reviewing attacks ever invented, besides making an actual map, of course.

Shortly after, they noticed a group of naroozie making their way back to the village in a loud and undisciplined manner.

"This is for us, Hengway, let's go!" mind-spoke Cleavie, dismantling their temporary camp, in a quick stint of chaotic movement.

"I'm ready," he replied, checking that the site was completely cleared.

Hengway punt jumped towards the naroozie, stopping within attacking distance. He thought it would be helpful to be invisible. It worked; they were both invisible and he could feel the strong presence of Cleavie beside him.

Hengway concentrated and thought that it would also be just as helpful if all the naroozie in the group, except for the tallest one, concluded it would be a good idea to turn off the village protection field, followed by proceeding to act like startled chickens for twelve hours and eighteen seconds. In future years, when Hengway spoke of this moment, he called the transformed naroozie, naroozikens.

The plan was going well with Cleavie speaking directly to the mind of the tallest naroozie, convincing him to turn off the force field around the secure brick building. Everything happened at once. The leading group of naroozikens ran to the open door of a recently constructed wooden farm building, as a clutch of chickens would.

Hengway would have welcomed an opportunity to record what was going on but did not have the time or the technology.

Some fought each other to pass through the doorway and made such a noise of it that half the village woke up. Fifth legs flapped around like lost wings of doom, the owners of said feet moving backwards and forwards in pecking motions, their furry faces making them look like teddy bears being dipped repeatedly into a bucket of honey. Watching them clucking, pecking, and scratching in the sand for fresh worms was a sight to behold.

With the first field removed, the pair waited patiently for the second one to fall. Nothing happened. For quite some time nothing kept happening, which was a buzzkill for Hengway. Cleavie's patience got on his nerves sometimes, in a teammate kind of way. Wondering what was happening, they sidled towards the main brick building.

"Be quiet and stick to the plan!" reminded Cleavie. In her hand was her trusty, sharpened axe. Her mind was ready and, much like her axe, in the mood for a wee scuffle. She was in tune with the environment and fully prepared for a bout of unrelenting combat.

The shield compound exploded. The blast launched them off their feet and into the fiery ash storm that filled the night air, savagely landing them on their soon to be bruised backsides.

"Lucky you have padding," Hengway joked. The silence that followed was deadly and unforgiving. Cleavie glared at him with an aggressive and violent silence. A silence that gave every indication that it had no end. Cleavie then took silence to a new extreme; pinning down an uncomfortable Hengway in his search for an escape from her ferocious gaze. Luckily for him, but unluckily for others, there was another massive explosion in the village, redirecting Cleavie's fixation away from him.

The village was in total disorder. As luck would have it, Cleavie and Hengway were still invisible after the explosion. They noticed a tussle in the remains of the damaged brick building. A young human and an impling were fighting two older naroozie. Hengway and Cleavie advanced to the building with extreme caution.

Even though he disliked physical fighting, Hengway readied his spear. The young impfish raised its two hand-fins, revealing several tubes that poked out from underneath its scaly skin. Hengway had heard about the many joys of impfish poison, so he ensured he was out of range of such a deadly weapon. A liquid that glowed softly red in the night's smokey darkness sprayed across the eyes of the naroozie. Yelps in high pitches that could make flowers fizzle resounded throughout the burning village. The paired they were there to rescue saw this as a good time to escape.

Hengway and Cleavie conducted a very quick mind meeting, deciding to punt jump the paired back to Acae Castle.

Hengway appeared in front of the escaping impfish, where a staring competition broke out. It felt like hours before anything else happened, but it was actually a microsecond before Hengway grabbed the impfish's arm-fin and punt jumped them both, he hoped, to Acae Castle.

Meanwhile, Cleavie was having a small party of her own. She had appeared near the fighting and was trying to make herself visible when she saw Trinni for the first time in months. Trinni appeared in front of the human, a female, grabbed her by the arm, and gave a cheeky wave to a still-invisible Cleavie before trying to punt jump to a nefarious destination with the human.

Cleavie was a microsecond quicker. Outsmarting Trinni, she jumped a second back in time, grabbing the human before Trinni could escape. Cleavie was now in the Acae kitchen and fully visible. The human quickly flicked Cleavie's grip away, distancing herself from the dwarf, seeking safety.

Hengway was seated, chatting with the impfish regarding their latest exploits. Upon the appearance of Cleavie and her guest, there was no rush, nor were the occupants startled. In fact they were at ease with one another, "Hello, you two," said a relieved Hengway.

"I saw your sister. She tried to kidnap the human," said Cleavie.

"The human has a name, and it's Simone," moaned the starving Simone, who had since noticed the considerate table of food and drink presented beautifully on the kitchen table.

"A 'thank you' would be nice," murmured Cleavie. Hengway could feel the tension between the two and was anticipating the battle of wits that was surely forthcoming.

Simone tilted her head. "It seemed like she let you take me. She should have seen that move coming."

"Perhaps she did," Cleavie replied in a tone more sombre than usual.

12. A Cunning Plan

Jay and Naroi were seated in a punting vessel, a privately owned craft designed to accommodate six passengers comfortably while providing access to premium external communication technologies. Their failure at the dwarf testing site was still on their minds, as was their subsequent conversation with the naroozie high council.

"There has to be a better way to track who is paired with whom. If we could find out why younglings are being paired and how they select each other, we should have the key to finding them," reasoned Jay, who was nervously fidgeting in his astonishingly comfortable seat. Jay picked up a posh looking tray of food and began indulging himself.

"Are you ready to talk to these people?" Naroi asked Jay, who nodded and reluctantly left his seat. His stomach churning, he threw the remains of his meal into the bin on the other side of the cabin.

Though they were undertaking the gravest of tasks, they gave each other a grin when the remains hit the bin dead straight. No matter what, boys appreciate a good shot when they see it.

"Greetings, Naroi and Jay," said Enfki. Naroi had the features of his father. His hair was roughly the same grey colour, and covered his whole body, including his long face.

However, hair does not grow on dead skin tissue, so many scars stood out on Enfki's disfigured face. These marks, along with his belligerent attitude, made his presence feared by all who knew him.

"Hello, father."

"Hello, sir," said Jay. He moved languidly through the cabin and sat next to Naroi, his elbow leaning on Naroi's armrest. Enfki noticed that Jay sat next to Naroi more closely than was necessary but did not really care as long as they got on with the job.

Enfki flickered. Then he flickered again. He presented as a hologram projected onto a seat in front of Naroi and Jay. In the other seat, a hologram of Draggi appeared, seeming to be as annoyed as ten startled bunglebeasts at feeding time.

"I hope you are lending Captan Hartog a hand at the Academy," Enfki joked.

"He is still not happy about you removing his second favourite appendage," Jay remarked, knowing full well he left the joke open for further exploration. The boys and Enfki, who desperately wanted to add to the line of humour, noticed the annoyed visage of Draggi's face. Being astute war fighters they decided to withdraw and joke about the Captain's most favourite appendage a bit later.

"Appendages aside ..." This remark from Draggi caused more mirth, "Does he treat you well with lessons and the like?"

"To be honest, I think he uses it as a badge of honour. He treats me well but none of the teachers, including him, talk about matters other than education around Jay and me. Also, I mention that particular appendage as much as I can to others."

"Your son is quite proud of the fact you bested The Captain," Jay said.

"You should have seen how awesome the strike was..." Draggi brought a halt to Enfki's commentary, which everyone, absolutely everyone, in their social circle had heard numerous times. The story flipped on details from time to time, according to the amount of ale he had consumed.

"Enfki, we need to turn our heads, thoughts, and actions toward the next steps of our plan," insisted Draggi brusquely in a crackly voice. Snoopers listening to her might suppose that the crackling tones of her high-pitched voice indicated fear or anxiety. They would be wrong.

"Draggi, with all due respect, we need to hunt down my sister and find my brother Hengway, and some more paired."

"Jay is right, I believe. If we had a large number of paired under our control, the next step would be easier," Enfki added. "I can't help but conclude that the enchanters know a lot more about Trinni and her activities than they are admitting."

"We want control over the systems, especially beneficial ones. This control will increase our production of war materials and grant us full access to dwarf technologies and to any paired that can assist us." Draggi said. Her spies had lost sight of Hengway and Cleavie after they entered the Cellfast system. "The T-Life could not transmit into or out of the planets in that system. This poor communication made it difficult to stay in control of the situation."

"We should have invaded the Cellfast system a long time ago. We have lost the element of surprise," a PSSA observed from a distant location. There was no visual of him or any indication of the source of his voice's transmission.

"Are you mind-speaking?" enquired a confused Naroi, who thought mind-speaking was only for the gifted.

"The advantage of having an individual or indeed a completed pair is that, with some persuasion, some of their gifts can be harnessed for more suitable uses," responded the PSSA tensely.

This particular PSSA and his T-Life army had collected a lot of technical information concerning magical executants with intense skills. Capturing or blackmailing those who had paired put the army in a more positive offensive position.

They were now ready to take over the Cellfast system and to gain control of not only ancient and misunderstood technologies but also the resources held by those planets.

A PSSA appeared next to Draggi. This would startle someone who was vaguely normal, but her solid personality stayed true, and unlike her hologram, she did not flicker.

"I have impfish, T-Life, naroozie, humans and even dwarfs ready to attack. I recommend that Naroi and Jay go take care of Trinni and capture as many paired as possible whilst we attack planets in the Cellfast system," suggested the nasty PSSA.

The mood was tense. Enfki and his clan wanted a more aggressive invasion plan. The other clans believed the T-Life plan was aggressive enough.

Enfki hung his head and explained, "This war is for all naroozie. We must take control of technology, magic, and military power before others take it from us."

Draggi sighed. She knew this was the beginning of a war they did not need. She raised her voice ever so slightly and commanded, "Invade as quickly as you can with as little damage and loss of life as possible! I am not amused with whoever is behind keeping this silly rock from the enchanter's grasp."

"I took the liberty of starting the invasion yesterday. May we all feel glory," said the PSSA. Draggi fidgeted and grunted. It felt wrong. She composed herself, calmed down whilst trembling slightly. She was trying not to be startled but failed miserably. The PSSA was trying to take more power than he already had, and much more than he deserved. A flash of anger appeared briefly on Draggi's face.

Jay sat wondering about all of this. *Who really is pulling all the strings, and who is going to rule once it is over? Will Naroi be safe?*

"Who do you think really wins from all of this?" Jay asked as the holograms faded. He moved a hand over one of Naroi's foreleg hand-hooves.

"I think once this is all over, the real war will be between those who see themselves as victors."

The punt ship appeared on the outskirts of Yurning 7 not far from the capital's library. More punt ships in many different sizes appeared. Small craft holding four soldiers would appear, they would exit, and the ship would disappear, reappearing ten seconds later with a new batch of warriors. These attackers would be participants in the strike against the enchanter headquarters, hidden below the dungeons of the Yurning 7 library.

Once the order's group concluded, Draggi removed her robe and replaced it with a more common garment made of woven cloth and other inexpensive materials. She then ordered her assistant to get the steam craft ready.

"Don't worry about your silly conveyance. We decided to come to you," Tarlan said.

Much to her credit, Draggi did not flinch at the sudden appearance of Tarlan and Tuja. She dismissed her assistant and said to her visitors, "It is disappointing that I am the one that needs to take care of your children. As you can see, I once again excelled in achieving my goals."

"And here I was thinking I was the chief narcissist of the Enchanter Sect," Tuja responded.

"Well, you were, until you were dismissed along with your girlfriend here. The Enchanters tend to frown on mayhem, murder and unapproved mischief." Draggi said.

"Unapproved mischief is in the same category as murder now? That makes sense only to Enchanters. If it's for their cause, then it's all good," Tuja spat.

Tarlan, sensing the typical tension Tuja and Draggi created between themselves, tried to intervene before the attack spells started. "We have taken care of Trinni. She is now on a wonderful trajectory of violence and disruption."

Draggi sat on a plush chair and responded, "Good. As you were eavesdropping, you are aware I sent your two cretins on a chase for that rock. You two can go. The name of the game is to keep up with the Chaos Light deflection and concentrate on our real mission."

Tarlan and Tuja nodded, with disdain, and disappeared.

Universal domination is becoming so complex, she thought. Reflecting on the current situation, she smiled with pride.

Having Trinni under my control is excellent news.

13. Hidden Rooms, Secret Thoughts

"I ss a pleassant place here, and you hass large sspacess."

Hengway was getting used to the strange speech and grammar of the impfish. The common tongue was not its primary language; it usually spoke in an atmosphere that was high in oxygen and helium coexisting with a low nitrogen content. When in human atmospheres it caused them to slur and lisp when saying certain words.

"Glad you like it. It's a bit moody and cantankerous at times. The castle has considerately laid out some food for you, Walker-Nine." Hengway pointed to the food on the kitchen table. Fishy things enticing only to impfish were laid out on stone plates to make it easier to wash away the smell. Glass jars the size of two human heads contained a thick, opaque gas hiding their contents, which species other than impfish were quite thankful for.

"I iss famisshed ass ever. I sshould conssume." The impling moved its scaly body towards the nearest jar. Upon reaching the jar, its hand fins lovingly dipped into the gaseous mess. The beastly insectoid it pulled out had eleven legs and one great big eye.

"Oh, biff! He is going to eat it," mind-spoke Hengway to Cleavie, who was removing her weapons and staring at Simone who, Cleavie correctly presumed, was both scared and aggressive.

"I wouldn't worry about the nude one. The human worries me more," mind-spoke Cleavie. Cleavie searched for something to give Simone to calm her down.

"Another thing, it is not a 'he'. Impfish do not have an actual gender until just before they mate—" Cleavie was cut off mid-sentence by the human laughing at Walker-Nine. Cleavie thought it would be destination awesome if time could stop for a bit. And so it did.

Next stop, destination awesome.

"Ah, the whole stopping-time thing," admired Hengway. "What is it with Simone? Walker-Nine looks a lot calmer. And what do you mean by 'nude'?" Hengway's words exploded in a high, then low, squeaking voice as his brain tried to catch up with events.

"While you and Walker-Nine were becoming friendly, your sister tried to kidnap the human over there and punt jump to another system. I caught the human just in time and brought her here. Simone is clearly unhinged. I would like her hinged."

"Hinged. Right. Worry not, o wonderful paired of mine," Hengway mockingly danced across to her and knelt on one knee.

Cleavie considered her pair's playful manner and made a decision: "I have resolved to keep your body intact for now. It may become useful later," she smiled before she continued, "Though for what, I do not know." Cleavie went to Simone, moved her to a chair, bent her into a chair-like shape, and started time once again.

Simone fell back into the chair with a thud. "Wha? What happened?"

"Ooh, there you iss, Ssimone. Welcome back," said Walker-Nine. It still had the mostly-legged gas beastie firmly held in its hand-fins. Its oversized eye blinked rapidly as Walker-Nine put the whole creature into its mouth. The second set of strong teeth at the back of Walker-Nine's mouth made thumping, cracking, crunching, liquidy sounds. Hengway was horrified. Cleavie heard it all, but was still staring at Simone.

"I don't trust these two," Cleavie mind-spoke to Hengway.

"I don't particularly trust you two either," mumbled Simone, rolling her eyes and raising her shoulders momentarily. She saw some food suitable for humans, picked up a big leg of meat, and chewed upon it—the hinges of her sanity were finally appropriately maintained.

"What's the story with you two?" Simone sputtered, pointing the half-eaten joint of meat at Hengway and Cleavie. Cleavie and Hengway's fighting skills came to bear as they ducked and weaved out of harm's way from spittles raining at them from Simone's moistened mouth.

Simone was wearing armour and footwear that Cleavie thought were long out of fashion. In fact, this style was depicted in paintings of earlier times when workers were treated like slaves.

"Why are you wearing that old-style worker kit?" Cleavie asked flatly. "Also, do you have any manners?" Cleavie picked up a cloth napkin from the table and walked over to Simone, who appeared to be enjoying making Cleavie uneasy with her unique etiquette.

"You lot really are living with your heads shoved up your—"

"What Simone is saying is that there is much going on in the systems, which is being concealed. Workers' rights are non-existent, and servitude for life still exists," mind-spoke Walker-Nine in perfect common tongue, since it did not have to vocalise.

It grabbed another eleven-legged thingy from the jar and not so delicately crushed it in its teeth-rich mouth. It swallowed, sighing happiness as the beastie met its second-last resting place. Walker-Nine announced aloud, "I musst dress in ssomething ssuitable for uss company."

"Oh, please do. We wouldn't want you to upset Cleavie's delicate nature," quipped Simone. She grabbed a flask from the table and drank straight from it.

Getting no response from Cleavie, she leaned back in her chair and emitted a thunderous and stenchy burp. Everyone continued to ignore her. Cleavie and Hengway were staring, with open mouths, at Walker-Nine, who was examining the new, considerately placed impfish attire.

Due to the unique atmosphere of their home planet, impfish require custom-made masks to fit over their flat, elongated noses. Walker-Nine's nose extended straight to its thick blue upper lip. It had a single nostril, opening into one flat cavity. The mask's breathing apparatus included a plug positioned just below this cavity—a small cord wrapped around the neck and connected at the back.

The armour was more of a sweating device than protective clothing, ensuring the scaly grey skin remained moist even during the hottest part of most planets' multiple-sun days. Another device attached to the top of the armour, delivering squirts of oxygen when needed.

Hengway was about to ask a zillion questions. *How did they come to be paired? How were they captured? What powers do impfish have?* And a biffle-load more, except his friend Chorlie burst into the room, armed with a shield and spear.

Chorlie was as startled as everyone else. Armed humans formed ranks behind him in full Chosen battle armour, clearly not here for the feast. "I didn't think you would be here," Chorlie muttered. He was wearing the uniform of a junior officer of the Chosen.

Chorlie being promoted way above his incompetence levels, both amused and alarmed Hengway. "I live here. What the biffle are *you* doing here?"

"You are all under arrest. Your families have been involved in whatever caused this war. The Yurning Council would like to talk to all of you regarding the events of the last few days."

"You have elevated your intelligence a notch or two, you traitorous b'hoy," Hengway said.

"All a ruse, of course. Don't bother to try to punt jump. We have just activated an anti-jump field. Come on, Hengway. Hand over the code to the castle. This castle is important for our offensive push." Acae Castle was always a point of conjecture with the people of the Yurning system. A majority agreed that a military or magical force should be used for the good of all.

The universe that existed in that room travelled backwards thirty seconds in time for one occupant only, Walker-Nine. For anyone standing and observing, the whole event got a bit trickier. Walker-Nine could time-travel. Possibly backwards, possibly forwards. Possibly for greater lengths of time than thirty seconds.

These knotty issues were among the many items of interest that Simone and Walker-Nine were desperately trying to unravel before the naroozie captured them. Right now, there were two Walker-Nines and many angry and confounded Chosen wanting to arrest them both.

Cleavie felt the presence of the second Walker-Nine and knew this was about to take them either to destination awesome or to destination *what the*. Either way, she shuffled towards Hengway and Simone. "Get ready to move into the centre of the room!" she yelled loudly, not knowing who could mind read, mind-speak or any of the other strange mind ways of communicating. "One, Two—"

During the thirty-second gap, Walker-Nine had disabled the anti-jump field, told Cleavie to position Hengway and Simone in the middle of the room, and relished another eleven-legged snack. *This is way more fun than I could have imagined*, both Walker-Nines thought.

They all jumped early, of course, as everyone always does—it is a rule of half-baked plans and panicky students. The Chosen, Chorlie, and the second Walker-Nine all stood staring at the spot previously containing four executants.

The remaining Walker-Nine waved and disappeared. The table and chairs then did their duty, also disappearing. The castle began to systematically vanish everything that could be of any use to the unwanted occupiers.

The two hundred highly-armed Chosen found themselves standing in a cold, empty and very unhappy castle. Chorlie was very quickly about to enter 'destination butt hurt' with his superiors. The Chosen's care factor fell below zero.

"Wow, do that again! I would love to biff about with time. Imagine the bullies at Trav-Coll. I could go and p—"

"Hengway, I'm sure you could do a lot of things to your bullying friends. Especially a lot of things starting with P. I would also like to do a lot of things, starting with P. Punch, poke, peck, plus—well, a plurality of punishments," Cleavie professed. She had punt jumped them into her room in New Axe after paying the appropriate punt jump tax. Hengway had never seen the inside of it before and was shocked at its utter—

"Plainness; that's a word starting with P. Where are all of your posters and pictures and odd jars full of critters?" enquired Hengway, gazing around the room.

It was a basic, plain Cellfast room made from some flat and hard material with a shiny veneer resembling stone because it was lighter and cheaper to build with. He did notice two doors leading away from the room, one on the far wall and one to his left.

"How are you two going?" he asked Walker-Nine and Simone. He noticed they were laughing. This laughter was born of stress, anxiety, fear, and sudden, immense relief.

"You were awesome, Niner," Hengway said, trying to give Walker-Nine a nickname to be friendly.

"You hasss a lot to learn about impfissh. In factss I assssume numerouss non-impfisssh acrossss the systemss iss ssoon to learn a lot about uss very sswiftly," said Walker-Nine. "Calling me 'Walker' iss jusst fine. The nine isss a rank."

"His 'Nine' is the lowest, and 'One' is the highest. Walker here was sold into working servitude by its family after failing skills tests like your own. On the day of the Paired One Hundred, we appeared within grabbing distance of one another, and I could read Walker's mind. I could also read the mind of the naroozie trying to track us down," explained Simone, who found a three-legged stool to sit on and was picking bits of stuff out of her unruly hair and dropping it on the floor beside an empty bin.

"Thingss transspired sso sswiftly it could have been a dissaster. We sstayed esscaped for sseveral weekss but were eventually sseized," continued Walker-Nine.

Being ever the nosey one, Simone ambled to the plain wooden bed made with white sheets and white blankets. She sat on it and slowly put her hands on her knees in what Hengway thought was an uncomfortable resting position.

There was a harsh knock at the main door. Without anyone responding, it flew open, and two dwarfs in complete battle armour screamed through, effecting full battle rolls. Axes and fists went everywhere. The bearded dwarfs stopped, turned, and stared at a bemused four.

"What–when, why the—" one of them stammered.

"Settle down, you two!"

Cleavie and Hengway relaxed since they knew that bellowing voice.

"Knock it off and fetch the appropriate paperwork for Cleavie's new friends!" said Kalle Hammer Petafelt from behind the two alarmed dwarfs. Cleavie was glad to see her father.

"Greetings, my most respected parent."

"Well met, daughter. Hello, Hengway. Hello, you two. Welcome to the Cellfast system and New Axe. I must cordially insist that you stay near Cleavie at all times, or you may be arrested. A war has started which makes everyone fearful of outsiders."

"Isn't that always the case," said the ever-talkative Simone.

"Aye, lass. Except war gives people an excuse to act on baseless fears." Kalle stared directly at Walker, who stared directly back. Kalle's reaction made everyone nervous.

"Iss there any newss of the impfissh ssysstem?" Walker-Nine asked.

Kalle shook his head. "There is a lot you all need to catch up on. In fact, Cleavie, if you hadn't come back, we would have sent for you. Meet us in the control tower in thirty minutes." He turned and left swiftly in an atypical military manner. Just as Cleavie was starting to think he had grown a military conscience, Kalle turned around with both thumbs up and gave his daughter a sly wink.

"That, I take it, was the old man?" Simone asked.

"If you mean my father, then yes."

"Got some nice braids in his beard. He has a following in the worker camps. Word is he was quite a good soldier in his time, though some will say he was a soldier of others' misfortune. Word is, he didn't mind a bit of stealing if he could get away with it."

Hengway punt jumped before Cleavie could react. Walker slowed time and ran towards Simone. Cleavie's fist swung through the air, connecting with Hengway's face and not with Simone's, which was Cleavie's intended target. Not just a part of his face. Not just a glancing pass-through.

Straight into the meat and bones of his face.

Walker grabbed Simone, turned her around and tucked her safely against the wall.

"Nnnggguuhhh," was as much as Hengway could muster as time caught up to its usual speed. He glared at Cleavie, who glared back at Hengway.

"What?"

Hengway continued the glaring challenge with Cleavie until he accepted she did not have the good grace to be even a little bit embarrassed. *Still a good punch*, she thought to herself.

Hengway's eyes slowly, very slowly, rolled towards the ceiling. *Such a smooth, straight ceiling,* he thought. Help from others was nonexistent so he fell to the floor with a whomp!

Hengway groaned throughout the slow process of regaining consciousness. Realising that he was still on the floor, and that outside assistance had called in sick he grew concerned. Very much so, and he was suitably biffed.

"How dare you mock my father and my culture?" Cleavie demanded.

"When you see what your bunch did to my bunch, you may change your mind, hairy one," Simone rebutted with a sly smile.

"Enoughs! Sseriousssly? Do I havess to be the adult inss the room? We all needss to takes a can of sshut-the-biff-up and takes in what iss going on," Walker interjected.

"We were all paired, we all come from different parts of the system pool, we have the freaky powers, and our parents are coming unstuck at the hinges," blurted a biffed-off and woozy Hengway.

"Unsstuck at the hingess?" enquired Walker-Nine, though very quietly. Hengway's door-themed remark hung in the air, and was duly ignored.

"Not to mention a war has started to bring back naroozie control. There are some of us that run around nude, my sister is a complete nutter who might want to kill us, and my biffing mother is nowhere to be found. *Have I missed anything?*"

"Yeah. How about that freaky Chaos Light thing? That's pretty intriguing stuff," added Simone. "When we were in prison, everyone kept asking if we knew anything about that thing. Nobody did, of course." Simone was on a roll and thought she had everyone captured with her deep wit and sharp insights into current, and former, events.

Cleavie snapped, barrelling Simone into the room's small side door. Simone whooped with happiness when they crashed through the door as, funnily enough, the door became unhinged. They landed without ceremony, and Simone's laughter could have made anyone not stressed about the situation laugh along with her.

"The door has joined your parents and their unstuck hinges," she hollered and whooped. She pushed Cleavie away and held her hands up in a universal sign of surrender. "Enough, enough. So fun–oh, my, I–can't breathe." Simone collapsed one limb at a time until she formed a Simone-shaped puddle on the floor.

"Light, now!" called Walker-Nine. A faint point of light illuminated the room about a foot above their heads. "Comess in handy in prisson, lets me assure you," Walker said, inspecting Cleavie's private things.

Hengway took in the scene of the room. This was more of what he was expecting from such an uptight dwarf. Printed papers were affixed to the wall. String connected bits of paper to other bits of paper. There were maps of the systems, with notes and scribbles decorating almost all of them.

"I *knew* you were planning this. Impressive," mind-spoke Hengway. "Even Simone has shut up."

"Well I'll be! A genuine war-planning-room. You done good. This room gets my approval for a one-way ticket to biffing inspiration," Simone said as she herself summoned her own light source, which appeared a foot above her head but a bit to the right.

Cleavie stepped over Simone and flicked a switch. A light in the middle of the ceiling shone into every corner.

"You might have done that earlier," griped Simone. With a deep sigh, Walker and Simone switched off their magical lights.

"Welcome to the room of knowledge, o remarkable one," said a tinny voice from somewhere in the room.

"Must be a T-Life or a steam powered helper," said Hengway, once again, albeit all too often, to no one in particular. "That sounded like The Captain, though," he continued.

Cleavie had the good grace to turn a subtle shade of raspberry before saying, "Helper off!" A bingley-dooply-bop sound reverberated before the helper drawled, in what was definitely The Captain's voice, "Catch ya next time, gorgeous."

That silence. Oh, that special silence. Three strange people in your private place. Be it your bedroom or your special swimming spot. Or even when people discover you collect nerdy brown suitcases from a specific period. It could be that you know a bit more about stamps or coins than your peers would find acceptable.

The usually unflappable Cleavie started to flap. Just a bit. The tiniest flapping hinge, and Hengway could detect it.

"I hass known of The Captain, of courrsse. I hass never heard him ssspeak. Ssoundss ssexy," said Walker-Nine.

"I wouldn't say a word if I were you," mind-spoke Hengway to Simone. Simone's face contorted into a painful visage as though she were trying to suck on a pickled impfish snack. Her small, uninteresting nose started to poke out like an unwanted pimple, or more like a throbbing boil. She tried breathing through her nose, sounding like an asthmatic bunglebeast running through the ash cloud of an exploding bush on Waiface 3.

Cleavie, being the ever-present lodestone of obviousness said, "This room is hidden from everybody. I expect having two paired together is going to release some more skills we haven't discovered yet. Please, everyone, be very careful in what you wish for."

That silence in the room again. Walker-Nine did not know what the problem was, Hengway was new to the whole having-a-crush-on-teachers thing, and Simone was left to continue sucking her own face. Luckily, this sucking was now done more quietly.

They could hear something, or someone, walking through the corridor near the main bedroom door. Cleavie sent them all a mind message to remain quiet, and jumped all of them out of the secret room. *Hingeing the unhinged will guide the nature of this game*, she thought. She restored all of the hinges that were within her power, re-hiding the secret chamber right as her father, accompanied by a hovering T-Life, came striding through the door.

"Listen up! The Captain has been captured. Get ready for a wee bit of a tussle!" exclaimed Kalle. In times of war, Cleavie knew that her father was solid, but still enjoyed making light of the situation.

"You lot, the war is about to begin."

14. Accidentally Mostly Successful

"Draggi, please report on the Waiface 3 incident. Particularly, the incident concerning your neglect to identify a murderous spy," demanded a senior member of the naroozie war council.

Draggi paused to fortify her morale as well as her story. "Tarlan and Tuja should have seen this coming. The spy was a trusted servant for twenty years. He must have come to us when he was barely a teenager. Faithful all that time, lying in wait to..."

"Calm yourself!" demanded the head of the council. The rest of the council shuffled uncomfortably in their seats for two reasons. The first was that naroozie were not known for their interpersonal emotional intelligence. The second being it was never comfortable to sit with a leg protruding from the middle of your back.

"Do not blame us. I wasn't around for that period of time. Besides, you should have vetted your staff in a more thorough manner," spat Tuja. She was the only human involved in this meeting, although there were two famous dwarfs sitting on the sideline trying to be somewhat inconspicuous, which was impossible for two dwarfs amongst large furry naroozie.

The silence was broken as Draggi recharged her social battery and continued, "Biff you two. This servant was here for decades. Who knew he was an assassin? Not I. It was never even an issue."

"Have you tortured, sorry, have you spoken to other servants, especially humans that were close to him," an attendee asked from the main table.

"All of this is irrelevant. You keep saying he. You are mistaken. *She* ... is a very patient enchanter. This patience did not pay out for her as I believe she failed her mission." Tarlan now had everybody's full attention.

"Welcome to the council, Trinni," said Professor Smeltzit. Although she could physically see the members of Section Nine, Trinni could also feel the invisible presence of others, or even ghosts. Luckily, she always acted as though she was being watched—it was not paranoia if people were actually out to kill you.

"I have recently been on a long-punt which was accidentally successful for reasons I will report. I had intended to jump to Waiface 3 and conduct surveillance, and perhaps deal with the main troublemakers, but to no avail. I found myself on Waiface 3..."

"Which is what we required of you," Draggi interrupted Trinni's well planned debrief.

"I am eager to get back to the future. As you will find out, I have been kept from matters against my will, and this me is actually a future version of myself that was long-punted to the past. If I could have everyone's attention, you will save questions until the end as that will help us get through this debrief a lot quicker," instructed Trinni. The attendees nodded their heads and had a quiet giggle at Draggi's expense. Most of the room wanted what Trinni suggested, for it to be over as soon as possible.

"As suggested, I was to deal with two naroozie commanders on Waiface 3, so I punt jumped there in order to create a suitable plan. I was long-punted to the correct planet, albeit twenty years in the past." The crowd gasped and attempted to interrupt Trinni with a multitude of questions. She held up a hand and gave the attendees a poisoned gaze that demanded total silence. They did the gaze's bidding.

"Fortunately for me, even before the recent sense magic revolution, my magic worked better than I expected. I created a backstory and befriended people who worked for the Fnwah family. Tarlan was young and paid no attention to servants, especially non-naroozie servants."

"My time there was wasted. My failure was somewhat dampened by study and research; however, it was fruitless nonetheless. I had access to the enchanters, although I did not tell them who I was."

"Why did you not inform them of who you are, or at least ask for help?" asked Draggi.

"You cannot punt within a long-punt. I usually have to wait to be long-punted back to the exact spot, and time, I started from. Rarely does it help me to tell the enchanters who I am. They assume that I am a spy, a heretic, or simply crazy. So, I continued studying and practising necessary forms of magic in private."

Smeltzit lifted his hand to garner the attention of Trinni without getting berated for interrupting her. She nodded. "I thought only males were allowed to work as a servant, especially at the Fnwah lodgings."

The attendees gasped in amazement as Trinni became a teenage human boy. Before they could ask questions she could have considered bothersome, the boy who had formed before them gradually aged. They watched as he became older and older until he resembled a twenty-four year old man fully outfitted with a poorly considered haircut and an atrociously over-managed beard.

"**W**elcome to the kitchens of the great house of Fnwah," the cook announced to Trinni disguised as a male. "Listen to me, Casus! The Fnwah family is generous to good workers but relentlessly brutal to slackers, drifters and ne'er do wells." There were a few snickers from the other new lodge staff, however, the clever ones studied the ground with stern intent and remained silent.

The duties were mundane, and it took a lot of effort on Trinni's part not to use magic for the most boring tasks. Setting hearth fires in the kitchen and main hall, cleaning rooms, and worst of all, shopping with the cook all had to be done the old fashioned, magic-free way.

Years passed. Trinni had to modify her Casus avatar as she herself grew older. During this time Tarlan, her original target, was growing up in a different part of the lodge. Trinni was a lower servant, so she had no access to the Fnwah family or their children.

One morning after a long, difficult winter, Trinni decided that, bollocks to space and time paradoxes, it was best to kill Tarlan when she was a teenager. It was either that or punt jump the cook to the exploding bushes. *These long-punts are a long nuisance*, she thought, all day every day.

Tarlan and the family held a weekly dinner where the kitchen staff worked tirelessly for days, preparing exotic foods for an expansive buffet. The expense of this buffet offended many, especially Trinni, as the money could have built hundreds of farms for many families.

Trinni discovered that Tarlan always insisted on a peculiar dish of frogs and snails that others with more astute tastes, failed to consume. Trinni spent more than a year orchestrating the attack. On the day of the banquet, a mischievous, random, untimely schedule of events played against her. A guest ate the eccentric dish while Tarlan was off with a boy called Enfki. The guest suffered a slow, painful death by poison, so the taster along with the assistant cook were executed using the same method.

"**...S**o, to cut a long story short, I attempted to kill Tarlan at least fifteen times and failed at each attempt. Knowing I could not punt myself out of the long-punt, I kept studying, planning, and failing."

"You did have one success though," Smeltzit commented. "I believe it caused disruption and may have stopped a naroozie and dwarf alliance."

"Indeed. It was after the mysterious death of the cook. I had been there for years when Tarlan and her husband had a child which I now understand is my brother's lover. I was a part of the furniture by this stage. I tried to contact the enchanters chapel but was told to go back to whichever mental institution I came from."

The enchanters' delegation began talking amongst themselves. "We hasss addressed the issue of longs-puntss and communicationss with enchanter chapelss, academies and other enchanter lodgess," said the impfish adorned in an ornate robe. She was older than the others and wore a human short sword as well as sense-magic webbing.

"Long-punts have been found to be effectively linear," Trinni explained. "There were occasions where an enchanter might speak to me in the afternoon, and I would immediately find myself waking up in my room the next morning. When approaching the enchanter again, they remembered nothing of our conversation and would completely dismiss me. The enchanters have no knowledge of this anomaly. They are not to blame for it."

Professor Smeltzit spoke, "Please expand on how during this time you were still involved in your brother's escapades."

"I would come and go. When I say I was stuck there, that is not entirely correct. I jumped a few times to places where I had to negotiate, fix or kill something. Some of my fruition, and some driven by ... shall we say other forces. More of that will be detailed in later briefings."

"Yesss, back to the ssuccesssful failure, pleasse." The impfish was more inquisitive than interrogative—even impfish enjoy a good story.

"I had another opportunity to kill Tarlan. Pardon my memory, but I have experienced a lot, so details do catch fire from time to time. I killed Tarlan's lover by mistake ..."

"That's just before Tuja and Tarlan hooked up and created a nuisance!" blurted Draggi.

Trinni turned her head in a slow dramatic manner. "She was very miffed."

Everyone in the room went impatiently quiet.

"I tried to discombobulate a punt but only managed to kill one of the two. So a successful failure," Trinni added with a mischievous smile.

"A successful failure that gave us the motive for Tarlan's maniacial behavior and started the relationship between the tyrants. And with that, we will adjourn for now. Thank you, everybody." Smeltzit said.

The attendees were excited to ask Trinni a plethora of questions. There was only one problem.

She had already disappeared.

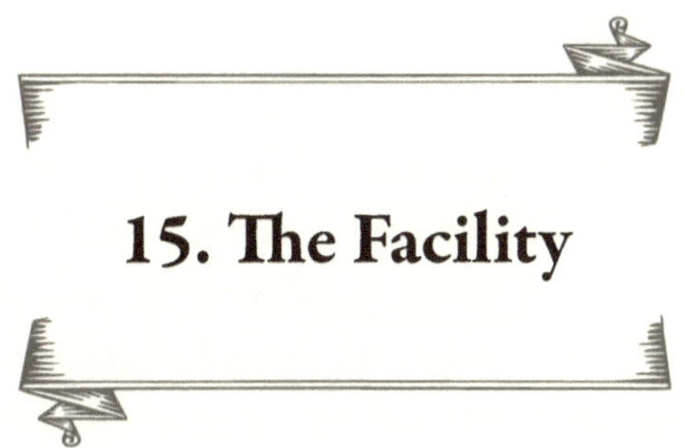

15. The Facility

The completely hinged four sat in an environmentally controlled command post on a small moon just outside a planet of the Gas Field system.

Before they left for the moon, the four attended a debriefing on the nearest planet.

"Thank you, Kalle. I hass been briefed on the locasssion and know thiss ssatellite quite well. It wass alwayss off-limitss to our younglingss for generasssionss. Sso mosst know the area very well." Walker-Nine gestured towards a table in the middle of the room above which floated a large map of the Gas Field. The slowly rotating map displayed the small dark sun and fifteen planets which filled the system, only it was difficult to tell any of them apart.

The four were assured that spies had discovered a device which could expose all who were paired, known and unknown. This device was capable of jumping the paired to a previously unknown position.

Kalle had not slept in days. His appearance and general stench suggested he needed a long shower and some longer rest.

Leaning over the table he sighed. "This device could be an extremely dangerous weapon. We don't know anything about it or its actual capabilities. We have to stop whoever, or whatever, is controlling it. The Gas Fields are mostly unknown to us. Fortunately, we have a new friend who can help us out in this area. I need you to search for anything out of the ordinary." Walker-Nine nodded to Kalle in readiness to guide the group to the place in question.

They had been on the moon for three days and were watching one particular punt jump port. Hengway had made the mistake of reading a little too much about the Gas Field System. He tried to keep Cleavie out of his mind-speak zone, and Simone from actually speaking. *Me thinks a change of topic is in order*, Hengway mused.

"Walker, why don't the impfish change the names of your planets and system to what you use instead of using the ones given to you by these explorers?"

"Not sso many people care about uss to assk ssuch a quesstion," Walker-Nine responded, keeping its eyes on the jump-port about five hundred feet away. The four had been there longer than their attention spans were built for, and they were getting beyond restless.

Much to Hengway's surprise, he had become an informal group leader, but members mainly acted alone, especially Cleavie. The plan was straightforward, which was all Hengway could muster at this stage.

The plan was to watch the spaceport for suspicious groups who usually fought their opponents but now seemed to engage them in shady deals. *At least we can stay under the radar for a few days and figure things out,* Hengway thought.

"And you still haven't answered me," he said to Walker whilst scrutinising a small box with multiple views of the spaceport on the screen.

"Iss not a ssimple matter to disscuss. Ssome ssay the impfissh ssenior counssel doess not wissh to sshare our hisstory or our future with otherss that assesss life'ss exisstencse sso worthlesssly."

"Oh, the dwarfs value life. They keep a price list of how much each is worth at every worker-camp," Simone happily chirped.

Before anyone could tell Simone to shut up, especially Cleavie, an unexpected ship punt jumped into view. This ship was not your typical silver box. Punt ships had no need to be streamlined, or to travel through space or atmospheres, so they are usually designed in the shape of a boring day-to-day round sports ball, however this one was long with rounded, ridiculously smooth edges. The ship was a sleek black with an even blacker disruptive pattern spattered along the hull.

"Well, I think this counts as something out of the ordinary," whispered Hengway. His three teammates knew what this meant. They packed their kits, readying themselves for action.

From within the ship frantic sounds of scratching and yelling echoed through the fuselage, violently vibrating the hull. Without warning the back end of the ship disappeared, revealing a ramp connecting the grassy landing zone to the edge of the ship.

"What do we do?" cried Simone.

"Quiet! We watch, wait, assess, plan, and only then commit to action," Hengway said decisively, surprising even himself. The four of them watched the ship intently. "Cleavie, time for one of our new skills," Hengway said. He and Cleavie closed their eyes.

"Where are we supposed to put this chunk of metal?" grumbled a grossly untidy naroozie.

"They're gonna send some help and that," replied an even untidier human.

"So, this works then," affirmed Cleavie, mind-speaking to Hengway. One skill they had been practising was mind projection. Using this technique they could walk around the target area, whilst seeing and hearing everything. Travis had explained that, according to vague rumours, some paired could even feel and touch when projecting.

This is good enough for now, mused Hengway. "Yep. Works well enough."

"Bring out the prisoners," said the stinky human. "Hurry up, ya b—" She was cut off by the noise of chains clanking and prisoners moaning. The ramp lit up with electrical lights, making visible the captives being pushed, shoved, or otherwise unwillingly encouraged to move down the ramp. If any decided not to comply, they were prodded with laser-sticks normally reserved for farmers to use on recalcitrant livestock.

"Count how many prisoners there are, Cleavie!" called Hengway. His first thought was to ensure that the device used to capture the paired was present at this facility, so they could find the bloody thing and proceed to blow the biffle out of the device. With these prisoners' being present they would be unable to take that path without causing injury to the innocent.

"Hengway–oh, biff." Cleavie sounded distracted. "Hengway, I tried to mind-speak with them to find out some information, but–oh, no!"

"Try not to be too dramatic," he murmured. Cleavie was usually annoyingly straightforward and tended to avoid drama, which he liked very much.

"They are *all* paired," Cleavie continued. They have been used to operate the artefact. Some paired have died trying to escape. Hengway, this needs fixing!"

Cleavie perceived a change in Hengway and, in the midst of her horror, was somehow delighted to observe his maturer approach to difficulties. His military and fighting skills were a little better than before, and she could sense a stronger mind.

Inwardly, however, Hengway was petrified. *See these soldiers! Consider these paired! Tired, hungry, and clearly poorly treated.* Hengway gathered his thoughts. In a moment of light, the plan drew itself together. It was a plan that began... now!

The team gathered around Hengway. Hengway took his time to stop and assess. With considerable personal insight he said, "I have stopped time and assessed. We have to behave as a team." The team, as it were, was thoroughly impressed with the time-stopping thing. They gazed at Hengway, attentive and completely intrigued.

"This is our plan. We damage the device beyond repair and free all the captives. I will be the first to attack and the last to stop fighting. I will leave no one behind."

"By my guess, there are twenty captives and ten guards." Hengway mind-projected the location of the ship's landing place. Every part of the scene was revealed in detailed slow motion.

They saw it as a bird-like view, and also heard Hengway's voice as though he was in their own minds. The scene drifted forwards focusing on a metallic door, in a dream-like motion. "This is the main door to the facility where they intend to place the device."

"Let's make this simple—" Hengway said, speaking at length, detailing a plan that turned out to be nowhere near simple.

The plan, against all conventional military wisdom and experience, proceeded adequately even after the initial interaction with the enemy.

Simone punt jumped into the ship and performed a textbook right-cross, knocking out a guard. This led to an immediate all-in brawl, with Simone making new friends amongst the guards. The type of friends who do not mind a kick in the shins as a sign of friendship.

Walker-Nine had been appointed backup, and punt jumped into the rear of the prison-ship. Cleavie soon joined. Finding mud on the floor that the cleaning-bots had missed, they quickly smeared camouflage onto their faces, and immediately grabbed the end of the long chain connecting every captured paired. Cleavie mind-spoke to all of them, detailing the steps to follow. They all acknowledged the plan by staring at her in wild surprise whilst nodding unanimous assent.

"Simone is having a quiet word with the guards. The plan is still good to go."

"Thanks, Cleavie," said Hengway.

All good plans, even bad plans, should have backup plans–even if those are worse than the first plan, and so on. Hengway had heard his mother say this in last year's military tactics lessons, and now he wished he had listened to the many others that had tried to give him advice in the past.

The guards started to get the better of an exhausted Simone. Hengway instructed her to punt jump back to his position. She did so with some sorrow, but it was a good call. The main door to the facility began to open.

The door's hinges bucked and squealed with disuse. The door swung upwards using a system of wheels and pulleys, beyond the raised door they could see the captured paired huddling closer to one another to protect their new members, for which Cleavie and Walker were wondrously grateful.

"Get the device in there so we can get out of this disgraceful place," demanded a guard who was better clothed, better bathed, and considerably better fed than the rest.

"Stay alert! Disappearing prisoners get my goat," blurted the overfed leader of the guards.

"Mmm, goat. I would love a bit of goat-stew about now," said the first raggy human.

The guards' banter gave Cleavie and Walker-Nine the time needed to blend in. The guards' stupidity also distracted the not-so-stupid ones, who had always considered their leader and his favourite guard a bit queer.

The device floated off the ground using the power of the artefact within, and moved towards the main door of the facility. The guards had to act quickly to shift the prisoners. Prods and kicks and shouts and spitting and slapping and generally every other cruel method of enforcement took place. The prisoners were made to proceed to a smaller door next to the main entrance. They were escorted, with violence, through the doorway not made for a crowd.

Hengway and Cleavie had practiced their next skill only a few times under Travis' supervision. It failed more often than it worked. "Ready to go," Hengway said to Cleavie, who was in a hallway two hundred feet away.

"I can't see a thing, Hengway. They put hoods on us. I have told everyone to make sure they are all touching."

Making a quick decision, Hengway punt jumped next to Cleavie.

'Hesitation causes thinking. Thinking causes doubts—by the time doubts come, you are dead. Don't hesitate!' The Captain would advise, always without hesitation.

Hengway could not help but gaze around at the hooded captives. He grabbed Cleavie's hand. The punt jump was much harder than usual, but it worked. The freed paired were now in Cleavie's room. Many vomited, some passed out, and one impfish started bellowing the foundation-song of its people then broke into a burst of deep, gurgling laughter.

"That went better than I thought," said Cleavie. "Time for the next step." Her small room contained paired of all types and sizes, squished together like a school-kid's sandwich on a hot summer's day. It was cosy, not nearly as gooey as the sandwich, but cosy nonetheless.

"No time to moan! Cleavie told you what you need to do next. Get ready! We move in ten seconds."

The room turned into a scene of chaotic order, like a murder of drunken crows fighting for one last piece of flesh. There were legs, hands, fins, and a few tails swishing about the room. Chains were removed, ropes were cut from flailing limbs. The idea was to find your paired if you could. If you could not locate your paired, hang on, because all was about to go off-centre.

Hengway was impressed that everyone had handled this so well and so quickly. He knew he had to maintain momentum and keep everyone busy and alert. The group's next punt jump occurred like the previous one but with far less drama.

Hengway perceived the consensus of thoughts through the haze of inarticulate moans; *Why return to the place of danger we just escaped?* He mind-spoke to all directly, "This is the main push. This must work, or we will never be free of this device." On that counsel, Hengway punted everyone into position.

Meanwhile, Cleavie, Simone and Walker-Nine had other tasks. They had jumped back into the facility and were sufficiently messing around with guards to discover vital information. The guards were far from happy, with some flopped over, dead.

They beat-up the remaining guards, magically made them believe they were small slippery fish, contented chickens, or disused house bricks, and ensured that the guards would not upset anyone in the near, or distant, future.

The three then entered the main control room. Before them were screens and panels dotted around a large command table displaying maps of other systems, with a huge map of the Cellfast system and New Axe displayed prominently in its centre.

"They want a chunk of your hometown, Cleavie," Simone noted. Simone was striding towards the large table when Cleavie advised her to stop. *This doesn't feel right*, thought Cleavie.

"I actually agree with that thought. This is completely biffed. Where are the control room guards and the traps? At least some nasty dogs would have been a bit more realistic," said Simone, who was expanding her mind-reading capabilities as far as they could reach. "There is at least one other in here. Hard to read her mind, though."

A small figure appeared behind them in enchanter armour. "Hello, you three, nice to meet you. Or should I say, bad to meet you? You have upset my plans."

Recognising who the interloper was, Cleavie commanded, "Jump now!" So they did, with extreme enthusiasm.

16. What Now?

The Weekly Voice.
Tuja Acae, on the hopeful future for the Yurning System.
Owning planets with adequate environmental conditions and rare minerals once helped make humans powerful, and this is how humans will gain control again. We need to work with the dwarfs of the Cellfast system to regain dominance. The naroozie, other humans and now the impfish have started an all-system quest for dominance and economic strength, which will be difficult to stop. We must once more protect the Yurning system and make our race great again.

Jay remembered his mother's article well, and knew that it likely caused most of the difficulties they now faced. The words *control* and *powerful* conjured up images better left forgotten. Unfortunately, species of all colours and flavours will want to think that they have rights over others at some point in their history.

Tuja came from a long line of people who entertained such beliefs, and with like-minded associates, they pushed for humans to become dominant once again.

Jay stood guard outside the Yurning 7 library, where the enchanters were said to be keeping captive paired. Jay did not understand Trinni's role in all of this, but his father certainly wanted to know what was going on when he urged Jay to spy on both the enchanters and the naroozie.

"The Chosen have assigned you an important task. As you know, Trinni has been acting strangely and has developed some unusually wide-ranging skills very quickly since your mother disappeared." The conversation with his father took place a few weeks after the day of the Paired One Hundred.

"The Captain has been hailed. We believe certain tribes of the naroozie are involved in creating a disturbance. There are only two or three naroozie tribes that would be interested in creating an intersystem council to control the systems. We need to know who in the senior naroozie ranks feels as though there are better options than a racially autocratic form of government."

Forthwright studied his son's bemused face, "Your activities will be unknown to those who do not need to know. It may appear to others that you have become traitorous, which is what we want them to think."

"I did have plans for the holidays, you know," joked Jay, giving his father a sly grin.

"It's good to keep a sense of humour, though please know that this is a genuinely dangerous mission. Your mother is absent without leave, Trinni has decided to evolve into a magical rogue, and your brother has found it necessary to mutate into a powerful magical force without my permission."

"I was going to reluctantly congratulate him, I must add. I suppose I'll need to keep him at arm's length for a while?" Jay responded, knowing full well he always wanted to keep Hengway at arm's length.

"Correct. There is a naroozie boy we need you to get close to. His parents are respected in the tribes, and he has been marked for high positions."

That conversation felt like a million systems and a million years ago. Naroi had proved to be very easy to get on with, and now his heart was starting to get in the way of his task. Naroi was being just as manipulated as everyone else in this mess.

"I hope this silly Chaos Light thing is in here," Jay said to Naroi, who was sitting on a rock examining the architecture of the library. Jay contemplated Naroi's physique, which was looking as good as ever, which always annoyed Jay—annoyed him in a good, distracting way, which annoyed him even more.

"We have sent in detectors. They should start transmitting shortly," commented Naroi, smiling back at Jay. Although Jay was unwashed and human, he still looked all right.

"Jay is a spy," his mother told him. "I know," he had replied—a spy spying on a spy invading the headquarters of the system's most prominent spies.

The pairings threw a spanner into the machine, though. It was a pity it was not all kept a secret. Rumours swirled that there had been many pairings over the centuries. The story was that if one did not find his or her, or its, exact pairing partner, their own magical ability would be somewhat diminished. This machine or device forced the pre-paired to be punt jumped together, which would kick off a mass pairing event. An event that had never been seen before.

"You ready, partner?" Naroi asked Jay as he picked up a gun. This gun was worthy of a name. *The Hunter*, *White Death* or some other lame thing given by young warfighters to well-designed things. Naroi, and naroozie in general, had respect for items of excellence with value and purpose. In regard to all of these things, he gave his gun the honorific title, 'The Gun'.

The joke was lost on most people, but naroozie, in general, thought it was as funny as that time they had invaded a whole system in three days and not a living thing was left. Oh, the laughter. *Those were the days,* mused Naroi, as he headed towards Jay, who was picking up his spear and personal sword.

Unfortunately for them, the naroozie military command promoted the two lads. They were placed in charge of a highly trained force of over one hundred fighters who were all armed and, in some cases, legged or finned, way beyond what would be considered overboard. Some of them had the appearance of ordinary soldiers about to go into battle. Others appeared to be untrained and possibly coerced into their current predicament. All of them had backpacks full of rockets and other bits and pieces sticking out of belts and pockets.

Jay examined a squad near him by the library, marched over, and began yelling orders in a way only a military leader could muster, "Drop half of that junk and get ready! Let's get you sack of bunglebeast droppings performing like a team of war fighters, you miserable sorts!"

Naroi decided Jay's yelling was a great example to follow and practised the same technique on the other squads. "What time is it?" Jay asked his T-Life war support droid. The droid replied that it was ten minutes to lunch.

"You mean launch, right?"

The droid was rather embarrassed. "Oh, yes, of course. Fifteen minutes to launch."

Jay was not amused as much as the droid was embarrassed. He poked around the pouches on his leather belt, producing a gun. Pointing it skywards, he shot a projectile straight up into the air about one hundred feet. The projectile exploded in a green flash. There was no need for a declaration of attack now as they had made enough noise to wake everyone up to ten systems deep.

"Let's go in and inspect the headquarters."

The army—well, not really an army; Jay and Naroi only commanded ten squads—the force was ready to attack—more than ready. The nature of their structure and training meant that the soldiers generally managed themselves. This method was immediately proven a disaster as they charged the wooden doors of the library in an embarrassingly disorderly sprint.

Stupidity and disarray ruled. The first ten or so soldiers fell straight into deep pits. A dozen others were shot with goo guns and transformed into green glowing ash that tended to stick onto anything then burn through it. Clothing, armour, skin, bone–anything that was not magically protected was eaten by this ash.

Jay ordered them forward. The soldiers lined up looking weak and disheveled. One of the enchanters from the library mumbled a command and pointed both palms at the brick and wood frontage. After some shakes and some strange whining noises, the wall crumbled, creating a ragged breach. The dust settled as the enchanters fell back behind the main line of fighters.

The murderous green ash dissipated. Waiting for the next surprise did not take long. A beast the size of a small farmhouse came stamping out of the newly enhanced entrance. Its enormous head was encased by thick metal armour pierced by four spear-like tusks, creating an impressive defensive bastion.

"Let's be getting this beastie," yelled a brave, probably insane human. She stepped up to the enormous beast, aiming her spear at its eye. A good tactic, usually. As she readied her spear, a dozen four-legged animals came out of the dark library interior, attacking her. *The brave should be a little bit more wary,* thought Jay. His mother always used to say, "no prizes for dead heroes." They had lost about twenty-five soldiers, and they had not even entered the front door.

"This is absolute biff," Naroi complained. The remaining forces fought the beasts in a lengthy fracas, rife with screams and the general noise of death and destruction before the beasts were killed.

"The enchanters' surprises are a constant amusement," bantered Jay. Together, they prodded a wretched soldier into the dark opening.

The soldier crept tentatively, step by tiny step, into the large room. In typical library design, it had a vast empty space at the front which contained nothing but floor. The area was empty aside from an empty easel tipped on its side, which worried the first soldier. He stopped and assessed the situation. He reported that he was alive. A fact that did not stop the panic of the following fifteen soldiers who stepped in behind him.

"Fantastic, team. We made it through the front door," said Naroi. He expected nothing more than traps all the way down into the dungeons.

"Let's get this sorted. There can't be too many traps le—" Jay's sentence was rudely cut short by a flaming log shooting through the air lengthways across the room.

Explosions caused the ground to tremble and created a fog of war existing of various pieces of wall, metal and body parts. More experienced or suitably flexible soldiers were leaping and jumping and ducking and positioning themselves away from the blazing battle zone.

Jay picked himself up, trying not to laugh nervously at the wreckage before him. Soldiers were strewn everywhere. "The best of the best. The highest trained individuals in all the systems, I was told." He took a deep breath and shouted, "Get up! Stand fast and take ranks!" His voice echoed off the stone walls. Glowing charcoal and ashes of various species fell dramatically over soldiers as they formed ranks in a military and orderly fashion.

"How about some lights." Jay's command sent T-Life droids into a frenzy as they flew towards the roof. The first droid that found the roof exploded in a multi-coloured display of defeat. Pieces of the droid rained down upon the soldiers.

"This is biffing bad news for us," remarked Jay as he looked for an advantage.

"We knew the considerate architecture would be smelly poo packets, but this is getting extreme," Naroi grunted as he flicked bits of burnt creature and T-Life off his now very dirty armour.

"Ha! We haven't even entered the dungeons yet." A hard silence crept over the sounds of moaning, crashing, and burning. It started near the downward spiral staircase in the right-hand corner of the room, and mercilessly spread throughout. *Wouldn't be an enchanter event without some new biffed-up magic tricks*? Jay thought. Lighting droids flew and did their job over the stairs.

"Ye lads have been taking yer time." Travis leant on his battle hammer, giving the air of a man with no worries or concerns at all. "Ye'd better get some of yer highly polished team doin' that ta sort out the remaining T-Life I've left for ye."

With a nod of Jay's head, the assembled troops tried to hurry down the stairs. None were actually hurrying with any noticeable speed. Impartial observers might even have interpreted the soldiers' hurry as a remarkably slow dawdle.

"Dinna worry, ye fearless warriors. The considerate magic of the defence and offence systems hae been switched off," assured Travis the Truthful. The soldiers gained their professional bearing, marching down the stairs once again at a better pace.

"Ya two an me need tae huv a chat once dey ave finished jiggling their swords down dere. This whole mess is going tae purchase a one-way ticket to a biffy, baffed, bizarre town." Travis stood in magnificent glory with his war kilt and trusty hammer on full display. He was splattered and smeared with dirt and blood, and a small part of his beard was smouldering, smoke gently escaping the confines of one of his many braids.

Jay glanced at Naroi. Naroi glanced at Jay. They turned back to regard Travis in silent wonder.

Finally able to form a sentence, the two asked at the same time, "Who the biff are you?" and "What the Biff are you?"

17. Duck

Hengway had single-handedly jumped all the paired back onto the moon in the Gasfield system. He waited for everyone to be in position. "On my count of two, we move this thing. One and Tw—"

During the sound of two, the device started to leave the moon. It was being disassembled as though a vast, invisible hand were taking it apart. The outside pieces disappeared. Then, floors, internal bits, and other cable-like things went the same way. The device was being dismantled to keep paired undiscovered and therefore safe. That was the theory, anyway.

Hengway felt Cleavie jumping towards him and was not surprised to see Walker and Simone jumping with her. "You are a tad late for the fun," he stated.

"Your sister is trying to kill us and is probably behind this whole biffing fight," Cleavie responded calmly.

"Can't see the resemblance myself. She sure has a bit of get up and go, though," added Simone, who for once appeared a little frightened.

"I am surprised you didn't call her 'plucky'," Cleavie said, accompanied by a wry smile. "Hengway, we should go back and get her. You two, stay back there and help the others move that device!" She ordered Simone and Walker-Nine. Their quick, affirmative replies slightly shocked Cleavie, who was expecting some push-back from Simone.

The control room was completely devoid of light, unlike the darkness found outside when two moons are glowing. It was the smashing into furniture and doing yourself a mischief, kind of dark.

"Biff, it's dark in here," declared Cleavie, master of the blatantly obvious. Both of them pushed their senses out into the dark, searching for solid or sharp objects and, more importantly, things with heartbeats. A live nasty sister would be good.

"Where is she?" mind-spoke Hengway.

Cleavie activated a small device that she switched on with her mind. It flew out of her back belt pocket and hovered a few feet above her head. She would have used PSSA, but he did not have this upgrade installed. Through mind contact, the device showed an image of heat from living creatures. It showed only two heat sources other than theirs. She turned the device around and moved it across the control room, anticipating the nasty surprise she knew was lurking somewhere.

It lurked in front of them immediately, so it was clearly not very good at lurking. The T-Life was huge, it roared at the paired inferring that it meant business. It had weapons for hands and had just turned on flashing lights meant to distract attackers.

"I hope this excellent tactic works," Hengway said as he leapt towards the first T-Life. The T-Life did what was unexpected. It did nothing. It did nothing without a care. The T-Life then did the next unexpected thing. It did nothing with absolute commitment to do nothing. To become the champion of doing biff all, with elegance and ease.

Hengway thudded into the T-Life. Luckily, he had taken notice of his lessons with Travis and felt for a small switch behind the T-Life's knee. If indeed it had a knee. The T-Life saw a great opportunity to skewer Hengway with its spear hand. It raised its hand above Hengway's head while he was desperately clicking at the switch. The T-Life stopped motionless. The spear was a bird peck away from piercing his skull.

Hengway rolled away and leapt to his feet in a rare military moment of his. Cleavie was standing in the middle of a pile of T-Life parts.

"Nice move. Where's that brat of a sister of yours?" The room was quieter now. The flickering darkness and the possibility that there might be more surprises hidden among the creepy halls of this place kept the two from making a sound. Cleavie used PSSA to light up the space.

They checked the maps and documents. Cleavie found a large red bag labelled "Waiface Project". Hengway started shoving anything that appeared to be official into a bag.

"Stop! That's a stapler," Cleavie said. "It keeps paper together. Put it back! Just take things with official stamps and posh things like that!"

"I have never seen so much paper. You could feed a small village for a year on the money it costs to obtain this much paper."

"This war is about more than power and control; it's about—"

"To get a lot more interesting for you two," said Trinni. She had some nasty friends with her. A mix of war fighters of notable talent. She probably handpicked the nastiest, non-hair-washing, nose-picking and boogie-eating individuals that have ever existed.

Hengway considered it a great idea to punt jump to Cleavie's room. He tried to make it happen but ended up a few feet from where he had started. He glanced over at Cleavie and saw her buzzing in and out of sight, zagging and zigging, adjusting her movements to zigging and zagging, to no avail. She must have flickered in and out five times before she stopped trying.

"We need to get out of here," she said to Hengway in a tone that did not give away her internal panic. She tried to mind-speak and failed. She presumed that Trinni had put some magic, technology, or a considerate combination of both in place to prevent such shenanigans, except for her good self, of course.

Hengway was magically snaffled into a vast, invisible field, tossed through the air, and thrown into a table at one side of the room. He tried his wobbly legs and was hurled across the room once again, hitting the wall full-on, face and nose first.

His considerate armour helped reduce the sting a little bit on his body. His face, however, was not covered, and he felt the full force of the wall. He tried again to punt jump and landed a few feet from the wall. Blood from his broken nose flowed onto his armour. The armour did not like this and flicked it onto the floor. He was in pain, he was bleeding and his eyesight was impaired. *At least I am alive and on my feet.*

Hengway hadn't carried a weapon in a while as he did not really like them. He wished for one now. Nothing happened. He thought it would be considerate for a spear to appear in his hands. Nothing happened, except it happened in a more forceful manner. Considerate magic, normal magic and paired magic were clearly out of the fight, for them at least.

"Got a plan?" he yelled across a very busy room.

Trinni was circling the large table headed towards Cleavie. Cleavie had her axe in her hands and was entertaining two large, filthy, stenchy humans. They had black armour and were swinging swords at her with an intensive amount of enthusiasm. Their nefarious intent was to cause as much damage as they could muster. Cleavie avoided these swings searching for an advantage.

Hengway concentrated on digging deep into his mind for answers. The fact that his sister was causing all this could be dealt with later. They needed to get out of this situation quickly.

"Your mother sends her regards," said Trinni with a wink. She moved fluidly across the floor. It was as if she were on wheels or perhaps floating in an unnaturally steady way. "Let's finish this!"

she snarled, raising her hands and rushing towards Cleavie. Sparks flew between her palms. A ball of light slowly enlarged as she raised her hands above her head. Cleavie waited for an interesting death but Trinni seemed slow on the attack. *I need to help them*, Trinni thought. She came up with a plan and executed the strangest diversion push she had created thus far.

Hengway heard a command deep inside his brain. *Spear incoming! And Duck!* Having been paired for a few months and having seen many strange things, he trusted the order and rolled to his left.

The spear did that funny *boing* thing into the ground that all spears should do when they miss their target. Fortunately the duck missed him and splattered on the wall, feathers flying hither. There was no time for tithering in this fight. "Thanks for the warning," he mind spoke to Cleavie.

"Wasn't me," she mind blurted.

Momentarily confused, his attention was brought back to the here and now as he leapt to his feet and was immediately smashed in the face with the butt of a sword hilt, which also happens in the best of heroic fight scenes.

Hengway glared at the horrible human just in time to see him make an awkward surprise face. He crumpled to the ground like a politician's promise after an election. Walker-Nine was holding an impfish hammer, a speciality weapon of their culture. Hengway spun around and saw Simone trying to get to Cleavie to provide assistance. Hengway picked up the spear and threw it directly at Trinni.

Trinni shook her head at him whilst winking. The spear stopped just short of her and stood horizontally. Without warning it decided to be a fork. Being a spear was losing its shine, as far as the newly born fork was concerned. Hengway observed this utensil related threat and began a forcefield push but was surprised when the fork dropped to the ground, harmlessly. Trinni said, "Wait..." but was interrupted.

"Jump now!" Cleavie screamed. Hengway grabbed hold of Walker-Nine and punted, using the last remnant of magical energy he possessed.

Trinni thought that an actual planned long-punt was in order. Her mother was starting to irk her incessantly. Before that she needed a chat with Draggi.

Draggi did not seem bothered by Trinni's appearance at the Enchanters Dungeons. The dungeons were protected by highly complex magical field spells, charms, artefacts and some big guard dogs, for good measure. Trinni cared not for security systems. She patted a huge dog, because she cared for animals. The poorly named Mister Muffins wagged her tail.

"Hengway and Cleavie are increasingly difficult to save from themselves. I had to chuck a duck at my brother."

Draggi turned around to look at Trinni to see if she was in a jesting mood. *The motion was redundant*, thought Draggi. "A duck? Okay." Draggi replied. "Did the chuck-a-duck technique achieve your goal?"

"Yes. He ducked. I have decided to approach our requirements from a different angle."

"Do not inform me of your approach. Walls, quite literally in some cases, have ears."

"I will probably need help."

Draggi nodded in agreement and said, "I agree. I will let him know."

Trinni patted Mister Muffins behind her huge ears and disappeared.

"She is a nice one, that! Woofingly dangerous, but nice." Mister Muffins observed. Draggi nodded her head in agreement.

18. Mother, Daughter, Lover

How did my father end up with this woman? Trinni thought to herself as she witnessed her seventeen year old mother bully yet another victim at the newly created enchanters college on Yurning 7.

This long-punt was becoming ... well, too long, and Trinni had been mulling the idea of seeking further guidance on how to stop her mother's future indiscretions.

The initial cunning plan was to travel back to when her mother was younger and kill her then. This was of course not as cunning as first envisioned. Twas a plan fraught with flaws and time paradox issues that enchanters typically fought to avoid.

Trinni watched on as Tuja walked by with her entourage. A young Forthwright Acae sauntered past the coven of enchanters and smiled delicately, if not nervously at Tuja. Watching her parents' initial encounter should have been 'cute', or even 'romantic' to Trinni, but alas it was not. To Trinni's surprise, and to her group of friends, Tuja smiled back without a terse word or a smidgen of nastiness.

The moment Tuja lurched past Trinni, all she could see was a naroozie boy who seemed to meld into the walls. He was seen as a loner, and staff and students did not, and could not, think about him if he was not directly in front of them. Trinni was glad her magic worked on this long-punt, having created a glamour push as soon as she arrived.

"Well, I am here," a voice said in her mind.

Trinni looked around and saw only students and the occasional staff member. "Where are you?" she asked.

"I am in your dungeon. Nice place you have created here," Professor Smeltzit said.

She punt jumped to her dungeon which had been considerately created by Acae Castle on her arrival some months before. "I am glad to see you. I was going to send you a message tomorrow."

"You did. You write it tonight. I receive it in seventeen years' time from the enchanters college records department, who surprisingly will not seem interested in why they kept a letter for so long." Smeltzit sat on a large sofa and lit a pipe. "Nothing has changed in the future, so I take it you cannot bring yourself to kill your mother?"

"I have most definitely *tried* to kill her. Either magic or the enchanters college or something I have not foreseen prevents me from doing so. Last week I actually shoved her off the bridge that connects the college buildings."

"Oh my. That usually does the trick. What happened?"

"I turned around and she was... well... back where she was before I pushed her."

"So I would imagine you gave her another shove?"

"Several. Each time we just time-bounced back to where we were previously."

"Time paradoxes are a confusing intellectual challenge. I would imagine magic has something to do with it. Have you tried something outside of the college grounds?"

Trinni gave him a look usually reserved by seasoned grandmas to inflict upon their grandchildren. "Of course, Professor. I am not a naive youngling anymore."

"Ah, yes. Twelve years of age with decades of experience. Shall we try together?"

"That is why I am about to write to you."

"Yes I know. I have the letter here. *Come and help. Nothing is working.* Short and to the point. And here I am." Trinni looked at The Professor and smiled. Before he could say anything they punt jumped to a steam carriage station where Tuja and friends were waiting for a steam conveyance to take them to their respective abodes.

Surveilling the group from the opposite platform, Smeltzit and Trinni waited, aware of what each other was thinking. Pushing Tuja into an oncoming tram was the obvious choice. They changed platforms and steadied themselves behind the gaggle of teenagers who ignored the two would-be assassins.

The Professor mind spoke to Trinni, "Are you not worried about blinking out of existence if your future mother dies?"

"I am," was Trinni's reply. The Professor looked at her and saw a new face with an older, experienced attitude running defence in the background. "It is what it is. I have seen things over many decades. I even met an older version of myself. I have a feeling I will be okay."

The Professor, trusting Trinni's usual sincerity, was less concerned than the situation warranted. He created a push that propelled Tuja into an oncoming steam tram. Time skipped back five seconds. Trinni said, "I believe we just time-blinked!"

"Indeedy, young lady. We seem to be the only ones that noticed." The tram was once again entering the station and he gave Tuja another magical nudge. Once again they found themselves sent five seconds into the past. Trinni tried. And failed. Repeatedly.

They tried numerous techniques to throw Tuja under the tram, all to no avail. At one stage Trinni tackled Tuja into the oncoming tram and in turn got run over and was time-blinked five seconds to the past.

After a long ponder Smeltzit said, "This is rather interesting and I am sure we could experiment all day, though I do believe it would be somewhat of a futile activity. We should depart from here."

Trinni nodded and, for her own amusement, she pushed the whole gaggle into the oncoming tram. They blinked back five seconds and Trinni and Smeltzit walked away from the platform. Once they were clear of the tram station and were relatively unwatched, Trinni punted them back to her secret dungeon at Acae Castle.

Back on the platform, Tuja stepped onto the tram, adjusting the bracelet her mother had given her some years prior. "This is a considerate bracelet but will self-destruct after it has done one task for you," her mother told her at the time.

Tuja did not understand what it meant then, but now she believed it was related to considerate magic and wanted more of this magical power.

The bracelet was quite hot to the touch and seemed to be humming. It continued to hum while it gained temperature very quickly. Trying to take it off, she fiddled with the clasp with increasing urgency as the vibration showed increasingly violent intent.

After grappling with the artefact that selflessly saved her life on so many occasions, she tossed it to the ground, whereupon the humming stopped and it disintegrated into a pile of dust. It considerately blew into the sky with the wind, leaving no trace of its existence.

I want more of that. I want all of it, she decided, and planned accordingly.

After the failed attempts to stop Tuja from destroying the world, her daughter and Professor Smeltzit decided to consolidate their plans and patiently wait.

It was a wait of three years. Trinni patiently spied on Tuja and her family. She tried to create a relationship with her would-be father to gain more information.

The glamour push she cast when she first arrived was far more successful than initially thought. Each time she spoke to people under the guise of a male naroozie, she was simply forgotten. *I need a less effective push next time,* she mused as she watched Forthwright and Tuja engage in courting pleasantries one afternoon at college.

She cast a hearken push and listened to her future parents' conversation.

"I would love to go to the solstice picnic with you. It would be lovely for our families to meet." Tuja said in a tone that Trinni, if she did not know her mother, would have taken for charming.

"That's great, as both of our families are going, they can meet. You look lovely..." Forthwright was cut off as Trinni ended her eavesdropping push. This could get creepy. *I hope it doesn't, though.* She continued watching them and had an idea. Follow Tuja home.

After the academic day concluded, Trinni did indeed follow Tuja home. She lived in a small cottage on the edge of the city. Trinni's grandfather had seldom been around so she knew little of him. Her grandmother died when Trinni was physically younger, or so she was told, so she was surprised to see her alive and well.

"Did the Acae boy ask you to the picnic?" Tuja's mother demanded as she walked into the kitchen of the cottage. Trinni had cast another hearken push and was loitering outside the house, still very much forgettable with her glamour push in full naroozie effect.

"He did. We will get closer to that family and their money."

"And that castle of theirs. We could be using that castle to make a lot more money than we could ever need."

"I will marry him and it will all be ours," Tuja cackled. Trinni' grandmother reached her hands out and embraced Tuja.

"That's my girl," she whispered gently. "Is your friend still coming over? Draggi, is that her name?"

On hearing the name of her mentor, Trinni dug deep into her magical knowledge. *What push or spell can I use to see what is going on in there. Invisibility push? If only I had a mini-PSSA or a spy-bot,* she thought.

"You do get them mixed up. Do all naroozie look the same to you? Wait...don't answer that. No, my very good friend, who is also a naroozie, will be staying over for the night. And yes mother, she is also rich."

Trinni was now desperately creating pushes to see into the house. *It must have a magical field that defuses pushes and spells.* She surmised correctly.

Then the obvious solution flashed before her. Sunlight hit the window above the front room. She squinted as the reflection hit her eyes. Through the glare, she noticed a bin. She moved it over to the window and stood on it, peering into the room. *Note to self, just because you can create magic does not mean magic is the only solution.*

She nearly fell off the bin in surprise when a young naroozie walked straight past her and tapped on the cottage door. Trinni was nervous, in her own way, but yet mind-bogglingly intrigued by this visitor. The door opened and Tuja ran towards her. Trinni stared with amazement as she watched Tuja hug a young Tarlan. They kissed. Then kept kissing. Then... kept on kissing. Finally they broke away and entered the cottage.

Trinni once again poked her head over the window sill.

"Hello Tarlan. We have a lot to talk about. You will see this long game we are following will eventually ensure we become quite a formidable team... wait, I think we have an unwanted guest!" Trinni's future mother exclaimed. A second later the windows turned black and the house became invisible.

"It is that weird naroozie boy!" yelled Tuja.

Before Trinni could be turned into bunglebeast food by Tuja's mother, she punt jumped away, placing herself beyond the realm of violence.

Professor Smeltzit was waiting in the dungeon. "What news?" he asked at Trinni's appearance.

"This situation is weirder than a truthful local politician. My grandmother and future mother have teamed up to control the systems with Tarlan."

"We knew that from the painting. We shall have to approach their removal from a different angle, in a different place and a different time. Shall we egress?"

"We most certainly shall. This has been another long-punt failure, albeit I have something weird and important to impart. After which, I have plan D and then possibly plan E to implement."

With their discussion complete, they disappeared. Acae Castle sighed to himself with a sense of loss. He knew in over a decade she would be back in his halls, so he considerately deleted her hidden rooms and waited.

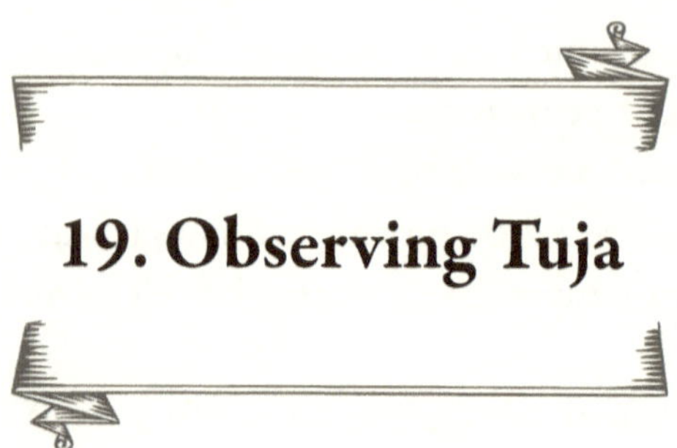

19. Observing Tuja

T*-Lifes were never to be trusted,* thought Forthwright as he finished his tenth night in a cell. The previous night was spent upsetting the guards as much as he could. He awoke on the eleventh day being dragged down a long hallway in a hessian sack by guards he named Dingbat One (D1) and Dingbat Two (D2). Stretches of smooth wooden flooring were randomly interspersed by uneven marble cobblestones. His being smashed against the cobblestones and caused large, pulsating lumps wherever it met the ground.

He tried to peek through the itchy hessian to detect any possible escape routes. There were doorways every twenty or so feet along one side of the hallway. He wriggled to get a better view and received some unwanted attention from D2 as a reward.

"Need a good kickin', do ya?" spluttered D2. To avoid giving them power over him, Forthwright gave nicknames to people he disliked . In this case, he picked a rare flying bat from the Cellfast system, which constantly got itself drunk on fermented fruits and crashed into walls of caves. He wished his dopey guards would run themselves into walls.

Forthwright would look his enemies in the eyes whenever he could. One time, a particularly nasty thing had seventeen eyes on a small body with ten legs. The creature was basically legs and eyes. He did try to look this beastie in the eyes but became motion-sick in an instant.

Anyway, this time at least, he had only a few unwashed humans and the occasional stinking naroozie to deal with, so he was more than delighted that his violent prison guards possessed the standard two eyes and four to five limbs.

D2 saw Forthwright peering through the sack, and kicked him as promised. It did not hurt, but he groaned anyway. This fake groan allowed him to shift enough to notice what was above the doors. Seats! Poorly maintained, but definitely a row of wooden seats.

Their placement and lax condition indicated they were probably benches of an arena. Forthwright moaned again and writhed in the sack to get a peek at the right side of the arena. The wall was flat and without openings. He risked another move and a kick in order to ascertain whether seats were to be seen on the left side.

His military intelligence allowed him to understand the situation, although it was not yet entirely clear. The arena seats seemed to be specially designed to accommodate creatures of different shapes and species.

Forthwright concluded this was undoubtedly an illegal fighting arena. Back in the days of the Second-Hand War, particularly unpleasant criminal enterprises had erected arenas wherein gladiators fought to the death for money, fame, and, sometimes, worst of all, freedom.

These arenas were usually found on Cellfast planets. Reliable researchers reported that those who owned the arenas kept their operations and knowledge of how they worked utterly secret. *What a great hiding place for a rebellion or an army before taking over a system,* Forthwright mused.

Outside his confinement, he could smell food, as well as folk mingling among their own stenches. Most of all, he could hear talking and the sounds of clothing squelching from the movement of their wearers. They were the sounds of a massive city, more significant than cities he had known elsewhere.

His hands found a loose string. The dingbats, as stupid as the real thing, had not adequately tied him up. *A big mistake in prisoner management,* he judged. Forthwright assessed the risks. The list of risks was so long that he decided to save time by performing only the risky act of saving himself. He needed to flee and find out what was happening.

He did not know what he needed to know, but he knew he would need to know it when or if the opportunity arose for him to know anything at all. The thought made him dizzy, but he had to do something to improve his miserable position.

He quickly tugged at the loose string. *Oh biff!* The bag tightened, his knees now pressed to his stomach. He realised he had decreased the space in the sack by about half. Maintaining his momentum, he moved both hands to the rogue string. He felt around it and found a small hole. He poked a finger through it just as the dingbats dragged him over another section of uneven cobblestones.

The bag split open when his finger didn't yield. Forthwright rolled across the hard stone floor, bumping his head a few more times. This new pain added to the extreme pain from the earlier bumps and his newly-bent finger, so he did not feel it that much. He inspected the size of the arena. Biffing huge with a closed roof and a fighting area hundreds of feet long.

Now free from the sack, he ducked under the predictable first punch from one of the dingbats. He surveyed the end of the arena and found himself in a vast marketplace. Then came an unceremonious punch squarely in the back, knocking him forward but not to his knees. He rolled to the left and ran, buying more time to seek a way of escape. He jumped to his feet and now stood beside armoured miscreants of every sort.

It was then he understood not where he was but in what he was standing. It was a military camp, most likely preparing for an invasion. Unfortunately, while he was lost in thought, the dingbats caught up to him. Needless to say, it wasn't pretty.

Forthwright woke up in the cell he had earlier occupied. They fed him–on occasion. He heard prisoners come in and out–sometimes.

An enchanter interviewed him at precisely the same time every day. These were fun times, as he always answered similarly: 'I am a teapot. Where is my tea? Have you smelled the colour blue?' or playful variations of these three sentences. He would be beaten a little and thrown back into his cell.

After the first few days of the interrogation, Forthwright started worrying about his sons and daughter. After being assigned the task of spying on Naroi, Jay had become withdrawn and quiet. His daughter Trinni began acting quite oddly, with sprinklings of insanity added for good measure. His wife, though, had a complete set of destination-biffed issues. Having the time to reminisce, he did so.

It was eerily quiet in the cells. An inner voice, an intuition, too much boredom, or perhaps just a feeling he should use this time wisely came over him. He waited for the guards to leave the area before he recovered the small device The Captain had given him in what felt like eons past.

He looked at the strange, tiny thing. If it had eyes it would have glared back with an attitude. *How does this work? More importantly, why does it work?* he thought.

"Work," he intoned, and the cell began to change.

Forthwright entered a dreamlike documentary, a most weirdly magical replay made just for him.

"I hope this works," spoke The Captain. "Enchanters and my good self have been able to put together the moment Tuja pinched the Chas Light. Enjoy!"

Forthwright could see a vision of Tuja. She was part of a small group that wanted Yurning to withdraw from the war, become neutral, and profit when it concluded. This was not out of kindness. Tuja would have fought the war if she thought Yurning would come out on top. By withdrawing from the war, she would let her enemies weaken each other, then she could take control.

The group, which consisted of enchanters and humans, gained considerable support across the systems. T-Life became a significant component of the group known as the Yurning United Party.

YUP started to lobby for Yurning to become the lead system in the known systems. The Gas Fields, the home of the impfish, was once seen as having no usable resources. When precious metals and rare gases were found on their planets and moons, their system became desirable. The impfish council were visited by YUP members who had, they claimed, only the impfishes' best interest in mind. The talks were led by Tuja and were deemed a failure. She was aggressive and not inclined to negotiate.

Tuja started publishing retaliatory newspaper articles and talking to armies and major business holders to gain support. Some months before, a derelict space tanker had appeared in the Cellfast system. Unluckily, a YUP member–*spoiler*: his name is not necessary since he is about to die–and his partner were the first to get to the massive tanker. After failing to talk to anyone from the vessel, they placed a vacuum seal over the side of the ship and cut a hole in the hull.

The pair took the risk of entering the unknown, unclear, unsafe, and a very fun bereft tanker. They found the command deck and the skeletons within it that had long since decayed.

The previously-unnamed YUP member pressed some prominent green buttons on a clearly important panel. They knew it was important because there was a large sign atop the machine that said, 'Important Technical Panel', just in case there was any confusion.

A green button is signified across the systems as a good thing to press. That is unless you are a public servant on the Yurning planets. For their engineers, green indicates a potential problem and red means all is good to go.

In this case, the board lit up like The Captain's smile, flashing multiple colours with loose bits of broken glass tinkling to the floor. The unnamed YUP member glanced around the chaotic control room, his helmet lighting only a small patch in front of him.

Somewhere in the distance, a small, noisy motor kicked into life. More lights began flickering around the YUP intruder. A small shadow moved across the doorway they had just entered, giving him just enough time to see his partner racing out of the command room, her arms flailing like mad sports fanatics after a winning goal.

The fleeing partner–*spoiler*: name also not necessary as she is only in the story for a bit; *other spoiler;* she doesn't die–raced towards the hull.

The unnamed YUP member who hadn't fled was left reading the writing on the walls: –aos–lig, –eth, –ill. This was not a lot to go on. Even more lights started to glow. Now the flashing board was talking. The speech was so old-fashioned that he could understand only every third or fourth word.

The whole command centre was now fully lit, though suddenly he wished it were not. He noticed something on the large green screen at the bottom right corner of the command panel:

"29, 28, 27..."

He wanted to avoid it, but his inner voice told him to examine the wall. His more reliable hidden voice told him to run away, but he could not help himself–he further analysed the writing on the walls until, more importantly, he discovered what the writing was written with.

Skeletal remains of arms and legs were haphazardly piled beneath the writing. The lettering appeared to be black, until he got close to a light source. It was dark purple, or very dark red at least. Some would even call it blood-red.

Whoever wrote the words had used the dripping limbs as self-inking pens. *The words! Worry about the words,* he thought, trying to not imagine the gruesome method by which they were written.

The Chaos Light means death. Kills all who touch it.

"15, 14, 13..."

"Oh, biffle, it's a counter," the not-so-bright and unnamed YUP member said to himself. *Time for a quick sprint,* his little brain suggested. His legs were way ahead of his thoughts. They had started running long before he begged them to.

"8, 7..." continued the counter.

His also-unnamed partner, who had earlier made her escape, did not bother waiting for the unnamed and now un-alive YUP member. She examined the package next to her; The box was labelled '*Chaos Light*' and it was about the size of a large box of jelly babies. The Chaos Light was an incredibly powerful tool in any hands–either the right or wrong hands. Its very existence was perpetually debated in college halls and public houses throughout the systems. She expected Tuja Acae would be interested in it, and supposed it could, in fact, be the Chaos Light, having now mastered the art of the blatantly obvious.

Forthwright's dreamlike magical experience ended with the anonymous YUP woman saying "Time to sell this to Tuja and run as far away as this ship can take me."

Forthwright sat in his dusty and cramped prison cell, musing on this miraculous event until his ponderings were concluded. This was where history, and Tuja's involvement in it, became sticky.

As far as Forthwright was concerned, the first time Tuja had heard of the Light was when she was asked to track it down by the Chosen and the senior enchanters. The Captain, and others with more credibility points, now implied she had been involved a long time before that.

As Forthwright sat patiently in prison, he brooded and speculated. Then, when he had some additional spare time, he cogitated. His thoughts grew darker as he tried to unravel Trinni's and Tuja's involvement. He also wondered what that YUP dude was called because he would need the name if he were to write down the new history.

20. War and the Whooomp

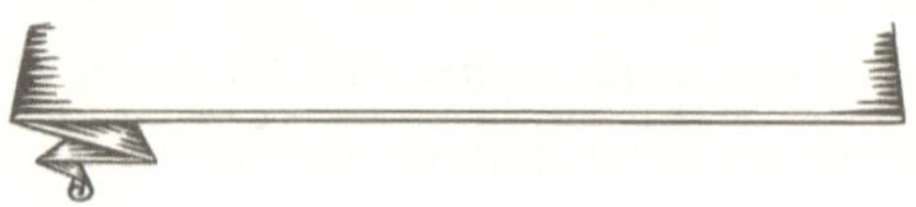

Wars are pretty stupid. Firstly, one could get injured. It is commonly opined that wars are started by people who want something they could not get through reasonable negotiation or fair purchase.

The lines between good and evil are wibbly wobbly when it comes to greed and violence. Usually, the winners of said war write the history books, and the losers, after reading these books, start planning for the next war to get even for a dispute they have already forgotten. Secondly, as stated earlier, wars are stupid.

"You see, lads, wever youse like it or not, we gotta work togever, at least on Yurning 7," said Travis, standing in the middle of the enchanter's main meeting room.

Jay and Naroi were still stunned by his presence.

"Tha two aggro naroozie tribes attack, tack, tack tha planets in the Gas Fields. Nah ta mention tha outlyin planets and all. Them are killin off all tha grunts and capturing biffers leftover ta work in da fields and factories."

At the time of Jay and Naroi's recent attack, the enchanters had already displaced themselves to safer surroundings. Additional security measures were put in place to slow them down. Once the library was secure, it was time to prepare for the refugees who fled from the attacked planets.

"I understand that the library will be used to house those fleeing from war zones, and the college has been authorised for fighters and displaced civilians," Jay explained after eavesdropping on other soldiers. He was tired and confused. And hungry. Mostly hungry.

"We need to report this back to our seniors and see what our orders are," suggested Naroi to Jay, ignoring Travis who he felt was being a bit too bossy.

It certainly was not Naroi's intent to be a part of a losing army, and he assuredly considered there was a better way to make their wishes happen. "Come on, Jay, let's get moving!"

When Jay and Naroi had cleared the library dungeons and were out of earshot, Jay said, "I think that strange dwarf thought we were on his side."

"I was thinking that stumpy biffer was a bit suspect. Let's find out what's going on with your brother and his girlfriend," Naroi said, draping his fifth hand over Jay's shoulder. They headed towards their small punt ship, a Nova VII model which was capable only of intra-system travel and could accommodate only two.

"My mother still wants us to spy. I don't trust her, even though she is my mother," Naroi said quietly.

"She probably doesn't trust you either. Let's go and see my brother and see what's worth seeing!" responded Jay. They proceeded to the punt ship on the landing strip busy with the many impfish arriving from the Gas Fields.

"If this is what war looks like, I may stick to farming and fishing," said Jay, before realising an impfish was standing right behind him, tap, tap, tapping his feet-fins in disgust.

"Oh, this is much worse than war. In a decently planned war, fighters know where their next meal is coming from. They know what's going to happen tomorrow. This is much, much worse." The sombre tone and brutal reality set the scene for a reflective few minutes as they jumped to Trav-Coll, once again taking on the role of spy.

"**B**ring in the weaponss and sstow them in the third classssroom on the left!" hissed Walker-Seven. Trav-Coll was now being used as a training and military headquarters instead of conducting skill tests for students. Hengway had been asked to take command of the paired, and Walker-Nine was promoted from Nine to Seven in impfish rank.

Walker-Seven was doing most of the leading since Cleavie and Simone had been captured. Walker-Seven's last sight of them was when an unknown traveller raised their hands beside Cleavie and punted all three of them away. Simone and Cleavie had been abducted right under their noses.

Hengway tried to follow the punt as carefully as his magic abilities would allow. Instead, he accidentally punted to his favourite place by the river. "What the actual?" he exclaimed. As soon as Walker-Nine could explain what had happened, he punted back to the command room. They were too late.

The punt jump trace, he had learned through experience, was not his best push. Punting created a magical stream for only a very short period. Cleavie was far better at stream tracking than he was, and he just could not follow that particular punt.

The saved paired began their training immediately. Many were given the uniforms of their native tribes and armies. Others preferred to stay relatively neutral and form teams of paired which were not tied down to traditional tribes or sects.

The explicit goal was peace and ultimate safety from the tyrants' reach across all systems. The unmentioned goal was to capture the Chaos Light and deal with it accordingly. *Who will dictate how and when the wretched thing is utilised will be a question for another day,* Hengway thought.

The feared object could fit in a generic box and be carried by one person, which was a tactical nightmare. Walker-Seven considered it odd that little was known about what the damned thing looked like. You could sit next to it, perhaps, or use it for a game of utensil wars unknowingly.

The next mystery was its function. "What doess it acsssually do?" Walker-Seven asked aloud while standing in the head teacher's room, talking to the empty room in general and did not expect an answer.

"I guess you are talking about the Chaos Light," Hengway said, who was sitting on a chair in the shadows.

"Bah!" Walker-Seven's head wobbled slightly, as impfish heads do when startled. "Were you invissible?"

"I was indeed. I didn't mean to scare you. I am in here escaping all of the rampant stupid that has recently surrounded my good self."

Walker-Seven tilted its head to the right. Its tongue emerged and rested on its razor-like front teeth. Hengway always found this amusing. He had read that implings only did this when they were nervous, though he did not know what precisely Walker-Seven had to be nervous about, as fate would dictate, he was about to find out.

"Sstupid what?"

"Stupid everything. I am impatient. The place has taken a one-way ticket to destination fu—"

"It hass been two weekss ssince they were sstolen. You ssee we iss organissing. Mosst of the paired iss waiting for you to assumes command."

"What do I know about commanding? I don't even like weapons. I definitely do like punting away from trouble. As they say, it's not what you are jumping to; it's what you are punting away from."

"No persson ever ssaid that. If ssomeone did, it iss ssilly. You musst sstop paddling around in your own sself-pitiess and sstart assssembling planss." Walker-Seven navigated around the lisp like a lost recruit with no map or compass.

Walker-Seven was angry, its blue lips protruded around its full mouth of shiny white teeth. Hengway did not want to upset Walker, but...

"My father is missing. My brother is some kind of super spy. My mother, whom I miss so much, is also missing, and my sister is some kind of magical mega-witch with all kinds of skull-blowing skills." He jumped up and pranced around the room. The room was large, but it contained boxes upon boxes of rations and uniforms that made angry pacing rather difficult.

"I puzzle whether sshe could blow sskulls. That sshould be awessome," said Walker-Seven. The impfish was now out of its depth. It had endured this same conversation for days now. *There was no movement in Hengway's train of thought, which was late and out of timetable order*, Walker-Seven thought before being interrupted.

The noise started a few hundred feet away. It sounded like laser fire and shouting. Hengway immediately urged Walker-Seven by mind-speech to freeze time. Time complied as instructed.

Hengway knew he had about thirty seconds. He punt jumped.

He returned with a very disgruntled naroozie in armour, but weaponless. He punted again.

The naroozie just stood there immobile in the shape of someone playing air guitar.

Hengway came back again with someone who could have been mistaken for an older version of himself. Their hair was long, and they had not shaved in some time. Both newcomers stank.

Walker-Seven was impressed. Hengway had defused the situation in under thirty seconds. The two intruders staggered forward, tripped over each other, then sprang to their feet.

The naroozie used his fifth leg to make the advance to his feet much quicker than Jay. Naroi and Jay stood still, staring at Hengway in disbelief. Walker-Seven was waiting for Hengway's next move.

"Do you recognisse thesse sstinkerss?" the shocked impfish asked.

Hengway lurched forward and punched Jay. He rubbed his bruised hand while Jay continued to stare at him. There is always an uneasy pause when brother hits brother.

The shock of violence usually makes people think quickly about fighting or getting the biff out of there. However, when the punch hurts the puncher more than the punchee, it turns into a clown-less circus.

"Really, brother?"

"Do you want another one?"

"You should stick to your magic stuff. You biff at fighting," japed Naroi, who was enjoying the circus, although he did not much like clowns. He thought they should take advantage of the situation and gain the upper paw. Jay sensed a move from Naroi and leapt quickly towards Walker-Seven.

Naroi was happy to give Hengway a belting and rolled forward to initiate his attack. The world moved slightly, and the stinkers found themselves hovering over a boiling lake not of their choosing.

"Where did you possition them?"

"That moon you mentioned in the Gas Fields. The one where everything is hot and nasty."

"Hengway, they can't breathe there for long."

"Yep," he said with a smile. He gazed at Walker-Seven who crossed its hand-fins and moved its head to one side. Its tongue poked out and rested on its sharp teeth.

"Fine." The stenchy two appeared back in the room, floating a few feet above the ground, reeking of steamed dog fur. Hengway felt alive for the first time in weeks.

"Hello, brother. What brings you back to our lovely place of higher learning?"

"Thought I would hang around with my little brother to hear any news of our parents," Jay responded, trying to sound as calm as possible. Of which he was failing with award winning ease.

Walker-Seven snickered at the hanging-around gag.

Jay and Naroi dropped heavily to the floor.

Hengway blurted, "You seriously stink. There are cleaning establishments everywhere. I have no news. I do know that you two are somehow involved in this mess. Or your stinky boyfriend's parents are!" Hengway stated, pointing at Naroi. Jay and Naroi picked themselves off the floor and sat in considerately-placed chairs. Neither of them flinched at the 'boyfriend' comment.

Hengway supposed that their secret was blown. He attempted to examine the contents of his love-life and opened an empty box. As yet, he did not understand what all the fuss was about. Walker-Seven would pick a sex when it found itself in a relationship, and Hengway felt that in good time nature would do its thing.

For now, he had other things on his mind. "Are you working with Trinni?" he demanded.

"No—" Jay was goaded into talking by Hengways' gruff approach, but Naroi intervened.

"None of your business!" Naroi barked.

Jay was annoyed they had not thought this through. Hengway was not in this to be powerful and rich. All he wanted was his nice little family with its annoying, controlling, considerate castle. "Listen up Hengers, we do—"

"Don't call me Hengers, or I will drop you in the boiling lake."

"All right. *Fine*. We don't know what's happened. I was sent to spy on Naroi, and Naroi was sent to spy on us. Everyone started attacking everyone else. There are about three separate war fronts at the moment." Jay stopped and noticed the unnatural silence. *This scene is going to biff,* he thought.

Naroi started softening as he got used to his companions' new behaviour. He tried a new tactic: "It appears to me that this is going to the toilet."

The others chuckled, breaking the tension.

"Look close enough," he continued, "We naroozie are more refined than you rough around the edges humans and impfish." Walker-Seven enjoyed being acknowledged and bobbed up and down.

"My tribe, and therefore my mother, simply desire open trade with all systems. Domination is always negotiable. My mother has been talking to the governing bodies of the most influential systems for some time."

"Jay, the thing is, most of the trouble is directed at our family. Trinni has gone rogue and is starting firefights all over the systems. Our recalcitrant sister invades villages, steals anything that is not nailed... well actually she just steals everything, nails and all. After the village is bereft of anything vaguely useful or valuable, she moves on to her next set of victims."

"Ssome folkss are calling her the Casstle Sspirit," added Walker-Seven. "My name, by the way, is Walker-Sse—"

"Sorry, sorry. Pardon my rudeness." Hengway hurriedly interrupted to stop Walker-Seven from revealing the secrets of the universe. He wanted this situation to be solved quickly.

"Jay, Naroi, this is Walker. Walker, this is Jay and Naroi. I don't trust you two. Travis thinks you may be helpful, so I will let you hang around, *if* you wash. Be aware though, that there is no money in what the paired are doing. We are trying to find and release captured paired, including Cleavie and Walker's other half."

"Isn't it nice and quiet without the dwarf, though," Naroi asked with a slight hint of his customary scorn.

Wwwwhhhhhhhoooooomp happened.

It was not just any kind of *whoomp*. It was the mega-awesome, amazing, shocking-skull-drilling *whoomp* that indicated times were about to get interesting.

All four moved together while their ears rang like a steam-tram's bell. Hengway could not punt jump since the *whoomp* had skewed his sense of direction. He could not even be sure where the *whoomp* came from.

Naroi took the lead. "This way!" The other three followed him as quickly as they could. When naroozie run on four legs, they can cover ground with extreme haste. Naroi knew he was quicker, so he stayed near them whilst scanning ahead for trouble.

They reached a section outside of the main Trav-Coll building, which contained supply tents and equipment. Now, it contained an additional dwarf. A young dwarf. A heavily armed young dwarf. A young, heavily armed dwarf who was on fire.

One of the nearest paired raised hands, and a stream of water poured over the burning dwarf. A young, heavily armed, previously aflamed dwarf lay wet and angry in the debris of tents and other costly kit.

"Bemovingyaselvesquicklyifiwasyouoryouwilldie," gabbled the dwarf. He quickly got to his feet and scampered as only a recently aflame, wet, angry, heavily armed gabbling young dwarf could do. Everyone stood agape, most trying to unravel what he said.

"Did he say *move*?" one paired asked.

"*Quickly* was hidden in there somewhere as well, I think," commented another slow responder. During this meeting of the 'not-that-bright', the quick learners were rushing away from the *whoomp* following the dwarf.

"I just heard *you will die*," one of the plethora of slow learners screamed behind them.

Just above the disaster zone, a vast circle opened. Hengway remembered from lessons at Trav-Coll that it was a very old magical system-portal. This was the way that humans and dwarfs first travelled around the systems. Usually, travellers wore protective suits to stop arriving aflame. The mega-*whoomp* was the hole's closure, causing a system rift. Hengway knew all of this and told Walker-Seven to stay and wait.

"We can help with the next unfortunate traveller," he said aloud. Those who heard him, dug deep inside themselves for one last jolt of enthusiasm. The newly invigorated war fighters stood around him, hands raised and war hammers at the ready.

Whhhhhoooooooooooooomp!

Not as skull-cracking as the first *whoomp* but just as loud and alarming. The ground moved slightly to the left, then came back again with a whipping motion and a cracking sound.

Hengway was expecting one of a paired. A lone, frightened paired searching for safety.

The ten warfighters who landed in the middle of the Trav-Coll grounds had more weapons than a small army and were far from what anyone was expecting. Two humans at the front had old-style Cellfast guns—big black ones with lots of bullets hanging from a belt on the side. They fired into the gathered crowd.

The Trav-Coll paired had been training for some weeks in attacking and defending, so they were able to punt jump to safer positions or duck behind anything solid.

The invaders were led by naroozie and consisted of representatives of every species except for the impfish. The lack of nasty impfish made Walker-Seven very proud.

Attackers moved aggressively towards the hiding paired. Hand-to-hand fighting took place, except where spears and other sharp things were available.

Paired used the tactic of punt jumping their attackers to places chosen to cause despair or possible death. Two naroozie ended up in the scorpion pits of Yurning 1. Meanwhile, Walker-Seven sent two very aggressive T-Life fightbots to a desert plain on the fourth planet in the Gas Fields system where there was no way to recharge.

The fighting was intense and involved a lot of shouting at the enemy, ducking from the enemy, running towards the enemy, running away from the enemy, running back towards the enemy, and shouting at the enemy once more.

After the remaining attackers were dispatched elsewhere courtesy of some well-placed punt jump magic, Walker-Seven surveyed the scene. "Okay, everyone. Sstop moping about. I don't ssupposse there will be another tracking punt jump. Be ready if there iss. Ssecure the area and assisst any wounded to the aid-sstasssion."

"Umm, we, we don't, we don't have an aid-station," stammered a frazzled naroozie at Walker-Seven.

"Congratulationss on volunteering to esstablissh ours new aid-sstation! Take that tent and getss at it. Movess, movess!" commanded Walker-Seven who had once read that keeping people busy during and after emergency events gave them purpose and also kept their minds busy so they would not dwell on the horrors they had just witnessed.

Walker-Seven inspected the scene and was quite surprised that there were very few critically wounded. Those that remained were getting on with restoring defences without too much fuss. *Where was Hengway*, it wondered. "Hass anyone sseen our fearless leader?" it yelled into the crowd.

"Over here. Quick!"

Walker-Seven sped through the camp and found the voice, and Hengway.

"He's been shot. I've been keeping pressure on the wound. I had to drag him over here to keep him safe." The small human who held Hengway was almost in tears.

"You iss doing an outsstanding job," Walker-Seven hissed. "What iss your name? Sstretcher bearerss to me!" Walker-Seven wanted to keep the human occupied while it summoned assistants to carry Hengway to the new aid station. Walker-Seven was hoping at least the tent was clear so it could treat the wound in a quiet and clean environment.

"My name is Elayne. I can help him. I need my paired. She is—"

"There you are. Oh, is that Hengway? I just heard someone had set up a place for the wounded," said another human girl. She was wearing light metal armour and held a metal gun in one hand. Her violently red hair fluffed in all directions from underneath a dull but rigid helmet. Elayne's paired raised her hands, and both Hengway and Elayne rose a few feet from the ground. "Give 'im a push then, fish-face," she said to Walker-Seven.

"That's not called for, Helsin. Just keep us in the air and be civil!" demanded the flushing Elayne. Not all were fond of the impfish, and some had no trouble in letting people know of their backward thinking.

Walker-Seven nudged the floating pair, pointing them towards the tent. It caught the eye of the bullying Helsin and bared a plethora of sharp teeth. Helsin poked her tongue out in defiance of the aggressive gesture.

Hengway was unconscious and bleeding heavily. Helsin floated him and Elayne into the tent, gently placing them on an equipment crate at the shelter's side. Five other wounded, with broken bones and scratches, were lying on makeshift tables, with some others just lying on the grass.

Walker-Seven inspected Hengway and said to Helsin, "We hass no ssurgeon here. They iss all ssupervissing the displaced paired at the library. I musst go and kidnap one."

"Don't worry about that! We have a party trick you may like. Your paired is in safe hands," said Helsin.

"We iss not paired. Each of our paired wass sseized. Sshow no concern for that nowss! If you can help him, you sshould do it ssoon." Elayne was now covered in Hengway's blood. *This scene is starting to unhinge,* thought Walker-Seven.

"I am going to let go. Then we start straight away. The bullet is still in him, so we need to extract that first," said Elayne to Helsin, who had put away her sense of humour and was now concentrating on Hengway.

Elayne let go. Helsin immediately held out her hand. Elayne grabbed it and took hold of Hengway's right hand while Helsin took his left. They formed a triangle. Walker-Seven continued as a reluctant bystander.

Everyone in the tent froze and watched the make-shift surgery. Elayne was floating two feet above the ground, glowing midnight-blue, somehow more brightly than her unruly hair. Helsin was also floating, but she was glowing mustard-yellow.

Hengway screamed with Gusto. Gusto realised he was not wanted in this scene and was escorted out, still screaming, by other medics. Hengway floated above the crate and started to glow fire-orange. The tent was a multi-coloured disaster, much like an artist's palette. It was also becoming quite hot.

Walker-Seven came from a very cool environment, and heat affected impfish more than the others, so it created a protective force field around itself. It also deemed it a good precaution just in case they exploded, which was a definite possibility. Walker-Seven said, "I hope you iss not disstresssing him."

"Of course we are hurting him. We are taking a bullet out of his guts, not baking him a cake," yelled Helsin, who had her lovely attitude back. The heated colour display continued in relative silence.

The colours were fierce. The heat was close to overbearing. Every now and again, a paired would run in to see what was going on before being shushed and pushed to a corner with Gusto, who was far too enthralled to scream.

Hengway screamed again. There was a slight pop as the bullet extracted from his wound fell onto the crate. The intense display continued as the wound slowly closed. The concentration from Helsin and Elayne was immense, leaving most of the observers quite impressed.

"What-the-biff-happened-where-am-I?" Hengway blurted suddenly. The unnaturally bright colours of all three started to fade and, eventually, the glowing stopped.

"You will need to rest and drink a lot of fluids," Elayne said.

Hengway gazed at Elayne, then around the room. The memory of his being shot and being in a lot of pain came streaming back. "That hurt," he said faintly. He sat up on the crate and scanned the tent for familiar faces.

Jay and Naroi came out of a closet.

"Why didn't you two helpss?" demanded Walker-Seven.

"This is not our fight. You lot had it under control, anyway," stated Jay scornfully with a hint of added sarcasm. Hengway stared at him long and hard.

"I don't know what to do with you, Jay," grumbled Hengway. The observers in the room were waiting for the next drama to unfold as the air carried a tense attitude.

"What makes you think you have any right to tell me what to do?"

"I am in charge of the paired in the Yurning system, and you two fit that description."

Jay and Naroi turned and surveyed each other. Then, they haughtily examined Hengway. "We aren't paired. We are just... close, that's all," replied Naroi.

"You can be such a fool at times," blurted Jay at Hengway.

Hengway chuckled, and Walker-Seven joined in. "What's the joke?" asked Naroi.

"You mean to ssay that you two iss never even ssenssing?" said Walker-Seven through a big sharp toothy grin. "You two may be boyfriendsss or whatever, but you are alssso paired. Pairingss are happenngss everywhere. Pairingss esscalated dramatically after the day of the Pairedss One Hundred. Thosse assaulting ssskills you possssesss that jusst popped up overnight, what is the ssource of that, you ssupposse?"

"We can't mind-speak or punt jump or any of that stuff," stuttered Jay. *If I am paired, I was ripped off in the magical skills department,* he thought.

Naroi and Jay disappeared.

The castle had foreshadowed their arrival. It had readied washing supplies and fresh attire just as they entered the dining room. Jay was a little shocked, whereas Naroi picked up an apple and spied a wine flask with two goblets.

"I have to say, I am glad we are paired. It will allow us to spend more time together," Jay said. He undressed, washed, and put on the fresh garments considerately supplied for him before turning his attention to the food and drink.

Naroi sniffed his garments and armour, found them still adequately disgusting for his short term needs, and poured some wine into the goblets instead. "I don't care for the perception of other biffers who have no right to judge. I will say that I am glad our mother's busy activities have ensured they stay out of our relationship. Paired or not, we would have spent as much time together as we wanted, regardless of a magical connection."

"That is true. On another note, those biffers are trying to take over a crap load of planets..."

"Not to mention kill us all," Naroi said.

"If my mother is going to murder me, I can't think of anyone better than you to be murdered with."

"Thanks, I think. I am glad I was asked to spy on you lot. I see it like this, if our mothers are to be murdered, you are the person I would love to murder them with."

They admired each other, star-crossed lovers, paired and together. Jay touched Naroi lightly on the shoulder, smiled at him lovingly, and said, "You gonna give me wine or not?"

Naroi and Jay reappeared, their mouths filled with beautiful fresh green apples. The crunch attracted everyone's attention. "Guess what? We *can* punt jump. I just went to my house and got this from the kitchen." The tension dissipated as the bystanders returned to whatever it was they were doing before the *whoomp*.

"Now that we have that sorted, you two need a job," said Hengway. Walker-Seven smiled its toothy grin.

After Hengway spoke to his brother and Naroi detailing his plan, he turned towards Walker-Seven.

"Let's go fetch our paired, shall we? They have had enough of a holiday."

21. Best Laid

After a productive meeting of paired, Hengway found himself pondering a decision. Half the group insisted they find Trinni in order to locate the remaining prisoners and free them. Walker-Seven was amongst those outspokenly eager to fetch them. Hengway was also keen to rescue Cleavie, but he had to consider the others as well.

The second option was a more calculated, tactical approach: find The Captain and formulate an attack plan. This would give them time to gather more information on where the pairs were being held, by whom, and why.

"Listen up, team!" Hengway was getting used to the leader gig and had regained his confidence following the fight with the murderous bastards who came through the system rip.

"My team will find The Captain. We will use every communication method we have, old technology, mind-speak, and so on. Go to villages if you have to and talk to those that like talking! Go to taverns and public houses in order to find out what the local shady characters are up to!" he commanded.

"I sshall take another team to ssearch for the paired. We sshall use the ssame tactic that Hengway jusst desscribed. Any quesstionss?" said Walker-Seven, knowing full well that everyone already knew the plan.

It was challenging to keep information confidential from soldiers with the ability to read minds or transform into small insects. Consequently, no questions arose.

Hengway sensed the time to move had arrived. "Try and avoid conflict. Stay alive!" The room moved backwards a microsecond as most of the fighters disappeared. Jay and Naroi were left alone. They had not agreed to help and definitely did not want to get involved in anything organised by Walker-Seven or Hengway.

"Let's go see whether we can make some trouble," suggested a smiling Naroi to a smirking Jay. They disappeared.

"This plan is getting a bit wonky," Hengway remarked as he leaned over a flat map, with Walker-Seven leaning on the other side.

"We have searched in all the places marked in green. Which is almost everywhere," he explained.

Hengway's ears started ringing. He rightfully presumed some magic was coming at him. He turned and raised his hands just in case. Walker-Seven saw his defensive move and grabbed a handy war hammer.

"You haven't checked everywhere, baby brother," said Jay after he and Naroi punt jumped into the room. Jay threw a crumpled piece of paper onto the map and added, "Your beloved Captain has gotten himself into some mischief."

Hengway picked up the paper and read it. "I thought you two would have run off and been punt jumping into treasury vaults all over the systems."

Hengway passed the paper to the confused impfish. Walker-Seven read the note and nodded at Hengway to indicate he knew what they had to do. Walker-Seven read the title once more,

'*The Captain – Fight To The Death!*,' sighed and concentrated on the planning session to come.

"We have decided to at least help find our mum and dad."

"Very nice of you. Do you happen to know where this arena is?" He did not trust them. It was tough to trust Jay at the best of times; as for the naroozie, not a chance.

"We do know where it will be tomorrow." Jay raised his hand, and writing appeared at the bottom of the paper. They were system coordinates they knew far too well.

"Our planet!" exclaimed Hengway. "Quite near the castle too."

"They iss there to get the lasst coin from punditss that like thiss kind of rubbissh. Alwayss in timess of trouble the gambling placesss will try to exsstract the lasst of the family fundss from the disstracted poor," said Walker-Seven. This was one of its more profound moments. The other three stared in astonishment.

Hengway brushed off the shock of the moment."Okay, we need to focus. Get all our forces together. There may be more than a tad of spying going on, and I also believe that a lot of T-Life are involved."

"Hengway, I think Naroi and I should go to find mum. If we follow the trail of Trinni and start asking questions about where all the T-Life are, we may find some clues to her whereabouts. The enchanters have abandoned the dungeons in the library for a reason. It was a perfectly designed killing field. I'll send word if we find anything."

Jay leant over and grabbed Naroi's hand. It was a natural bond that people in strong relationships used as a comforting reflex. Hengway was stunned. That was probably the longest and most sensible sentence he ever heard from Jay.

"I think that is an excellent idea. Stay safe, brother!"

Hengway switched his gaze to Naroi. "Both of you, stay safe!" As Hengway turned to talk to Walker-Seven, Jay and Naroi punt jumped out of the room.

"Organise a planning meeting for tonight. We will attack tomorrow and save The Captain."

Hengway stood in Trav-Coll's makeshift tactical command centre, planning the rescue at the arena. After asking for help from all the high councils, he was told they were on their own. "You paired have enough magic to last a lifetime," declared the Yurning high council.

Hengway and the remaining paired took the hint and started planning.

They came up with an excellent plan.

Then they threw the plan into the bin.

They planned again. They threw this one into a fire pit.

They calmed down and planned once more. This plan, on the surface, was less rubbish than the others, so they allocated tasks. The rumours were that punt jumping was stopped by a protection field in and around the arena, just as the Cellfast system used.

"That's not correct," said Phil, the dwarf who went '*whoomp*'. Many paired called him *Whoomp* behind his back, but never to his face. "I saw a lot of people punt jump around the ship."

"When were you there?" "And how were you there?" "What was it like?" Those and similarly unhelpful questions flowed rapidly from the team. Hengway ignored them all.

"You could have told us you had already been there. I don't care how you know this stuff, but let's go through this again," thundered Hengway so the whole planning team could hear.

22. Arena of Death

The Captain was growing weary of the daily beatings. He remembered long ago, he used to yell at his crew, 'The daily beatings will continue until everyone is happy.' It was not so funny now as the daily beatings did indeed continue, and he wasn't happy. They were becoming tedious, and, with the familiar couple of punches to the face and a set of predictable kicks to the ribs, familiarity was breeding contempt.

Every time the guards interrogated him, they had the same silly question, "Where are the rest of the paired?" which was always answered with something like, "Your mum's pants are purple in summer."

These witty responses, learnt from his time with Forthwright, were then met with more customary punches and kicks before he was thrown back into his cell. *Torturers these days have no imagination*, he thought.

He carefully stepped over to the door. The trek did not take long as his room was square with each length slightly longer than his outstretched body. The cell had a hole in the ground with a straw mat for a bed. He did not go anywhere near it. It was constantly damp and smelled as if it were alive, and moved every now and again. How it was always wet was a question that kept him busy during the dull down-times of his days.

His main mental focus was to escape from—well, wherever he was. The guards were changed every few days and checked on him sporadically, never methodically. He was frail from the daily beatings and lack of food. They fed him once a day with a soup that dirty dishwater would be exceptionally proud of. On good days the soup had crunchy bits in it. He was not interested in what the crunchy bits were as long as they stayed down.

He knew he could not hold on forever. Time was ticking and tocking away. There was a hustle and bustle of movement within the walls of his prison. The door to the cell flung open, slamming against the stone wall. A super clean, lovely-smelling human appeared within the strong door frame. He probably used actual soap and water, which was unheard of in this place. The human was carrying a tray of food that smelt like heaven. *A meaty, spicy kind of delicious heaven,* he thought deliriously.

The human placed the tray on the ground and turned around in a fancy military fashion. Now holding a pure white tablecloth, he stepped over to The Captain. With a lavish ceremony, he fluffed the makeshift napkin before tucking it into the Captain's dirty and bloody tunic. The Captain was amazed! Just what the biff was going on?

"Eat well! For tomorrow, you fight. You fight and die," chortled the human. The human then gave The Captain a sheet of newspaper.

"Thanks for the toilet paper," he said. "Bit too late, though."

The human gave The Captain a fake half-smile, made one of those fancy about-turn moves, and marched out of the cell. Unseen hands slammed the door shut.

The Captain stared at the food. This was not his first last supper as a condemned man, although he found it bizarre that people would feed someone they were about to execute. Must be a ritual, an old charter, or...something.

"Where's the knife and fork?" he yelled at the door. The tray held five pots with lids, a bowl of freshly baked bread, lots of fruits and other yummy bits and pieces.

"I'm not falling for your trap, ya biff-goats," he yelled at the door, deep down knowing full well he was most definitely going to fall for this trap at some stage. He just did not know when.

He heard a whisper, edging into the realms of creepy, "Eat the food! It's safe. Then get some sleep! You are going to fight a monster or dragon or beast just as horrible tomorrow."

"What?" was all he could muster. The detached, eldritch voice recommended that he eat the food, and who was he to distrust a peculiar unknown voice?

"Who are you?" he asked as he lifted the lid of the first pot. The wyrm did not answer.

He was expecting live snakes or a spring-loaded spike. He found fresh roast chicken sprinkled with spices and a sweet sauce that glistened like fresh honey. His curiosity regarding the voice took a back seat as he dipped his disgustingly filthy hands into the pot and hungrily gobbled down the food.

After he had eaten as much as he could, he wiped his hands on his filthy tunic, making it more disgusting than before—but better smelling. He looked around for the newspaper and found it half under the tray. His artificial hand was starting to glitch because he had not been maintaining it as he should. He picked up the paper with his real hand and read the headline.

The Captain – Fight To The Death!
The notorious Dwain "The Captain" Hartog will fight a horrifying
beast of death tomorrow in the arena. Thunder and Lightning, the
commentating duo of destiny, will be on hand to give their customary
insights to each fight to the death.
Don't miss this exciting event—

I have not been called Dwain Hartog in a long time. It's going to be an interesting day, thought The Captain. He glared at the straw 'bed' and saw it move slightly towards the wall. He decided to lie down next to it and get some rest.

The Captain woke to an intense banging on the cell door. He rose with his usual shaky hips, tingling backbone, loose teeth, and bifflingly painful neck. He nurtured unsteady feet but was still able to inspect the wreck that was his cell. Any leftover food that remained on the tray was gone. In fact, everything was clean, as though it had been licked to a shine.

He braced himself against the wall and took further interest in the room that had never been so clean. The straw bed appeared bulkier. A slight movement near the end of the room indicated that something was in the cell with him. Something that could eat food from plates without making a mess.

The noise that had woken him was not coming from his door. With ears on the door and eyes aimed at the back of the dank cell, he waited for something to happen. Nothing happened, and it continued not to happen for some time, as it is wont to do.

"For crying out loud, are you just going to stand there? Try to escape at least. This is beyond dull," said a strangely croaky voice.

The Captain had been in many odd situations, and this experience added to his Catalogue of Interesting Times. "Nice to meet you. Would you like to come into the light so I can see you?" he asked, moving his head slightly towards the tray.

He could hear one of his teeth playing the fighting utensil song of Yurning 5. *I love that song. I wish I knew what the teeth wanted me to know*, he thought to himself. *Was it 'danger, enchanters in the area?' No, can't be. 'Danger, tavern is about to run out of rum?' Nope. Oh, biffle*, he thought as a rare stone wyrm slithered from the straw bed and curled itself into a ring. It stank, it slimed, and it coiled about two feet tall.

"How's it going?" casually enquired the slippery fellow prisoner.

"Well, apart from having a talking wyrm living in my cell, I am as cool as a very cool thing," replied The Captain, who was formulating a cunning plan in regards to grabbing and strangling the creature.

"Your tooth has stopped playing music. Can I have your teeth?"

"No, you cannot have my teeth. What do you want?"

"Your teeth and your legs."

"How about we agree on one thing up front? No body parts are going to be offered to you. At all. Ever. What you will do, though, is explain to me how you got in here and how we are to get out."

"Not unless you let me eat your leg! Just one leg. I'm not greedy. I will tell you how I got here."

"Listen up, my slithery, wyrmy friend. Tell me what's going on, or I will..."

Slime spattered across the ceiling as the wyrm expanded to three times its size and pushed The Captain against the wall. A now huge, toothy grin was directly in front of The Captain's face, which was not grinning. It was, in fact, grimacing, and his thoughts focused on how to dispatch his unwanted guest before it grew any bigger.

"What exactly do you think you can do to me?" the wyrm enquired.

That is a good question. It would be wise to stop being the smarty captain and slow things down so I can think of a way out of this slippery situation, he thought. *Maybe the guards will come along, and this wyrm will eat them instead.*

Before The Captain achieved his preferred outcome, the wyrm grew smaller, returning to her two-foot size. The shrinking ceased and she felt that the worst of the shrinking was over. She was wrong. She had shrunk to the size of a newly born bunglebeast and was unhappy with the system and everyone within it.

"I think Mrs Wyrmy has been getting a bit too big for her—well, boots, as it were."

"Please don't hurt me. I will tell you how to get out of here if you let me eat some of you. I get stronger and smarter when I get food. I have been small and near death the last few weeks, living in your straw bed. I ate the rest of your meal last night, and now I am smart and strong again."

The Captain raised his eyebrows under the stinking hair that now covered most of his face. Bits of blood, food, and straw were present, but this did not bother him, as his hair looked like that most of the time anyway.

The door clicked open. "Have you idiots forgotten how to slam prison doors open," The Captain chided. 'The four humans who stood before him were the type that ate far too much beast meat and lifted far too many heavy things. "You, out! The arena wants death," demanded one of the guards.

The Captain turned around to study the wyrm. She was gone. He had the feeling that the wyrm would have tried to eat him if it grown strong enough for such an undertaking. *If only she were here now to eat those idiots,* he thought.

Before The Captain could say anything witty or suicidal, he was made to float a few inches above the floor, amusing the guard that executed the spell. As he floated outside the door, he kicked another guard into the cell. The hiding wyrm sprang up and shoved its growing body against the door, closing it before anyone noticed a guard was missing.

The corridor looked a bit different than usual as he floated along. He was usually taken right for his daily beating, but this time, he floated left. The walls were cleaner and had lights, making it a better-lit passage than he had become used to. Others floated in front of him. "Captain, is that you?" a voice he could not mistake came from somewhere close behind him.

"Forthwright Acae. What brings you to these wonderful surrounds?"

"Not a great deal, my old friend. Resting and being beaten. How about your good self?" responded Forthright, taking deep breaths through the pain of bruises and cracked ribs.

"Oh, very good, thank you. I thought I would try sitting around and nearly get eaten by a stone wyrm. I have taken the opportunity to have my skull bashed every day, and I have also starved myself," explained The Captain, who was far less relaxed than he sounded.

"I always wondered if they were tasty, those wyrms. I have been taking part in the same activities. I do believe that our next round of events is not going to be much fun either," replied Forthwright.

The guards were playing a demolition derby game with the floating prisoners. Knocking each other's prisoner into the walls or, for more points, endeavouring to hit another guard to inflict physical damage. The prisoners dared not complain. The guards would have ignored them anyway, that's if they could hear anything over the din of bored-guard mischief and mayhem.

A blinding light lit the way ahead.

"You are about to meet death in the honoured arena. The first two fighters will be on in five minutes," announced a guard who had reluctantly detached herself from the prisoner smash game.

The prisoners were floated into a larger room with a stone bench across one side. "Gentlemen, please note," the guard mocked, "on the other wall, there is a weapons rack that easily accommodates some of the largest, nastiest and loveliest death devices ever conceived."

The rack was empty. "Only joking! I should have said *accommodated*. You lot will be lucky to be equipped with a blunt spoon," laughed the guard as she swaggered towards the door. Embedded solidly in the middle of the wall was a large claw stained with blood, giving all involved a sombre premonition.

It would have taken a beast of immense size and strength to lose a claw to such a formidable wall, The Captain thought...correctly.

The guards walked to the far side of the room then turned to face the prisoners. The prisoners dropped to the ground without warning, and were then shoved roughly onto the bench.

"Where are our weapons?" asked one of the prisoners scheduled to fight first.

"Ahahhahhahahaah," came a gurgly laugh from a large dwarf. The Captain noticed he had very few braids in his beard meaning one of two things. He was either an outcast or a traitor.

The dwarf threw his head back as he laughed, revealing burns to the right side of his neck. In dwarf systems, the neck was burnt as a punishment. This was usually the part of the beard where the warrior braid would be severed and displayed to all other dwarfs to signify that he was irredeemably disgraced.

"Well I'll be a burnt hair piece. Looks like we have an Unclaimed and Unwanted. I thought you would have made yourself scarce a long time ago," mocked The Captain. Forthwright knew The Captain was insane, as did everyone who ever met him. The situation was about to get more hectic.

"Burnt hair piece? You are bonkers," rumbled the dwarf. He was confused and angry at first, but after some solid thinking, he smirked. It was one of those smirks that meant you had tried to offend or bully someone, but they knew something you did not.

"I know something you don't know," the dwarf guard said. "You are well and truly biffed." A roar started low and deep. A roar that lasted fifteen seconds, ending in an ear-splitting scream that cascaded through the doors to the arena. The Captain had the good manners to appear a tad concerned when the dwarf said, "Not so smart now, are we?"

The dwarf approached the first two prisoners and gave one of them a small axe. It was a small wood-splitterwith the blade notched and blunt. The other human put his hand out, expecting a weapon for himself. "What do you want? Oh, you think we can spare the gold for more weapons? No, my lad, it's a share system here. We like our prey–sorry, *prisoners*–to be sociable. Sharing strengthens one's heart and community spirit."

Without warning, the doors flung open, the guards shoved the two wary prisoners out into the arena, and the doors slammed shut.

"Can we get drinks and a snack cart while we wait?" Forthwright asked casually. He did not want The Captain to be the only one taunting the guards.

The fast-flung rock hit him hard on the side of his face.

"Good throw, Notso," said a fellow guard.

"Notso?" jeered The Captain. "What's your surname, freak: Clever?" This insult did not compute for either of the guards. Notso's brain was ticking, but clearly bereft of tocking. The guards came to the conclusion that they may have been insulted, so they stepped forward with their spears to cause a bit of pain.

The Captain and Forthwright leapt at the same time towards the guard nearest them. They thought they were up close and personal enough to start trouble. This, much to their dismay, did not occur. They were returned to the bench, slightly tenderised.

The guards' laughter was loud and persistent, but the racket did not stop the prisoners from hearing the fight going on in the arena. The occasional "Oh, run, duck!" or "Over *here*!" were shouted through the brain-busting roar of something awfully big. The duck knew better and flew to safety.

"How did you two punt jump us in? Is it a protection field? Come on, tell me. I won't tell anyone else." The Captain said, trying to learn the magic's source. He leant over and attracted Forthwright's attention.

He mouthed the words, "Have you seen any magic here?" Forthwright moved his head in the generally accepted manner for 'No,' which in this system was diagonally from back right to front left.

The relative silence was sharper than any spear. Horrific sounds of eating, crunching and squelching. A burp. It sounded as though the deadly critter had finished its meal.

"I take it that those mouthy dwarfs are calling the fights?" asked The Captain. Before Forthright could answer, the crowd roared, 'Thunder!' followed by, 'Lightning'.

Forthwright sighed and rolled his eyes. "At least crowd loves them."

"At least we are going to experience our horrific death with some interesting commentary," responded The Captain.

"My sons love them. I happen to think fights to the death are pretty much self explanatory and don't need ridiculous comments from those windbags."

"I like them..."

The Captain was interrupted by a loud voice booming through the arena "Give it up for the beast of pain!" Sporadic applause followed the loud voice's demand before the crowd resumed their 'Thunder!' and 'Lightning' chants.

"For our next display of deathtertainment, we introduce the six-headed beast of eternal agony," Thunder announced.

Lightning added to her husband's announcement, "Don't forget your snacks at the considerately placed snack bars at twenty different retail points in the arena."

Considerate technology would be lovely, thought Forthwright as all the remaining prisoners except for him and The Captain were shuffled to the door.

"Hey, where's our weapon?"

"I love this bit; can I say it, Notso?"

"Sure."

"As we said before, you stinky bags of blood, we want you to get along as a force of togetherness. The axe is out there somewhere. Good luck!" The doors were again flung open, through which prisoners were kicked, shoved, and viciously encouraged to enter the arena.

"You two are next, and you won't like what you are up against," said Notso, with a big stupid grin on his big stupid face.

At the arena, Walker-Seven and eight other paired were disguised as older pundits wanting to gamble and watch victim gladiators get squashed by sharp and noisy creatures of varying sizes and temperaments. After all, blood sports and sports ball were the pastime of idiots throughout all time and all systems.

From the outside, the arena resembled a small farmhouse. This was obviously an illusion. The long line at the older clients' entrance gave away the ruse. No authority was interested enough to stop the illegal fights since a massively complex war was being fought

Walker-Seven's team went unchallenged as they casually shuffled through the security apparatus at the entrance. Would-be spectators had to drop an item into a chute in front of the T-Life officer as the entrance fee. The T-Life would vibrate a little. Blue light would stream out of cracks around the sharp edges of his square body. He would then either accept the fee, or ask for another item, and might behead anyone who was being less than generous.

All manner of items were presented. Whether they were acceptable depended on where the spectator originated, how wealthy they were, and where they intended to sit. Obviously, gold, silver, and chocolate bars were presented—yes, chocolate! Chocolate was as rare and sought-after as the finest gold in the developed systems. It was a known historical fact that more wars were fought over chocolate than gold, which, of course, is not surprising.

Walker-Seven's group did not want to stand out, so they offered candleholders, parcels of rare foods, and other items that would appear average. This was the less cunning component of Hengway's cunning plan.

The arena inside gave one an uncanny impression that it was infinitely large. Rooms and hallways fish-boned from the main entrance. The magic was far older and superior to considerate architecture and was owned and operated by whoever had access to the main control room. The control room was hidden within the deliberate confusion of hallways, making an invasion or take-over difficult.

Now inside, they were told they could punt jump within the arena's confines so long as they had been there previously. This was a good escape plan, but it did not help with exploring the arena itself.

Walker-Seven nodded at an impfish and naroozie paired. Together they could briefly turn the impfish's scales into flying spy devices. Wherever the scales traversed, they could punt jump because, in theory, they had already been there.

Another paired was responsible for the creation of a punt field. Punt Fields were accidentally discovered by a paired who were trapped in a no-punt force field.

The guards and the village vanished, resulting in their confinement for several days. They decided to create a force field within a field to facilitate a punt jump. The technique was successful, allowing them to escape, leading to the identification of a new paired skill.

The two paired joined up to form a team of four, leaving their commander alone. Walker-Seven could feel Simone close by, which did not make any sense, though not much had made sense lately. Walker-Seven allowed the thought to sit on its mind until the team's mind-speakers picked up the mental transmission and let the others know the captured pairs were probably in the arena or the cells.

An empty room off a quiet hallway was found for the punt jump field, which was a success. Hengway was the first to jump through, quickly moving away from the field. He held a sword in his hand and wore metal armour, playing the part of someone who just flipped the war-fighter of the year switch.

"Where the biffin' biff have you biffing been?" mind-spoke Cleavie from her cell. Thankfully, when mind-speaking, you could not actually yell. Otherwise, Hengway would have been mind-deafened.

"Hengway. Is that you? Is Walker with you?" Simone's voice came through far calmer than Cleavie's.

"Simone, it's not polite to eavesdrop so quietly. Walker is with me, and so are a lot of well-armed paired. We did not know you two were here, so you were not a part of our plan. Stay where you are; we will get to you soon."

"Don't you leave me here!" ordered Cleavie, desperately wishing she could mind-yell.

Hengway knew he could not do all of this. There was simply too much. Time stopped, and he could hear Walker-Seven dealing with something unpleasant.

"Snap out of it and move now!"

Hengway could not make out who had spoken. It might have been Simone, Walker-Seven, and Cleavie altogether for all he knew.

The impfish with the spying scales located the cells of Cleavie and Simone.

Hengway punt jumped to Cleavie. She looked like—

"I can read your mind. Be careful what you think next!" He grabbed Cleavie by the shoulder and punted out of the cell, straight to Simone. Cleavie and Hengway grabbed Simone, punting her to Walker-Seven. The four of them jumped back to the main entrance.

Things in the arena were heating up. Guards were jostling to see more blood. Huge creatures were ridden through the arena's winding corridors. The poor creatures were being used as attack weapons.

Their aggressive behaviour and willingness to bite their handlers indicated their lack of enthusiasm for the unkind treatment.

Cleavie disappeared. She reappeared three paces to the right with a bloodied battle axe. "Don't ask!" she said as Hengway gave her a questioning gaze. He quickly agreed not to ask. Cleavie reappearing with blood and bits of bone spread about her person was alarmingly common and never to be questioned.

In the arena, the crowd began to notice a lot of unwanted movement within the spectator section and decided to be someplace else. They soon realised there was only one way out.

The hastily departing crowd provided suitable cover for the paired to explore the arena without suspicion. Hengway and Cleavie stood in a corner by the entrance, monitoring what was going on and searching for any sign of The Captain or for a way to the control room.

The main arena had been found. They punt jumped there without delay. The scene was mayhem, like 'Free Bunglebeast Burger Day' at the Trav-Coll refectory, except Burger Day did away with the whole fight to the death thing decades earlier. There were humans in the fight pit running around in circles, trying to avoid the substantially sized multi-headed beastie. Hengway and Cleavie worked together to put out a mind-find on The Captain. They were both stunned when they found someone they were not expecting. "My father is here!" exclaimed Hengway.

"The Captain is also here with your father," Cleavie happily observed. During another unplanned absence, Cleavie cleaned her axe, put on clean armour, washed her beard, and appeared to be better fed thanks to a bone of a large bird dangling from the bottom of her beard.

Wanting to be helpful, Hengway indicated she had something in her beard. She smiled at him and moved it so it showed more.

Hengway shook his head, not knowing if it was a cultural thing or a Cleavie thing. *Probably both*, he thought.

"I will ask someone to go and see what else, and who else, has deigned us with their presence," Cleavie said, still smiling about her wonderful beard ornament. "We need to go and get your father and the Capt—."

She was interrupted by the doors at the far end of the pit splintering open into large shards and bursting halfway across the huge arena. Thunder and Lightning continued their observations even though the guards and crowd were in varying states of disarray.

"One of the victims in the pit has had a one-way disagreement with the arena door and is well and truly biffed," Thunder observed.

"The large beast has seen the captured prey and is making its way to its next meal," roared Lightning. The wyrm noticed the commentary box and took an instant dislike to the dwarfs within it. She picked up a body in her mouth and spat the corpse at the dwarfs. It crashed through the wooden boards and splattered into the rear wall, missing both dwarfs by a beard's hair.

Forthwright and The Captain came hurtling out of the doorway, their arms flailing. They headed for the beast, which was attempting to gorge itself on everything within reach. The crowd noticed their comedy duo was unnaturally silent, so they raised a chant to get them once again engaged in the arena's current events.

"Thunder! Lightning!"

"Those two are an embarrassment to dwarf kind," Cleavie commented.

"I kind of like them." Hengway said. After a pause, he continued, "That's strange."

Cleavie nodded in agreement. "The pit must have an extra protect-a-field around it." After several attempts, Cleavie and Hengway discovered they could not punt jump into it. They ran towards the lower edge of the seating section and physically leapt directly into the pit.

"Some short human and a silly dwarf, who should have more sense than leaping to certain death, have indeed leapt into the buffet area of the beasties. *Buffet,* I tell you!" yelled Thunder.

"Buffet! Buffet! *Buffet* for the beasties!' Lightning joined in, wiping the remains of the human missile from her beard and tunic. "As Thunder always said, *the deaths must go on.*" The crowd roared, "Buffet! Buffet!", time and time again.

The surviving prisoners, including Forthwright and The Captain, were now huddled together in the middle of the fighting pit with the many-headed terrors circling them. As was to be expected, they were pondering in which dramatically brutal way they were going to die.

The beast moved away from the now unguarded exit, creating an enticing opportunity for escape. They prisoners were continually turning their horrified gazes between the clearly ravenous beast and back to the broken door, splitting their attention between certain death by beast and a probably worse but still certain death by spear.

"Can our moving feast make a break for the open door?" Thunder bellowed to the crowd.

"Run! Run!" Lightning yelled. The crowd joined in, though most of the crowd missed the new chant so it sounded like they were chanting 'Ruffet'. Sure enough, the whole crowd started chanting 'Rough Hey'. Nobody had any idea what it meant, but chant it they did.

Hengway and Cleavie sprinted towards the prisoners, immediately noticing a terrible scene: a giant wyrm with a head no less than twelve feet wide and twelve feet long slithered into the fighting pit. "Wow, that is a biff load of teeth," Hengway yelled as he recoiled.

"Distance between those teeth and us is quite a non-negotiable proposition," Cleavie yelled back.

Thunder turned towards the impfish in charge of the fight schedule. The official stared blankly at Thunder and said, "That monsster is unplanned. The guardsss are reportingss conflictss all over the arena."

Lightning took the initiative, "Welcome to our corpse chucking wyrm. Firm Wyrm is what we shall name it. Let's see who Firm nibbles on first, shall we?" Lightning was hoping to start a new, sensible, chant, but to no avail. 'Rough Hey! Rough Hey!' continued the raucous crowd.

The Captain spied the slithering beastie and sighed. "By the way, Forthwright, that's my bed-wyrm. The biffer has enlarged herself somewhat."

"That's great, Captain. What did you feed it?"

"A guard. And not a very tasty one, I would have imagined."

"O Captain, my Captain," the wyrm bellowed, slithering across the pit. The other beast was still intent on eating the large group in the middle. There were seven possible dinners, two diners, two weapons and no magic.

The other paired were watching from the seats. Hengway yelled out instructing the others to keep searching for the control room, and not to enter the pit. They disappeared, with caution.

Hengway felt Cleavie's mind. What was she doing? There was a very low chatter coming and going inside her mind. "What are you doing? I sense that we are about to get killed, and I would appreciate some help." The beast with a plurality of heads came sliding towards the group with gnashing teeth, a few heads snorting, and at least one head pointing the other way, laughing.

Enough of this, Hengway thought. The beast froze. It could not move anywhere, though its body was still swaying in place but all heads turned to Hengway. He had its full attention.

"Will the beastie eaty the silly humanie!" roared Thunder. Lightning gave him an incredulous look. *That statement was as silly as it gets*, she thought. She was soon proved wrong as Thunder continued, "Who is a nice lots of heads beastie? You cute widdle fing." The crowd fell silent waiting for the cue for their next chant, because they sure as hell weren't going to chant 'widdle fing' for the rest of the day.

Lightning raised her hands and started clapping above her head. The crowd followed. In true crowd fashion it started off as a cacophony of poorly timed claps, but eventually formed into an constant rhythm.

After one clap Lightning yelled 'Eat!' On the second clap she yelled 'The!' and on the third 'Human!' The crowd entered into the vibe of the chant and after a few loops of the three chants, 'Eat the human' became a musical within itself.

Those biffing dwarfs, Hengway thought. He could still hear Cleavie's mind chattering away, except the noise was growing louder and more intense. He glanced at the wyrm, and it, too, had stopped moving. The Captain and Hengway's father were also staring at the wyrm, waiting for it to come their way.

"What the biff is happening?" Forthwright asked the arena at large.

"We have the dubious honour of witnessing a beast standoff. I would have thought we would be snacks by now," observed The Captain.

Thunder wanted to continue with his silly chants but Lightning wanted the opposite so the crowd continued with their favourite chant of this day. Clap. 'Eat!' Clap! 'The!' Clap. 'Hu-!' Clap. 'Man.'

"Everyone, shush!" demanded Cleavie. The crowd obviously could not hear her, but most certainly would have ignored her if they could.

"Son, what are you doing?" Forthwright was watching Hengway walk directly towards the beast whose heads were now all aligned in a triangular formation.

Thunder finally got a chance to yell, "The human is walking towards his own death," he yelled. The crowd stopped the chant, which was replaced by mumbles and sounds of confusion and some of delight.

The beast opened all mouths on all heads. Without hesitation, Hengway said, "Good girl. Who's a good girl?" He put out his hand to pat one of the lower heads. There was a clash as the other heads tried to get some attention. Hengway gave each head a pat. Some of the braver prisoners took this as a good sign to wander over and start paying the beastie some attention.

"Who wants a belly rub, then?" murmered one of the rescued prisoners, gaining a few chuckles from the others.

It was gradual at first. Easy to miss. "Are these things getting smaller?" asked Forthwright. Cleavie approached the wyrm.

"How about The Captain? Can I just eat The Captain, Cleavie?" enquired the wyrm.

"No, you biffin' well can't," replied The Captain.

"I'm afraid that's not a part of our deal," said Cleavie.

"What deal? They *are* getting smaller. What's going on? Hengway, answer me! Cleavie—" The Captain stopped asking questions and just smiled his colourful, toothy smile. "Ah, you two are talking to the beasties. Nice skills!"

The multi-headed beast's name was Jane. Jane was a long-time member of the arena community and, as it turns out, a system navigator. The wyrm was called Ramussa.

"Jane is over five hundred years old and is rather smart. We were discussing the finer points of inter-system fartism in the arena," said Cleavie.

"Fartism? You made that up!" exclaimed The Captain. He was now sitting on a seat in the arena, drinking from a flask of water, *alas,* and generally trying to calm himself down.

"It sounds like a funny thing, but it is quite a serious component of system physics," said Ramussa. "There are some systems that have Fartial Arts. I couldn't make this up."

The Captain gazed at Ramussa, he still could not get it all straight in his head. "I have heard of you before. You, Ramussa, are a talking wyrm who doesn't have to eat people, but can? You are also one of the owners of the Arena? And you have an actual sense of humour?"

"That," she chuckled, "is correct."

"In fact, there are many creatures who actually own and run the arena; however, you were taken hostage by these nasty individuals some time ago?"

"Correct again," said Jane, who was sitting on Cleavie's lap. Cleavie and Hengway were resting while all the other paired were reassembling.

"We were just about to eat everyone when Hengway and Cleavie worked out that there is more to us than teeth and big stomachs," said Ramussa.

Hengway interjected. "Those gobby dwarfs up there. Can you sort them out please, Ramussa?"

Everyone that heard Hengway's questionlooked at Thunder and Lightning. Confused, the crowd looked at the commentators. Ramussa said, 'You two are finished for the night." Thunder and Lightning disappeared with zero argument and just as much fanfare.

One step away from creating a stampede, the crowd started heading towards the exits. No longer interested in the day's events or the possibility of being disappeared by a weird multi-headed death beast, most of them thought the local inn offered fewer chances of death and mayhem, perhaps. An expeditious egress is always a solid choice when one finds oneself in an arena with multi-headed beasts, wyrms and deadly magical executants traipsing about.

Walker-Seven and Simone appeared, making an unneeded dramatic entrance. "We found the control room. We also found Trinni." A pause for an even more significant, this time justified, dramatic effect. "We also found another bigger problem," Simone revealed.

"Sounds like it's a big enough problem with just my sister. Well, what's the other problem?" Hengway asked.

"We think we know what and where the Chaos Light is."

23. Controlling The Room

Hengway always considered there to be five main types of conversation: food-related, fight-related, family-related, friend-related, and fart-related.

There were more types of conversation to be discovered. The sixth type] was getting a little unruly. For a start, it didn't start with "F". It began with, "We are in an arena that can travel through all systems and is run by creatures that can shrink and grow whenever they like. Also, your sister is trying to capture or kill the magically paired and is now in the control room of the arena. Oh, and your mum, Tuja, has the lighty chaotic thingy." A long sentence starter on any planet.

"So, we have to storm the control room, kill the witch—sorry Trinni—release the hostages, and have something to eat. I, for one, am famished," declared Simone.

"All of the nasty surviving prisoners are back in prison. They have a few cuts and bruises to remind them of the fight on boring nights," one young paired was telling an enthralled gathering.

The room gradually fell into quietness.

"Well, they'll have to work this out on their own at some stage. Might as well be now. I always thought there was a lot more going on with this whole pairing thing than our little heads could imagine," said The Captain, drinking from a new flask. He had returned from a brief visit to one of the many markets of the arena. The contents of the flask were unknown, but he knew he liked it.

The lack of screaming and biting indicated that the main event had come to a conclusion, and everyone and everything was a lot happier than earlier. Forthwright gestured for the flask and took a large swig, urging himself to be just as happy.

"Everyone listen up!" barked Hengway. All stopped talking. He had not washed in days, had dirty stubble on his round face, had no weapon, but now had a definite aura of command. Everyone else was heavily armoured in varying colours and types, giving the group a spectacularly roguish look. The weapons they brandished were intended for short-range engagements and bore the stains of recent action.

Other creatures of the arena appeared every now and again. Word was spreading that the guards were gone, and they could now regain control.

Hengway had noticed something strange about them. Cleavie was also pondering the oddness. There were creatures with many heads, no heads, heads on both sides of their body, huge heads, tiny heads and, on occasion, heads that actually fit the scale of the body. The thing was...

"Why is there no more than one of each of you?"

"We are each the last of our species," replied Jane, who was now sitting on Forthwright's lap and looking very comfortable. "Who would not pay a great deal to see the last of a species die in combat?"

That information hit the room like a dust storm. Most who heard this lowered their heads at the needless suffering creatures endured for the entertainment of others. "They won't be bothering any of you anymore, then," promised The Captain. That lightened the mood.

Heads turned back to Hengway. "You aren't bad for a bunch of no-gooders from various parts of the system. We had our problems before we became paired. Some of you have lost your paired in the fighting, or they were killed by your captors while you were in prison.

We have been through more than we should have seen. You are not being forced to stay for this battle. I don't know what is in that control room or what awaits us, but the room is heavily guarded on the outside, and you can expect worse within. Any attempt to punt jump in or send in a T-Life spy has already failed."

He paused for effect and continued, "It might be super easy, which would be awesome, but I doubt that will be the case." Hengway noticed his brother and Naroi in the crowd. It was the first time he was happy to see his brother, a rare, if not singular, feeling. He was also happy to see Naroi since he would surely be handy in any scraps they might soon find themselves. "I think this is going to get messy, so stay close and keep communicating!"

"For those who want to fight, we start the advance in five minutes; be ready!" commanded Cleavie, impatiently finishing off Hengway's speech.

Creatures that had been captives were to now become soldiers. They would lead the journey to the control room. A smaller group was tasked to check the lower dungeons for prisoners.

Hengway, Cleavie, Jay, and Naroi accompanied the group headed towards the control room. Forthwright followed his sons. The Captain opted to follow the group checking the cells.

"Hey, who can mind-speak with the boss?" asked The Captain, referring to Hengway. A paired of two naroozie each raised a fifth leg. "Stay with me, then; we need to remain in contact," he said, waving farewell to Hengway.

Hengway waved back, shouting, "Don't kill anything that doesn't need killing, please!" The Captain did not acknowledge receipt of this command.

Cleavie was relaxed and ready for the fight. After she was released—well, rescued—she had frozen time for a few hours, ate some food, bathed—twice, combed everything, and generally made herself a nice-smelling warfighter. Though she would never admit that she had taken the time for relaxation, even the most battle-hardened dwarf occasionally needed a little cleanliness and preparation before a murderous encounter.

Moving through the arena corridors which forked into narrow hallways, the first battle group was packed close together as they patrolled down and away from the fighting pit.

"Spread out!" Hengway yelled as he and Cleavie felt the first blast of heat. Unexpected rises in temperature, as a rule, came from a source that was almost always unwelcome–fire in this case. Those with force field skills put them to good use, raising fields around the team. The blast bounded up and through the narrow hallways as it hit each shield, finding a way to maintain speed until it ran out of fuel.

The hallway had already filled with smoke. The force fields kept the air clean, but the heat and dirt made the advance slow and messy.

"Keep moving!" Hengway shouted to the remaining paired. Hengway could sense something very odd. The hallway started to shake. "Can you feel that?" he said aloud. Before he could finish his sentence a few of the paired answered that they could.

"It's your biffing sister. She is such a pain in the backside," added Cleavie with a forceful stream of mind-speaking that was louder and clearer than usual.

"Okay, everyone, keep it down! Be clear: there are three, not one, very powerful magical signatures in the control room," Hengway shouted so everyone would understand. He then sent the message to Simone, who passed the information to the team searching the cells.

Suddenly everything went awry. One by one, Hengway's team disappeared. Cleavie punt jumped to him and created a mighty shield around them both. This was a good and a bad thing.

No magic or mind skills could reach them, which also meant they could not interact with their team. The dust, carried by an unseen source of air, kept moving out of the tunnel, creeping towards the control room.

Other paired who had the skill and the good timing to place protection spells around themselves were glad to see Hengway and Cleavie moving and followed them up the passageway. The air became clearer the closer they were, their shields joining with bright changes of colour and the crackling sound of small firecrackers. Being protected by a larger, combined magical field made Hengway a little less worried about the next move.

"This is the door to the control room," Hengway explained, feeling a little dim saying that. The entrance was a double doorway about twelve feet tall and just as wide. It was labelled in huge letters, 'Control Room' in red and bold. Sufficient energy for banter was missing in action, so they saved their witty asides regarding dull naming conventions for later. Hengway hesitated and glanced at Cleavie; she nodded towards the door and mouthed the words, "*Get on with it!*"

24. Great Escape

Observe! Events are about to happen quicker than Trav-Coll students heading for the lavatories after 'Free Bunglebeast Burger Day'.

Hengway's hand was shaking, as were his feet and legs Even his nose hairs were shaking. He gripped the door handle, so the door started shaking. He took a deep breath and flung open the door. It shook itself to a stop.

He found a large room with monitors and dwarf technology boxes lined up along a bench on one side. All sorts of miscreants were clicking away on small black devices that seemed impossibly thin. Letters would appear on the screens above the thin devices, making words. Cleavie let the force field drop. She needed to know if they could communicate with each other and, hopefully, the captured and paired.

"Oh, biffle," blurted Cleavie as the field of protection completely vanished. Hengway sent an immediate order. "Take defensive positions."

"The Captain and the others have found something, and they want us there," said Cleavie.

"Go, help them!" Hengway replied.

The room was quiet except for the tapping of the word-makers along the other wall. Naroi and Jay fell in behind Hengway as he crept cautiously through the room.

The room's occupiers ignored the visitors. At the far side of the control room was a dark, open doorway leading to another poorly lit room. An orange and green light haphazardly flashed every few seconds around the doorframe. Without a word, they hesitantly approached the dark, mysterious entrance.

"Hurry up, you three! You are going to miss the show," cried a voice from within the room.

Naroi knew that voice. *Shock!* That voice did not belong here.

"Do as she says, boys!" cried a second voice. Jay and Hengway gazed at each other upon hearing that voice. *Shock!*

Forthwright had come up behind his sons and whispered, "It can't be. What's going on?"

Popping and sizzling noises escaped the room. Hengway entered and stopped in absolute amazement. His father, brother, and Naroi followed closely behind.

"Mum!" exclaimed all three boys.

"Tuja?" asked Forthwright.

"Trinni?" said both Hengway and his father.

An illumination push from Hengway brightened the vast room, which was made of the same large stone as the rest of the fighting arena. In the centre stood Trinni, white-robed and unperturbed.

Tuja, the mother of Hengway and Jay, stood at a nearby terminal pushing coloured buttons on a box console. Tarlan, Naroi's mother, was fiddling with a metal helmet. It presented as a prototype with the mandatory wires and other technical bits poking from it.

"About time you all arrived. I left enough clues." Trinni said.

Tuja glared at Trinni and hissed, "Clues?"

The rest of her family looked at Trinni, all being somewhat as confused as Tuja. Trinni understood that she had let her guard down and took on a solid veneer once more, "Just in time for the show!"

There were so many questions to ask. Hengway examined the perimeter of the room and saw an endless row of grey metal seats in which zombie-like individuals were seated.

He slowly moved around the area, and since opposition to impede his progress was luckily absent, he gradually increased his pace to inspect the seating. His fears were confirmed. All of the missing paired were attached to the chairs. Some were tied using rope, and some had metal clips attached to their arms and legs. Others had protection fields holding them in place. They were all wearing the metal helmet prototypes.

Each helmet had a thick cable coming out of its side. These long cables were connected to a small box sitting on a stone altar in the far-right corner. The box occasionally emitted green or orange light, alternating between the two.

Hengway tried to punt jump himself and a few others out. Nothing happened. "Seriously, brother, that doesn't work in here. And besides, they are chained to the chairs," Trinni said. She glared at Hengway and mindspoke, "Try something else."

Cleavie was also in his overly populated mind. "There is some serious biff going on down here," she said.

"I'm a little bit busy. Would you like to come and help? You won't be able to jump straight into this room, though." A fracas could be heard from the other room, yelling and cursing, with a delicate sprinkling of horror, followed by the appearance of Cleavie.

"Took you long enough," he grinned. "Where's The Captain?"

"Dealing with about ten thousand soldiers hiding in the lower levels, with hundreds of thousands of prisoners."

"What is all this?" Forthwright glared at Tuja and demanded, "Where have you been? Why did you leave me? When did you become such a biffer? What's the point of this?" After not receiving an answer, he pointed at the box in the middle of the room and asked, "More importantly, why are these paired held captive? Why are they wired up to whatever that is?"

"I see that Hengway and his charming pet received our encrypted message. We made the war; we sold the weapons, and now we have the workers and enough magical power for the next part of our plan. The Chaos Light will allow us to create paired executants whenever we deem necessary."

"The best part of our scheme was we were keeping you and the rest of you miscreants busy dismantling a karaoke machine, whilst we were protecting the real artefact of value," Tarlan mocked.

Forthwright was aghast as he slowly realised what his wife was doing. "You are sucking magic from the paired to increase the power of the Chaos Light! You fiend!"

"Fiendish? Oh, I do like to be flattered," Tuja replied and continuing with her tasks at hand.

Jay and Naroi used the banter as a cover, moving quietly towards Trinni and their mothers. They did not know what they were going to do when they got closer, but they had to do something. The paired in the peculiar helmets were still squirming and groaning as light flashed from the box they were connected to.

"That's clearly the Chaos Light. Trinni is probably keeping the protection shield up, stopping us from punting. Cleavie and I will try to get the artefact. Everyone else will keep Trinni occupied in the hope she lowers her protection shield."

They all tried to mind-speak simultaneously, making mostly obvious observations but undoubtedly understandable comments. These included, but were not limited to, *our mothers are frauds, treacherous biffers*, and *what the actual biff?* Hengway told them all to concentrate on the task at hand. After some brief protestation, they recollected their thoughts. Hengway was desperately endeavouring to hang on to what was left of his drive, motivation, and sanity.

He wanted to lower the shield and start punting out anyone they could. The plan his mother had formed was dubious at best, but he decided he did not give a naroozie's fart what she wanted. He wanted everyone out–and safe.

Cleavie mind-spoke with as many of the paired as she could. Hengway edged towards the shiny thing in the box. Naroi cautiously edged closer to Trinni.

Trinni raised her hands, casting a 'fetch be quick' spell. She dropped her protective shield as a spear appeared in her hands. Naroi felt there was an opening to kill Trinni. He attacked immediately. "No!" cried Trinni as Naroi ran straight into the spear, imbedding itself in his stomach.

His mother briefly shuddered in dismay but quickly gathered herself and concentrated on the knobs and switches to her front. Naroi would have to look after himself or die a horrible death. *It was always good to give your offspring life choices,* she thought.

"I see you have a new weapon to play with," Jay said. Naroi did not respond as he grasped the spear with both hands, he was endeavouring to stay upright as each movement caused pain and dis-joy. Jay executed a spell that hurled the spear back to whence it came. Trinni smiled and said, "See you soon brother," then punt jumped to somewhere where spears were not being hurled her way.

Hengway dug deep mentally, formulated a plan, and slowed time. He did not want to stop it entirely because he needed to move others and to deduce what his mother was going to do next. He had a chat with the arena outlining his displeasure with it. The arena mentioned that things were not its fault and he should biff off.

The entire arena decided not to be there anymore. The fighters who were in the arena remained in place; however, the arena must have been floating in the air because everyone was hundreds of feet above the ground. No one was falling–yet. It was as though their bodies refused to believe the arena had decided to absent itself.

"Jump! Jump! Jump!" Hengway sent a mind-message to everyone and also yelled it as loudly as possible. Hengway spun towards his mother with the intent to punt jump her to somewhere uncomfortable, like a prison cell or a volcano.

She had what was possibly the Chaos Light in her hands. The box had "*Chaos Light*" written thereon in large red letters. Okay, he thought, it is the Chaos Light. She raised one relaxed hand and waved. "You arrogant terrors may have stopped us creating our paired war fighters; however, you will see that we are quite determined. We will return with an extremely powerful army," she said, after which, she vanished.

Cleavie was busily punt jumping the paired who were hooked up to the boxes. Her PSSA was reconnoitring the surrounding area and placing protection shields around those who were falling.

Hengway glanced down and saw thousands of bodies hanging in the air. They must be the prisoners The Captain and Cleavie had discovered. He was wondering what to do with them when he noticed he was falling. The air began rushing between his legs,making the *whoosh* sound that air likes to make when you do something as silly as falling from a ridiculous height.

The thousands of bodies below him stopped being there. Punt jumping experience at its best. He glanced around and saw Cleavie and Walker-Seven punting the last few survivors.

"Where are we going?" he asked Cleavie.

"Acae Castle. It considerately considered that we needed help and has operating tables set up for the wounded. There will be rooms to hold all of us. Let's get the biffle out of here!"

All of this took sixty seconds.

25. Never Ending

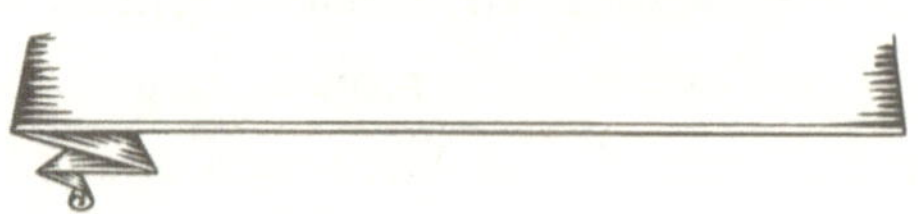

Bodies everywhere.

Paired punting in and out on important missions. Cleavie's mother coordinating medical matters with the dwarfs. T-Life moving about the castle, trying to document precisely what had happened.

Survivors lying in hallways on makeshift beds, volunteers dispensing food, and paired comparing notes on just how awesome they were. Formerly missing dwarfs and humans milled about in a daze.

It was a well-organised chaotic disaster. Naroi lay in a bed at the side of the dungeon room, being tended by some medics as Jay sat beside him.

"This whole situation is beyond biffed," Jay muttered, leaning back against the castle wall. His voice was sharp with frustration, yet there was an undertone of weariness that only Naroi could detect. "Our mothers—what are they even doing? Building armies, creating chaos across systems... It's like they've forgotten who we are. Or worse, they never cared."

Naroi shifted in angry annoyance but took time to answer. "You think I don't ask myself the same thing? I wonder if my mother—our mothers—were just using us as tools? Maybe the whole 'family bond' thing is just a convenient lie?"

Hengway wanted to intervene in the conversation but Cleavie mind-told him to keep his own business. He did not comply. "Our mothers will get what is coming to them. Very simple really!" said Hengway. Cleavie tutted in annoyance.

"No, you're right. You're absolutely right," Naroi interrupted, his tone laced with a sorrow that made Jay's stomach twist. "My mother raised me to believe in the honor of the clan, the strength of the naroozie. And now? Now she's plotting like a desperate warlord with your mother, pretending it's all for some greater good..."

Hengway interrupted, "What if it's just greed? Just power?"

Jay held his hand up so people would listen to his weak voice. "I used to think my mother was a visionary," he admitted quietly, his hands curling into fists at his sides. "She always talked about making our system great again. About protecting humanity, expanding our influence. But this... this isn't protection. This is tyranny. She's hurting people, *innocent* people."

Naroi sighed deeply, his usual sharp edge softened by the weight of Jay's words. "I knew my mother had ambitions, but seeing it play out like this... seeing the lives it has cost—it's hollow and shameless. This is no kind of legacy."

Jay hesitated before asking, "Do you think they even care about us anymore?"

Forthwright stood in the doorway, his demeanour was that of unnatural calmness. "Trinni is missing because of them. My summation is that your mothers gave up on us a long time ago."

Silence.

Professor Smeltzit appeared in the room. The busy occupants showed zero surprise. The movement of people and bodies was an accepted component of the chaos, however they did stare at him for waiting to tell them what he wanted. They knew he never showed up not wanting something. Finally he asked, "Where is Trinni? I need to speak to her."

Jay laughed, and before anyone could say anything, they heard a racket coming from one of the corridors leading from the main area.

"Let's go check out the noise," suggested Cleavie. They made their way down the corridor towards the loud scratching and metallic screeches.

"Sounds like chains," Jay said.

"Does your sister have any beasts down here?" Cleavie asked.

"I'm not sure I really want to find out," answered Hengway.

They felt the blast first. This was followed by a mighty explosion as a door flew into the corridor, the door was headed directly at Professor Smeltzit. Instead the castle considerately ensured its trajectory changed, smashing it into the opposite wall. Hengway instantly created a force field. Cleavie took out a small, one-handed battle axe from beneath her armour.

"Interesting! I thought the fun was over for the day," Cleavie said.

"Great deal of fun, to be sure," said The Professor.

"There's always fun to be found in my house," Hengway replied. Castle Acae shuddered.

Hengway cleared his throat."Sorry, there's always fun to be had in the castle we gratefully reside within." Hengway clenched his eyes and waited, but remained intact, so he took this as a sign that his apology was accepted by a very temperamental castle.

Another small explosion came from within the room with the missing door. Cleavie tried to read the room to determine whether she could sense any minds. She was sure someone was in the room, but she could not feel a presence.

"Who is out there? I will kill anyone who gets in my way." This voice came from the now smoky and dangerous room. The voice confused Hengway and Cleavie.

"Can't be," muttered Hengway.

"This place is as freaky as impfish food," whispered Cleavie.

"Hengway, is that you?" enquired the voice.

"...Yes," replied a naturally hesitant Hengway. He mouthed a countdown to Cleavie, and they froze time together. "Let's investigate the room!" Cleavie nodded in the affirmative, and they eased over to the newly vacant doorway.

The doorframe was busted entirely, and the door was scattered in splinters. Much to their astonishment, Trinni stood in the centre of the room, creating a blue fireball in her hands. Freezing time did not affect her. The blue ball vanished, and she put her hands on her hips.

"Where the biff have you been? Acae Castle would not let me out so I had to try and bust out. I left all the clues. I kept the tyrants away from you as much as I could. And hairy buffoons throw spears at me. Ungrateful I would say."

After a great deal of hugging, questions, further hugging, much laughter, some crying, and even more hugging.What remained of the Acae family eventually gathered around the table and began catching up on current affairs.

"After all the subterfuge, and the constant rescue missions plaguing this family, I have petitioned the enchanter council to help, though I do believe the enchanters have had a lot to do with our recent problems."

"Well spit it out, or I will ba... Actually, I may bash you anyway," Cleavie said.

"It is a long-punt story."

"You mean a long story?" snorted Cleavie.

"Well..."

Trinni told the story of her long-punts, how Professor Smeltzit told her to follow the light, and all the times she stopped her mother's plans whilst keeping her brothers and others safe.

"I must admit it seems like a great subterfuge but Trinni has a lot ahead of her," The Professor spoke in a calm manner. "As you are safe, I will leave now. Rest assured; I will be seeing you some time soon." With that, just as he arrived, he disappeared without fanfare.

"Strange man that. A good man, but a little too occupied with intrigue and mystery" Forthwright said. He sighed and turned to Trinni. "Why didn't you tell me your plans at least?"

"Things were moving so quickly that I had to follow the light. I had no idea who I could trust."

"You trust this family, that's who," Hengway said. He hugged her and she patted him softly, once, on the back. "Well maybe our mother needs a few doubts thrown her way," he added.

Everybody noticed her lack of hug acceptance so stood fast. Cleavie started to say, "I still think you are a..."

"Well, don't you lot genuinely look greatly, greatly enhanced!" boomed The Captain, interrupting Cleavie and soliciting a grimace from the still miffed dwarf in the process. He was wearing a shiny new brown coat with armour pieces covering the important body bits and a multitude of pockets. and he wore a shiny new sword on his left side. His hair was now washed and neatly tied back. The only feature that was unchanged was the mouth full of egregious teeth, as ugly and multicoloured as ever.

"Indeedy everyone, I've had a bath and washed all my places. I try to have a wash every six months or so, even if I don't need one.'" I have heard rumours about The T-Life starting to replace others with copies."

"It might also explain why our mothers are acting so oddly," said Hengway. Naroi nodded in agreement.

"I'm afraid not," declared Forthwright. "Your mothers are quite real and are in this mess up to their teeth. We believe that they started the war, as well as smaller conflicts to sell weapons to all sides in order to fund something terrible. They possess the Chaos Light and have enough magical capacity to do tremendous harm."

"What's our next step?" asked Hengway.

"We crown peace with law, we spare the conquered, and we subdue the proud," suggested The Captain, to some astonishment.

"I shall translate," Forthwright said. The others gratefully nodded in acknowledgement. "We fix what has been broken, help us all recover from the impact of the war, and help the paired," he translated.

"I have a lot of catching up to do," insisted Trinni. "I believe we need to start bringing wrongdoers to justice."

Draggi stared at Tarlan and Tuja in a cold, damp room, probably in a castle somewhere relatively safe. "You two are failures. Our plans are ruined. You should have controlled Trinni the way you said you would." She blinked. Blood dribbled from the sides of her mouth.

"I am really sick of your nonsense," Tarlan said as her sharp paw smashed through Draggi's breastplate, leaving her with Draggi's still-beating heart in her hand. "You have been a useful idiot up to now. Thanks for all the help, but we will take it from here."

Tuja walked up to Draggi, glared into her dying eyes and said, "You fool. Trinni was slowing us down on purpose. As foolish as we look now, we have all we need to continue our plans without you." Tuja watched the confusion on Draggi's face and smiled. "You had us kicked out of the Enchanters and used us to get the Chaos Light to research a paired army. Now you will die knowing you could have been a part of our army, but biffed around and found out."

Tuja took this as her cue to crush Draggi's heart with no emotion or remorse.

Trav-Coll was reopened with a special unit for paired to practise and to learn their craft. No sightings had been reported of the two mother tyrants who were responsible for so much pain and agony. No one really cared because they were glad to be rid of such nefarious characters.

Hengway and Cleavie were sitting in the refectory with Chorlie, whom Hengway had forgiven for the incident at the castle. For now.

"Where's Jay and Naroi?" asked Cleavie as she put her hand into her bag and brought out what appeared to be her lunch. She poked at it, and a bit of whatever it was plopped out of the side. She used her mind to float it to the bin. Her PSSA took her lead and shot a small ball of flame into the bin, setting it on fire.

"Both of you are showing off. Nice new braids, by the way." Hengway observed. "I don't know where they are. Perhaps having kissy-kissy time."

"Hengway, that's disgusting," wheezed Chorlie. He made a kissing face at Hengway. "What the biff is happening to me?" he rasped as he stared at his fading hands.

Naroi came screaming into the refectory, "I can't find Jay," he yelled in a frantic tone.

Time froze except for Hengway, Naroi and Cleavie. Hengway peered around the refectory trying to locate the magic's source.

A human slowly combined together in front of them. It was the opposite of what happened to Chorlie. She was wearing blue pants and an enchanter's robe that had been turned into a tunic. She had pouches at her waist and a small gun in her hand.

"Holy biffity biff. Trinni! Is that you?" Cleavie asked, as she recognised the blonde hair and the small nose.

"Yes, it is I. We need to get out of here. Now! Come on, hold hands!"

They gazed at each other. After they ascertained they were not going to gain any meaningful information, they turned as one to stare at Trinni.

"We need to wait for Jay," blurted an anxious Naroi.

"I already have him. Let's go! *Now!*"

They rushed to Trinni and held hands.

Hengway found himself vomiting on a rocky hill with the greenest trees he had ever seen. After his lunch exited his stomach, he glanced around and noticed that everyone else was just as sick as he.

"Okay, what the biff is going on, Trinni?"

"It was our mother who jumped the arena. Upon doing so, they have amassed a large army. She is now the ruler of an entire planet along with Naroi's mother," Trinni explained. Naroi and Cleavie moved closer so they could hear what was happening.

"They are using the Chaos Light to create mischief. I have been working for some time to set things right. I couldn't stop them, so I decided to get help."

"Where are we?" they asked as a single squeaky out of tune voice. The resulting cacophony sounded like a grade two choir.

"We are on The Planet. I have started helping the local academy protect younger executants. I need your help to stop our mother from killing everyone on this planet. Naroi you will be happy to know that the citizens have formed a military practice using sense magic and martial arts. Especially prevalent is the use of sound and smell from farting."

"Awesome," said all of the boys.

"Ewww," said Cleavie.

"Yes, the fartial arts are quite powerful. I am sure you will enjoy learning this new craft. Good luck!" On that note, Trinni disappeared.

Whoosh! The group was startled by the sudden appearance of two humans who looked as if they had been through a wildly out of balance washing machine. Twice. They gazed around, one of them said, "Hello, everyone."

"What the biff?" Cleavie said, who was now less startled and more alert.

"I am Karl. You will get to know me soon, I would imagine. This is Showie." Showie raised a gracious hand and said hello to Hengway and Cleavie.

"Well, Trinni never disappoints," observed Naroi.

"We are here to help you with your current mission," explained Showie.

"And who precisely asked you to do that?" retorted Cleavie.

"The Professor and Trinni. Trinni lectures at the magic academy here, and they decided you may be able to help with the matter of the recalcitrant mothers."

"Sounds like an adventure I don't really need. Let's do it!" was Cleavie's reply. She decided to take it like she always had—alertly, calmly, and then ruthlessly.

Hengway said, "We can all get to know each other later. Right now, we need to have a wee chat with Tuja and Tarlan."

www.ingramcontent.com/pod-product-compliance
Lightning Source LLC
Chambersburg PA
CBHW061540210726
48287CB00006B/2024